D1565281

TOTALLY
WORTH IT

Visit us at www.boldstrokesbooks.com

TOTALLY
WORTH IT

June 2019

Gerri

Happy Pride. Thanks so much for the support!

All the best

by

Maggie Cummings

2015

TOTALLY WORTH IT

ISBN 13: 978-1-62639-512-1

This Trade Paperback Original Is Published By
Bold Strokes Books, Inc.
P.O. Box 249
Valley Falls, NY 12185

First Edition: December 2015

CREDITS
Editor: Ruth Sternglantz
Production Design: Stacia Seaman
Cover Design by Jeanine Henning

Acknowledgments

I'd like to thank Ruth Sternglantz and the entire team at Bold Strokes Books for all the work that went into making this book possible.

I also want to thank my amazing support group led by my sister, Sheila, for her proofreading skills and her enthusiasm, which seemed never ending. Thanks also to my awesome friends and first readers, Kerry Symon, Melissa Begley, Alyse Pecoraro, and Judy Ekberg, whose encouragement and motivation helped me overcome my ever-present fear of failure. Last, and most important, thanks to my wife, Kat, who endured countless hours of conversation about fake people, was consistently expected to be a human thesaurus, and who, above all, believed in me from the very start.

For Kat

CHAPTER ONE

It's amazing how three little words can change your entire life.

That's what Meg was thinking as she stood in front of the doorway of her new house.

She had never owned anything before—she had always rented. It all seemed so…adult. Everything was happening so quickly that she hoped she had made the right decision. She vaguely remembered hearing somewhere that you were supposed to look at at least eight places before buying a house. This was only the second place she'd been to; maybe it was the wrong move. But every bone in her body was telling her it was right.

"Are you okay?" The voice came from the walkway of the house attached to hers on the right.

Meg took a deep breath before answering. Lost in thought, she hadn't realized she was still just standing two feet in front of the doorway, keys in her hand. She turned to see a girl about her age, with long curly hair pulled into a ponytail and curves that were visible beneath running shorts and a long-sleeve shirt. "Yeah. Whew." She breathed out audibly. "Just a little overwhelmed, I guess. I just bought this place. And I don't know, I'm kind of freaking out a little."

"Well, welcome. I'm Lexi. I live here," the girl said, nodding to the door she had been about to walk through.

"Hi, I'm Meg." She waved.

"Do you need help with something?" the new neighbor offered, rather sincerely, Meg thought.

She blew out another breath before answering. "No, I'm okay. I really just brought a few things over. I'm moving my stuff in this weekend, but I wanted to come by and make sure the keys worked and everything." She jingled the key ring.

"Well, you should probably check, then." Lexi smiled as she crossed the small lawn between the two houses. "Usually it's a big square key for the top lock." She took the keys from Meg. "This one, here."

Meg inserted the square key into the top hole and felt the lock slide smoothly to the left. She pushed open the door and instantly knew that her first instinct had been correct. Although she couldn't quite explain why, this was the right place for her. She contained her goofy grin and turned around to say thanks, but Lexi was already gone.

Shoving her keys in her pocket, she stepped across the threshold into her new home. She moved through the house precisely, remembering each detail as she had seen it the first time—the only time, actually—prior to plunking down her life's savings on it. As she passed through each room, she felt a calm coming over her body. She completely surveyed the first floor before climbing the stairs to the bedrooms. At the back of the house, she looked out the window at her tiny decked yard and couldn't help but remember the view from the first apartment she'd considered and the events of the clear June morning that had led her here.

Three months ago, Meg had paced the hardwood floors of a different apartment, giddy with nervous anticipation at the sheer possibility that she might be standing in her new home. From the window of the apartment on the twelfth floor, she stared at the lush treetops outlining the edges of Prospect Park while the Realtor and her sort-of girlfriend Becca murmured their approval from behind her. The view was unbelievable. It struck Meg that it was exactly like something you'd find on a postcard in one of those New York City souvenir shops.

The new construction high-rise was located in the heart of Brooklyn's Park Slope—prime real estate—a few short blocks from the park, mere steps from the bars and restaurants that she and her friends were constantly in and out of. Meg knew in an instant that if she bought the apartment, she would certainly have a lock on all the pre- and post-parties and, of course, Becca would love it. But the apartment only had one bedroom and she could barely afford it at that.

She might have actually taken the plunge if Becca hadn't been so goddamn adamant that it was worth the cost, none of which she would be contributing to, of course. Meg had brought Becca with her to see the apartment, figuring that's what you did with the girl you were dating. Plus she knew that Becca would go crazy for it. And secretly she hoped it might help push their relationship to the next level. It was a bad plan, and deep down she knew it. As it happened, Becca's remarks during the walk-through sealed the deal anyway.

"It's worth it. It's totally worth it. I mean *whatever* you're paying for it—it's worth it." She must have said it thirty times.

Probably if Becca had said *I love you*, it might have actually been worth it to Meg. But she didn't. Instead, she said *It's worth it* over and over. And finally, it occurred to Meg that it wasn't.

Their relationship ended pretty much right after they left that apartment. It hadn't even been that big an argument.

"You're not going to take it, are you?" Becca had more than asked, with a puss on her face.

"No, I don't think so."

"Why not?"

"Look, it's gorgeous. But it's a ton of money and it's actually not any bigger than the place I have now."

"But it's worth it." There it was again.

Apparently even the Realtor knew it wasn't going to work out for Meg and the apartment, or for Meg and Becca. Later that same night, she got a call from the woman, saying she knew of a listing she thought Meg would like. It was located in Staten Island. She made Meg promise to at least look at it before saying no.

Now, leaning on the window ledge of her new master bedroom, Meg laughed to herself, snapping out of the memory. She looked up with a smile, realizing she could see the top of the Verrazano Bridge, stretching the span from Staten Island to Brooklyn. In all her years growing up here, she had never noticed how pretty it looked with the sun setting over the Narrows. She crossed over to the sliding glass doors and stepped out onto her balcony—her balcony!—and rested her body weight on the wrought-iron railing, indulging in the irony. Here in Staten Island, she had a hot neighbor, who looked to be about her age and seemed friendly too. She had her own house—okay, it was a town house, but it sported three bedrooms and her own backyard. Most importantly it was set in the middle of a *frigging* lesbian community that she never even knew existed.

Meg's problem had never been with Staten Island, per se. She had always kind of loved the *idea* of Staten Island. Located south of Manhattan and Brooklyn, Staten Island was the smallest of the five boroughs which made up New York City and it was the most suburban in feel. She had spent the first eighteen years of her life here, and her sister and brother-in-law had settled here permanently after they got married. Plus, New York City was a mere thirty minutes away. So, theoretically, she liked Staten Island. She just never really felt like she belonged here. Because for all its proximity to the Big Apple, Meg knew firsthand that Staten Island was really more small town than big city. And the problem with small towns is, when you're a big gay, you stick out.

It was why she swore to herself that once she got out, she would never move back.

And yet, here she was.

Meg walked into one of the spare bedrooms at the front of the house, still reeling from it all. She shook her head, totally flabbergasted that she was suddenly a resident of Bay West, a lesbian enclave comprising 400 town-house-style condominiums on thirty acres of land at the tip of the island, just under the bridge. She was still floored that a place like this existed at all, let alone in small-town, traditional Staten Island. She shook her head again. She might never understand how it came to be, or how she had missed it for so long. Right now, she was just happy to be part of it.

Because as she looked out the window to the street down below, she spotted three women dressed in bikini tops and shorts, obviously heading toward the pool. As her gaze trailed their tanned legs, Meg was overcome with one single thought:

Now, this place—*this* was going to be worth it.

CHAPTER TWO

Meg looked around the room filled with cardboard boxes and wondered where exactly to start. She hated moving, every part of it. Sure there was the whole fresh-start element, but right now nothing about it felt fresh or new. That wouldn't happen until rooms were painted and pictures hung. Unpacking boxes was just work. Perhaps her cynicism was the result of just having gone through this exact process a year ago, when she re-moved-in to her Brooklyn apartment after subletting it while she was away at grad school for a year. In that year, she had moved to Philadelphia, gotten her MBA, moved back to Brooklyn, started a new job as a management consultant—really a new job within her continued place of employment, but still—and it had involved a lot of packing and unpacking.

Searching for a distraction, she glanced out the window and saw one of her neighbors, a woman named Jesse, working on her car in the driveway. She sighed to herself. It had started off so well when she had met Jesse two weeks earlier, on her move-in day.

With all the relocating Meg had done in the last year, she fancied herself an expert. Rather than wasting her hard-earned cash on professional movers, she opted to do it herself. She guilted her brother-in-law Matt into service but had apparently underestimated the amount of brute force it took to lug all of your worldly possessions, including one pretty big couch, down five flights of stairs. By the time they got to Bay West, both she and Matt were beat. They might not have actually been able to finish if Jesse had not come to their aid.

It happened as they were not-so-deftly maneuvering the couch from the U-Haul and fumbling toward the front door. A tallish brunette dressed in gym clothes ran over and put her hands under the base of the couch at the middle. She ushered them toward the house and grabbed the front door, holding it open.

"Is it just the two of you?" the stranger asked, as the three of them manipulated the couch through the opening.

"Yeah," Meg managed to breathe out.

"Hold on, let me just throw my stuff down and I'll help you with the rest."

And with that, her neighbor had helped move all of Meg's furniture, boxes, and the random junk one acquires over twenty-six years into the house.

It wasn't until her third trip from the moving truck that the stranger took a break to introduce herself. "I'm Jesse, by the way. I live at one-fifty-two across the street." She pointed as she used a shirtsleeve to wipe the sweat from her temple.

"Sorry. I'm Meg. Megan McTiernan." She knew it sounded overly formal the second it came out of her mouth. She tried to breeze past it. "This is my brother-in-law, Matt." Meg glared at her brother-in-law, who had barely contained his laughter. "Thank you so much for helping us."

"No problem, Megan McTiernan," Jesse had said with a friendly wink. "Come on, let's get those last few boxes."

Meg was pretty embarrassed, but not at all surprised. She could always count on herself to make a mess of a perfectly normal conversation with a pretty girl.

After everything was unloaded, Jesse hovered outside for a few minutes, giving Meg a rundown of the community. Logistics, really. She told her about the softball field, the tennis court, the dog run. She said their block was the best location within the development because of its proximity to the pool and the Commons building. When she mentioned offhandedly that she had lived at Bay West for over ten years, Meg was completely thrown because up to that point she figured they were roughly the same age. Meg tried not to stare as she conducted a thorough once-over. Meg was five-six, and Jesse had her by at least three inches. Her short brown hair was wavy and wild but showed no grays peeking through anywhere. She had nice eyes, an unusual moss-green color, and olive skin with no hint of laugh lines. Doing some quick math, Meg estimated early thirties, at the most.

Jesse seemed relaxed, straightforward, and in no rush to leave, but as they stood just outside the front door chatting easily, a car barreled to the curb aggressively, blocking the U-Haul in the driveway. The door opened and out sauntered Kameron Browne, president of the Bay West board. Meg remembered Kameron from her interview. She was big, brash, and bossy, not the kind of person easily forgotten.

"Just figured I'd come by to officially welcome you to the community," Kameron offered to Meg. She looked right past Jesse, barely acknowledging her presence as she greeted her coolly. "Jesse."

"Kam," Jesse echoed back, just as icily, before turning back to Meg. "Well, I gotta run. See you around, Meg." Before Meg could even respond, Jesse was halfway to her house.

Kameron handed Meg a contact sheet with the names and email addresses of the board members listed on one side and a calendar of events at the development on the other. Meg had about a million questions but didn't get a chance to ask even one. Kameron darted off to her car, speeding away from the curb just as obnoxiously as she had arrived, leaving Meg standing on the lawn by herself.

Matt took the first opportunity he could to rip on her. "So, Megan McTiernan, is that how you greet all the ladies?"

Really what annoyed Meg when she remembered that day wasn't that she'd acted like a dork when she introduced herself. She was used to that. Eating away at her was the feeling she had been given another opportunity to make a friend in the neighborhood but hadn't closed the deal. So far she had been living at Bay West for two weeks and had exactly two social interactions with the locals—first with Lexi next door, and then with Jesse across the street—and both had ended too quickly to even form the foundation of a real friendship. And she could really use a gay friend. Since her breakup with Becca, she had lost her entire social circle as well as her girlfriend. Okay, they were all Becca's friends first, and she never really expected to stay close with any of them, not really. But still she missed being included in whatever they were up to. This was part of the reason Bay West appealed to her. Certainly in a community of lesbians, she would be able to find a few friends. The fact that she might find a girlfriend in such a target-rich environment had crossed her mind too. Start small, she reminded herself.

Looking out her window today, she saw Jesse's feet hanging out of the rear driver's side door of her black SUV, her lean body stretched along the backseat. Meg wished she had the confidence to march across the street and strike up a conversation with Jesse, offer her help with her project, return the favor for helping her move, and foster the friendship she'd felt budding beneath the surface. The more she watched, the clearer it was that Jesse was struggling with whatever it was she was doing. Jesse had just plucked the owner's manual out of the glove box, giving it a quick scan before retreating to her house and returning with a screwdriver and wrench. Meg thought those tools seemed an odd choice for auto repair, but since she didn't know anything about cars herself, she certainly couldn't go over and critique her new neighbor—that would be just plain rude. Meg sighed, wishing she knew something, *anything* really about cars at all, something to give her a natural segue.

But she didn't.

Turning back to her boxes, she whispered under her breath, "Come on, Megan McTiernan, back to work."

❖

Lexi Russo was sitting at her dining room table, surveying the scene playing out beyond her window.

She glanced away from her laptop and over her shoulder for what was probably the hundredth time. For the last half hour she'd been watching the woman across the street struggle to completely collapse the backseat of her luxury Range Rover Sport. For the life of her, she could not figure out how in the name of God her neighbor was having so much trouble.

Her neighbor. In a few days, her boss. Her nerves rattled as she thought about it. Her mothers' former friend. Jesse Ducane was many things. Apparently handy was not one of them.

Lexi turned back to the computer and tried futilely to focus. Mere seconds passed before she peered out the window again. "Really, a screwdriver?" she muttered, forgetting she wasn't alone.

"What's that, honey?" her mom said from the kitchen across the open-plan space.

"Nothing, Mom."

"Are you nervous, honey?" The sound of a knife against a cutting board punctuated the question. "For your internship and everything?"

"Huh?" Lexi was only half listening, still utterly involved in the show outside. "Um, I don't know. I guess a little," she lied. She was terrified about starting her new internship, working for smart, sexy Jesse Ducane, whom she had idolized since she was a teenager.

"You know it's not too late to back out."

Both of Lexi's mothers had been dead set against her applying for an internship at Stanton Ducane, the law firm run by their neighbor, but Marnie had been relentless in her efforts to dissuade Lexi. The internship started next week and she was still lobbying hard.

"It kind of is." Lexi raised an eyebrow, challenging her mother. "Anyway, I don't want to," she added, sounding more defiant than she wanted. "I still don't understand what you guys have against her." She shook her head dismissively. "If nobody bothers to explain it to me..." She left the remark open-ended in hopes that it would elicit an explanation as to why both her mothers objected so staunchly to Lexi's good fortune, scoring an internship at the reputable up-and-coming law firm.

Instead, her mother remained silent, shuffling dinner ingredients around the countertop, deliberately avoiding eye contact. Lexi pushed the envelope. "Seriously, Mom, what is the big deal? You used to be friends, you know." Lexi'd meant to simply point out the fact, but it came out as a kind of taunt.

Marnie's head snapped up. "That's exactly why I wish you would listen to me." Her voice was clipped but controlled. "I know her, Lexi. She's not a good person." Looking back down, she reached for an onion, just barely maintaining her composure. "I know you think she's the cat's meow because she has a successful business, but that's not everything."

Lexi exhaled audibly, unable to cloak her chagrin. "I don't think she's the cat's meow, Mom," she said, rolling her eyes at the archaic expression. "I think, actually I *know*," she corrected, "that she's an outstanding lawyer. I don't know why you wouldn't want me to work for her."

"Because she's a sleaze." Lexi was taken aback by Marnie's contemptuous response. "She has no integrity, no sense of what's right.

Which is probably why she's successful at what she does." Marnie placed the knife down on the chopping block and walked over to the dining room table. She leaned her arms against the chair across from where Lexi sat, bent her head, and met Lexi's eyes.

"I know you won't be *that* kind of lawyer, that's not who you are." Her voice was softer now. "You are sweet and compassionate and kind." Her mother gave her a reassuring smile as she said it, but Lexi saw her purse her lips again as she turned away. "So I'm sorry, honey, but I just can't fathom what you could possibly learn from that kind of person."

Her mother had it all wrong there. Jesse's law firm did amazing things for all sorts of people. Lexi had done her research—more than half of Stanton Ducane's cases focused on civil rights issues. She had explained this fact to her parents when they initially protested her decision to apply for the position, and several times since then. She didn't have the energy for it today. With a long sigh, she checked out the window again as she closed the laptop and stood up.

"I'm going to take Butter out for a walk," Lexi said halfheartedly. Really she just wanted out of the conversation. Plus, she was still dying to get outside and get a closer look at Jesse.

As she put the leash on the old golden retriever, Lexi's mind wandered to a scenario where this impromptu walk resulted in an opportunity to assist Jesse. She could do it for sure. Since she was a kid, she had watched as her other mother Chris, an automotive engineer, fixed every car in the development. This informal education meant Lexi was naturally adept at auto repair. Whether the problem was with the engine or the electrical system, she could fix it. Jesse's current problem would be a ground ball for Lexi. She'd already assessed the high-end vehicle from a distance, factored for the make and model, and roughly estimated the year, and she was fairly certain the seat adjustment involved releasing a tether before pressing the button located underneath the base of the backseat.

In her fantasy, Lexi helped Jesse out and they shared a laugh, breaking the ice before next week's internship started. As she walked down the street, though, she knew she would never be able to pull off something so bold as approaching Jesse out of the blue. After all, she had lived across the street from the woman practically her whole life, and she barely had the nerve to smile or nod when they crossed paths.

In the warm autumn air, Lexi pondered her imminent future. She was nervous about her internship, sure. But she would be nervous no matter where she was working or whom for. That's just who she was. There was an added level of anxiety, too, that involved needing to prove herself to Jesse Ducane. She knew part of the reason was tied to the bad blood between her parents and Jesse. But it wasn't like Marnie thought. She wasn't acting out, staging some kind of rebellion. Jesse Ducane's law firm was one of the premier boutique firms in the city, and she just wanted to make a good impression.

While this was true, Lexi knew her motives weren't purely academic. Jesse Ducane intrigued her. When she was honest with herself, she acknowledged this small truth. Jesse was gorgeous and successful and completely out of her league. And even though there weren't that many years between them—twelve, max, if Lexi's calculations were right—that was enough. Enough that Lexi's fantasies would never amount to anything more, and enough, she feared, that Jesse would still see her as a kid instead of a twenty-four-year-old law student.

As she walked along, she convinced herself this was exactly why she had to approach Jesse today. She needed to show her she wasn't uptight like Marnie or even totally laid back like Chris. She was her own person. She would just walk over to her car and offer to help. It was simple. Jesse was having trouble and Lexi could fix it. They would be working together in a week. This was a nice friendly gesture, and one that would signal that Lexi was neutral in the cold war between her parents and her boss.

From halfway down the block, Lexi plotted her strategy. She could see the seats were still in place in their upright position, and Jesse wasn't even trying to budge them. Now she was standing with her hands on the closed hood, her shoulders hunched up, her clenched jaw and steely gaze revealing her frustration as she fixated on the hood of the car, obviously having thrown in the towel. Perfect. Lexi quickened her pace. She was less than twenty feet away, and her pulse was racing as she struggled to select the right opener from the ones playing out in her head.

Then it happened. Jesse looked up at Lexi and made definite eye contact. Bravely, Lexi curled her mouth up in a smile and raised her arm in a small wave. She watched Jesse's shoulders drop and her face relax as the corners of her eyes crinkled a little, a curious expression overtaking her demeanor. Jesse licked her lips and opened her mouth and Lexi could swear she was about to say something, but at that precise moment, a white Lexus turned the corner and pulled into the parking space right in front of Jesse's house, stealing her attention. A tall blonde got out of the driver's seat and called out to Jesse as she bounded up the driveway.

"Miss me?"

Lexi couldn't hear the answer, but she saw Jesse's face light up as she spoke and watched as the blonde cracked up with laughter in response.

With her plan sabotaged, Lexi crossed back to her side of the street and hurried to get in her front door. In her peripheral vision though, she could see the two women were hugging. She dared one last look and caught her breath at what she saw. Jesse's arms were wrapped around the blonde, and her chin rested on the woman's shoulder, but Jesse's clear green eyes were looking right at her.

CHAPTER THREE

Meg threw open the screen door and hustled out onto the deck. She was determined to use the barbecue at least once before summer was officially over. She just barely made it over to her sister's hand-me-down table and chairs without dropping all her utensils and her beer.

"Okay, grill, let's see what you've got." Hopefully some gas, she realized as kind of an afterthought.

Meg had been so busy with her new job in the last few weeks that everything else had pretty much taken a backseat. Unfortunately, that included setting up her new place and exploring the development and its residents too. One of these days she would make some new friends, she promised herself, trying not to get down about it.

At least the grill fired up without a problem. She opened her beer and sat down in the late afternoon sun, waiting for the grill to heat up. This really wasn't so bad, she thought, taking a swig of the cold beer. It was true she hadn't made any inroads into actually being part of the Bay West community, but at least she was still physically here. Nobody had come to take her keys back and give her spot to a better lesbian, one with an active social life or even a real live girlfriend.

"Hey, neighbor."

The voice startled her even though she recognized it right away. It was the girl from the first day. She'd been so busy feeling sorry for herself, she hadn't realized she had company in the adjacent backyard.

"Hey." Meg took her legs off the chair and turned toward the voice. "What's up?" She swallowed hard, immediately annoyed at herself for her lame, clichéd response.

"I'm Lexi, in case you forgot. I helped you with your key a while back…?"

"No, no, I remember. You just surprised me. I didn't realize you were out here."

"I would have said hi sooner but I was on the phone." She waved the cell phone as she walked across her own deck and leaned on the wooden railing that separated their yards. "Sometimes I come out here for privacy." She rolled her eyes and nodded toward her house. "So, how do you like it?" Lexi said with a huge smile on her face.

Meg froze for a second, embarrassed that she hadn't really experienced anything to like or dislike since their initial meeting a few weeks ago. She tried to play it cool. "It's good. I'm still trying to unpack half my stuff and get everything organized, but it's good."

"But how do you like *Bay West*?" Lexi asked the question with a knowing smirk, as if they were both in on a secret, because they kind of were.

"Um, it's good." Meg nodded her head to make up for the hesitation in her voice. She had never been a good liar. She shrugged. "Honestly, I haven't actually been around that much. I just started this new job. Well, not new, but sort of new. It's a long story." She shook her head at her habit of rambling. "Anyway, I haven't met anybody here or anything. I mean, except for you. Twice now. But you seem really nice," she joked, remembering after it was already out that she had also met Jesse from across the street. She wondered if Lexi knew her too.

"Oh, so you don't know anybody that lives here already?" Lexi asked with a note of surprise.

"No. Is that usually how it works?"

"I think so. I don't know, though, now that I think about it. It just feels like everybody here knows each other. It's like a word-of-mouth kind of thing." Lexi paused and seemed to consider her words. "So how *did* you end up here? Are you from Staten Island or something?"

"Actually, yeah. But I never knew this place was here. I've been living in Brooklyn for the last, like, seven years, since after my first year of college, and I was looking to buy a place. I was really only looking in Brooklyn, but my Realtor brought me out here." She smiled a little awkwardly as she raised the bottle to her lips.

"Hey, do you think she knew about it because she's gay or because she's a Realtor?" Lexi quipped.

Meg laughed. "You know, I never even thought about it. I was so overwhelmed by the whole thing. She said something in passing about an all-women community"—Meg shook her head, reminded of her own obliviousness—"but she totally passed over the main attraction and focused on how close it was to the city. She kept going on about it being right under the bridge, practically Brooklyn—that was her selling point." Meg smiled, giving a halfhearted vocal impression of the Realtor's blasé attitude. "It was probably a good move, because there's no way I would have believed her anyway, and her pitch did get me to look at the place." She leaned against the shared railing, resting her beer bottle on top of it, resisting the urge to peel at the label. "Anyway, I got here and started noticing all the little nuances. A rainbow flag here, bumper sticker there. But I still thought it was probably my imagination. Then, when we got to this town house"—Meg nodded toward her own unit—"this other woman met us to show us around. At first I thought that she was the seller, but it turned out she's one of the board members. That's when it started to sink in. She kept mentioning that there were all types of women here—families, couples, everything. As she was showing me around, she kept pointing to houses, saying *her wife* this, and *her wife* that. That's when I finally got it."

Lexi smiled knowingly. "The woman who showed you the house, her name was Mary, right?" Her voice was certain as she continued. "About forty, dirty-blond hair, down to about here?" She touched her own shoulder to indicate the length.

"Yeah, I think so."

Lexi smiled. "That's Mary Brown. That was your preliminary interview."

"You mean they were checking me out before they even knew if I was interested in buying the place?"

Lexi shook Meg off. "I think it's like, they want to make sure you're a normal person and stuff." She chewed at her full lower lip as she continued. "And also that you're actually gay. Supposedly, Mary's the best at judging people cold." Lexi paused for a second, considering. "Also, the thing with Mary is she's just really nice. I bet she does a good job of not scaring people away."

"So do you have to get a certain number of votes or something to get in?" Meg asked, still trying to understand the process.

Lexi shook her head, even though she wasn't entirely sure herself.

"I don't think so. I don't think it's a popularity contest or anything. I think the main thing that they're concerned with is you are who you say you are. You know, that you're gay and not an imposter or a voyeur or something. Like I said before, most people know somebody who lives here, so they have an automatic reference." She shrugged. "If you're completely new, I think they just want to be careful. That's when either Mary or Kameron comes to meet you to do a prescreen before the big board meeting. Be happy you got Mary. They're both nice, but Kam can be kind of intimidating."

Meg swallowed the urge to call Lexi out on that particular understatement, but instead moved on to more neutral ground. "So did this Mary person do your walk-through-slash-interview too?" she asked.

"Oh no. I didn't, I mean, I don't…I live here with my parents. My moms," she added.

"Oh, right. Okay." Meg was a little confused at first, and then totally disappointed as it registered. She glanced at the back of the house attached to hers, Lexi's house—Lexi's parents' house, really—and saw it extended a full floor above her own. Of course Meg knew that already. But now it made sense. As an end unit, it was much bigger than Meg's. All of the end and corner units were three floors, buttressing the two-floor units that ran between them. It made for a nice design for the development, giving it not only balance but also sort of a palatial look. Now Meg understood that the larger town houses served a functional purpose as well. They were designed for more people, a full family. She hoped her face didn't show her disappointment and embarrassment that she had simply taken for granted that Lexi was gay. After all, it wasn't that strange of an assumption, all things considered. And Meg hadn't said anything too revealing. But she felt stupid anyway.

"So…your parents are gay," Meg offered, attempting to push through her awkwardness and focus on the positive. "I just figured you owned the house. It was stupid, I guess." Meg hoped this covered the apology that she couldn't muster for assuming Lexi was a lesbian.

"No, it's okay. Please, I wish I owned this house," Lexi said wistfully. "No, I live here with my moms, my sister, and my two little brothers. But someday I hope to live here. I mean, not this house, my parents are never going to leave." She chuckled. "I just hope that someday, I would love to have my own house here. Bay West is awesome. I doubt there's anyplace like it in the world."

Meg couldn't hold it in. "Wait, I'm confused. I thought you had to be gay to live here. Is there some kind of grandfathering-in clause if you're from a gay family or something?"

Lexi burst out laughing. "No, no. I don't think so." She collected herself but continued to grin. "I'm sorry, I should have been more clear. I *am* gay. My parents are also gay, but I'm gay too. Wow, that explains the look on your face. It's priceless."

Meg let out a deep breath. "I mean not that it matters or anything, but you were my only gay friend here, and then you weren't gay. I'm just glad to have you back." She revealed her true smile.

"You're funny."

"Hey, I never even offered you a beer. Want one?" Meg started toward the house.

"No, thanks. We're actually going to my aunt's house for my cousin's birthday. They're probably all waiting for me. Rain check, though?" Lexi backed away from the railing toward her house.

"Sure."

As she was just about to pull the sliding glass door open, Lexi turned around. "Actually, my friend Sam and I are going to The Kitchen, Friday night. You should come."

"I don't want to crash your date or anything," Meg said, hoping she hadn't just killed her one social opportunity in recent months.

"Oh my God, not at all. Sam Miller is practically my sister. We've known each other since first grade. We've both got a crazy week coming up. I'm starting my new internship, she has some major project due at work. So we figure Friday, we'll reward ourselves. You should totally come celebrate with us."

"Okay, I'm definitely in then."

"Great. Give me your number and I'll put it in my phone right now. I'll text you with the details during the week."

"Great." They exchanged numbers. "Have fun at your aunt's."

"Yep, see you later."

"Later, Lexi." Meg headed through the sliders to grab the burger she had promised herself. She treated herself to another beer. She could hardly stop smiling even as she cooked her dinner for one.

CHAPTER FOUR

L exi sat at the conference table, thoroughly prepared for what the next forty-five minutes would entail. She lined up the legal pad in front of her and placed her reliable black rollerball pen on top, ready to take notes.

In a minute, Laney Stanton, the other half of Stanton Ducane, would enter the boardroom with Allison Smith, the only remaining junior partner who had yet to be assigned an intern. Placement meetings for the interns had started yesterday afternoon and were finishing up today, with Lexi rounding out the bunch. While it had kept her in anticipation, being last had its perks too. At least she knew the routine already from the other students. The meeting would be facilitated by Laney Stanton, who would go over some general guidelines of what was expected by the senior staff, and then turn it over to the junior partner, who would dole out his or her list of requirements. Based on what she had heard, the list varied drastically with each junior partner. But Allison Smith's reputation preceded her. Word had trickled down from the first-year associates to the interns by the middle of the week—Allison Smith was notoriously brutal to work for.

Adding to this particular run of bad luck, Lexi was totally bummed that in this entire first week of her internship, she had yet to even clap eyes on Jesse Ducane. Rumor had it she was working on some major case out of town which had kept her away from the office.

At least she had tonight to look forward to. Lexi made a mental note to text Sam and Meg after her meeting to firm up what time they would leave for The Kitchen. She was just starting to think about what she was going to wear when she heard the hollow sound of the conference room's glass door opening behind her.

Lexi straightened up and turned slightly in her chair, preparing to greet the two lawyers formally. Instead, she froze. Mouth agape, she watched Jesse Ducane enter the room alone, the door latching closed behind her as she cruised past Lexi and took the seat directly across from her.

Without a word, Jesse took off her dark gray suit jacket and hung it neatly over the chair. She placed a thin folder on the table and next to it the shiniest red apple Lexi had ever seen. Jesse opened the folder and silently perused the document in front of her.

Lexi looked at the clock on the wall and checked the door behind her again, wondering if somehow she was in the wrong place.

"Somewhere to be, Ms. Russo?" Jesse flashed a look from under her dark lashes, a wave of brown hair covering her raised eyebrows as she waited for an answer.

Lexi felt her mouth open, but nothing came out. She was paralyzed by Jesse's stare, those fucking incredible eyes that had locked with hers less than a week ago on the street. "I…uh, no. No, I'm sorry. No."

"Well, then. Let's get started," Jesse began. "As I'm sure you've figured out by now, you will be working with Allison Smith. Unfortunately, she couldn't be here today, as she is covering a meeting for me." Jesse spoke evenly, continuing to read the page in front of her. "This meeting is meant to be an introduction to the firm, to give you an idea of what will be expected of you, and of course to address any questions you might have at this point." Here she paused, looked up at Lexi, and waited.

Lexi remained silent, not really sure what, if anything, she was supposed to say at this point.

Jesse obviously accepted this to mean she had no questions and began outlining the particulars of the internship and the background of the firm.

Lexi couldn't help but be distracted by Jesse's long elegant fingers as she touched the edges of the file and fingered the short stem of the apple next to it as she spoke. Lexi forced herself not to think about what those hands might feel like on her skin, instead focusing intently as Jesse gave a brief but personal synopsis of the entire staff, complete with mini-bios. She finished with an homage to Allison Smith that painted her as both a genius and a saint, directly contrasting with everything Lexi had heard about her.

Lexi was still using every ounce of composure to cover her shock at actually sitting across from Jesse. She had none left to mask her surprise at Jesse's glowing endorsement of Allison Smith.

"Judging from the look on your face, you've heard otherwise." Jesse cocked her head to one side and leaned back in her chair, clearly waiting for a response.

Lexi tried to answer. But she was having trouble finding the words. Any words. She could feel her hands starting to sweat as she fidgeted nervously with her pen. She knew she was taking too long. "No, of course not," she spluttered out, realizing immediately that it was at once too little and too much.

Jesse pounced on her flimsy answer. "Well, Alexis, let that be your first lesson. Don't believe everything you hear. Get the facts yourself. Make your own decisions." There was something beyond condescending in her tone as she said it; it almost sounded like annoyance.

Lexi clenched her jaw as she felt the telltale tingle in her throat. A mix of anger and embarrassment. The twinge was always the first sign that she was about to lose it completely.

Perhaps Jesse noticed it too, because her demeanor softened. "Look, I know she has a reputation. And she is tough. But Allison is an excellent attorney. She'll make you work hard, but you'll be a better lawyer for it. Just don't take for granted the opportunity to learn from her."

There was silence as Lexi acknowledged Jesse's advice with a simple nod. It was the only thing she had done right so far.

"All right then, moving on. I'm sure you've heard the rumors that Stanton Ducane will be putting on two first-year associates next year. Those hires will likely come from this pool of interns. So you know what that means."

Everyone knew what it meant. It meant the entire internship was a competition for the two slots. With eight interns and two positions, there really wasn't room for error. And Lexi had just blown a meeting with the senior partner.

"Do you have any questions, Alexis?" Jesse picked up the apple and inspected it, the act indicating that the meeting was over.

"No." Lexi cut directly to the point so she didn't make another unnecessary flub.

"Okay, then. You are free to go."

Lexi stood up quickly and smoothed the wrinkles from her skirt. She collected her pen and pad and pushed the boardroom chair to the table before she took the few steps to the door. She was seconds from safety, her hand on the handle.

"One more thing, Alexis."

Lexi felt her stomach tighten at the sound of her full name, again, as she turned around.

Jesse was eyeing the apple, as if about to take a bite, but shifted her gaze to Lexi. "Why did you apply to work here?"

Lexi was startled by the starkness of the question. This was ground covered in the initial interview, which she had done with Laney Stanton, months ago. Lexi looked at Jesse blankly, not really sure how to proceed.

Jesse swayed a little in the large chair. "There are hundreds of law firms in the city. Bigger, more prestigious firms. You're at the top of your class. Why Stanton Ducane?"

Lexi wanted to say a lot of things. She wished she had the nerve. She would start by shoving Jesse's lecture right back in her face, telling her she chose Stanton Ducane because she was the type of person who made her own decisions and got her own facts. That instead of simply listening to her parents'—and other Bay West residents', by the way—insistence that Jesse Ducane was a typical arrogant lawyer, an opportunist, and a swindler, she had decided to find out for herself. She'd ignored the local rumors and hearsay, choosing instead to research the company and their cases, and had come to her own conclusions. In the end, she was so impressed and intrigued by what she had discovered, that she needed to be a part of it firsthand. That's what she might have said, if she had any balls.

But she had already choked so badly that she felt she had no choice but to take the safest route possible, giving the cookie-cutter answer that she had prepared for every interview since college. "Stanton Ducane is an excellent firm. You do solid, gratifying work. It's an honor to be a part of it at any level."

"Okay." Jesse crunched into the apple dismissively, clearly unimpressed by the response.

Lexi didn't exhale until she was halfway down the corridor. Drinks tonight couldn't come soon enough.

❖

The Kitchen was practically an institution in New York City. It was an enormous bar, packed no matter the day or hour. It catered to all ages, types, and styles of lesbians—girly-girls, tomboys, young, old, butch, femme, middle-of-the-roaders, and the vast majority that didn't fit a particular category at all. Meg always found that to be part of its charm, that there seemed to be room for everyone. She had only been there once since she and Becca broke up. For about ten minutes. It was during that experience that she learned being single was not like it is in the movies, when you walk into the bar by yourself and immediately make eye contact with some hot girl standing in the corner, who's sipping a cocktail like she's been waiting for you to get there. Not so. Pretty much if you came in by yourself, everybody figured that nobody else wanted to be with you. It didn't make you a hot commodity; it made you the plague.

Which is why tonight was so important to Meg.

She had spent forever trying to get her hair to look normal. Not that it looked abnormal, just that Meg always felt it didn't really suit her. It was a color that Meg's grandmother called true brown, which she wore in a chin-length sweep, framing her face. The old woman used to say it perfectly matched her true-brown eyes. Meg was never comforted by her grandmother's completely transparent way of trying to make her feel better about her boring looks. Her sister was real black Irish—dark brown hair, light blue eyes. Meg was insanely jealous.

After being ready for over an hour, Meg walked out of her house promptly at eight to meet the girls. She hated being late for anything. Of course she knew her eagerness worked against her in most social situations, but she couldn't help it. She often reminded herself there were many people in the world who considered punctuality a good quality, but it always made her feel like a gigantic nerd. The fact that lateness was cool was a universal concept, yet she couldn't get herself to go there. So she pretty much always arrived exactly on time; it was her own little compromise with the world. Thankfully, she found

Lexi and her friend already waiting, resting against the Jeep in Lexi's driveway.

"Sorry, am I late?" Meg asked, one hundred percent sure she was not.

"Not at all," Lexi answered. "Meg, Sam. Sam, Meg."

Sam went for a cool nod, but it was too late, Meg had already extended her hand. She cringed a little on the inside for having done it, but Sam shook her hand nicely and gave a little smile too, restoring Meg's confidence.

"My sister is going to drive us to the ferry. Save us some time," Lexi stated matter-of-factly.

With the ride to the Staten Island Ferry, the girls made it into the city earlier than expected. They took their time getting the subway up to Greenwich Village, giving Sam an opportunity to tell them about the group of girls she had met at The Kitchen last week, whom they were slated to meet up with tonight.

"So it was like the end of the night, last Saturday. And I was getting ready to leave, when I notice these girls standing by the bar and I could swear they were talking about me. So I go over in their direction, pretending that I'm looking for my phone or my keys or something. And it worked because right away one of them says, *Hey, you look familiar, do you live at Bay West?* I say no, but my best friend does and I'm there all the time. And the one who started the conversation, who's totally hot by the way, says, *I know, I've seen you there.* I'm like, of course you have, I practically live there. And then I mention you, Lex, and how you grew up there, and that your moms are like these lesbian pioneers with this huge family—that I'm practically part of—and on and on."

Sam leaned off the curb at the corner of Fourteenth Street looking back at the other two as she waited for the light to change. She bounced off the sidewalk as soon as the walk signal flashed, pushing her honey-brown hair off her face as she crossed the street. Her long, slender fingers matched the rest of her physique. She was a few inches taller than Meg, and her jeans and loosely fitted graphic tee accentuated her wiriness. She was so animated in her storytelling that her hazel eyes twinkled as she talked. "And this other girl, not the blonde who had started the conversation, but one of her friends, who seemed kind of quiet, pipes up and says with, like, absolute awe in her voice, *Wait I know you. Your friend is the girl who's always running.* And I say yes, because the truth is you do run a lot." She tilted her head and looked at Lexi. "It's so cute, she totally has a crush on you."

"Did you ever think she might not be talking about me?" Lexi said, the lilt in her voice revealing she was genuinely flattered.

"No."

"You know I'm not the only person in the neighborhood who goes running. What if she expects someone else?"

"C'mon, Lex. She knew exactly who I was talking about. I described you. And let's face it, you are the only twenty-four-year-old obsessive runner with long dark curly hair, two moms, and huge boobs who lives in Bay West. Believe me, she's talking about you."

"So wait, I'm confused," Meg interjected. "How do these girls know who you are?"

"That's the beauty of it," Sam answered. "They live in the development. They live at Bay West. They're renters."

"Do you know about the renters?" Lexi turned to Meg.

"I know that the units at the edge of the development behind the service road are all rentals, if that's what you mean. Is there more to know?"

"No, I guess that's it," Lexi said.

"Except that since we were teenagers, Lexi and I have been trying to get in with the renters, get invited to their parties and stuff, and now it has actually happened," Sam said with excitement.

"The thing is," Lexi tried to explain, "growing up in the development, it was awesome, don't get me wrong." She shook her head adamantly. "Being gay and living with two moms in this unbelievable lesbian community, it's amazing, I know. And I am grateful for it, I really am, but in a way I'm not really part of it, because I grew up there." She shrugged, her voice maintaining its desperate sincerity. "I'm always Marnie and Chris's daughter, you know? It's like I'm not taken seriously or I can't grow up or something. It's weird." Her shoulders dropped. "It's like I'm still trying to fit in. Sam and I always figured the renters would be the ticket."

"But you don't live at Bay West, do you, Sam?" Meg asked.

"No, but Lexi and I were in first grade together. I went over to her house once and basically never left. Seriously though," Sam said with a laugh, "Chris and Marnie are like my second and third moms."

Lexi continued her explanation. "The great thing about the renters is they're usually younger and sort of transient. So they're not really part of the larger Bay West picture."

"Meaning, Lexi can just be Lexi. And I can be her available, charming friend," Sam finished.

"And these two are going to be there tonight?" Meg tried to sound casual.

"Yeah, I've been texting one of them all week. They're coming with a bunch of their friends." Sam said it just as they hit the bar, providing a natural end to their conversation as they showed their IDs to the bouncer.

They quickly settled in a corner in the back of the front room, each armed with a cold beer. Sam took off to do a lap, checking to see if the renters had arrived, leaving Lexi and Meg to themselves. Meg looked around, trying to absorb every last tidbit of the scene that she had been absent from for so many months.

"What's up, Meg? You're all smiles right now."

"Just happy," Meg answered. She took a sip of her beer. "I haven't been out in a while. It's good to be here." She tried to sound nonchalant, but she feared the enthusiasm in her voice probably gave away how excited she was to be here, with friends. Luckily Sam appeared in the archway and waved them into the back room, sparing Meg the opportunity to further display her dorkiness.

As promised, a small group of girls hovered near the back bar next to Sam, nursing their drinks, trying not to look too eager to meet Lexi and Meg. Sam introduced them both as "my friends who live at Bay West," which Meg was grateful for. She had been nervous that she would look like a hanger-on, but Sam's introduction instantly made her feel like she was part of their crew.

A dark-haired girl who had been introduced as Julie was the first to break the ice. "So you're the girl who grew up in the development," she said, focusing her attention entirely on Lexi.

"That's me." Lexi lifted her shoulders and raised her drink slightly in mock-toast to herself.

"So cool. What was that like?"

Meg and the other girls listened in as Lexi gave Julie and the rest of them a condensed history of being raised at Bay West by her two moms.

Somewhere along the way Sam and one of the other girls—the blonde—fell out of the group and into their own flirtatious conversation, leaving Meg and Lexi holding court with the others. And Sam had been on the money—Julie was totally crushing on Lexi, and from the looks of it, Lexi was into it too. The rest of the night followed pretty much the same pattern. There were drinks and dancing with breaks for talking here and there. When they weren't in the same conversation, she and Lexi and Sam checked in on each other frequently, and it felt to Meg like they were a team.

❖

At two fifteen, Lexi was telling Meg and a very drunk Sam, who was openly pawing the blonde, her plan to get home, which involved Julie's cousin, a city bus driver, picking them up on his final route and dropping them off at the condos.

"Hey, there's Jesse," Meg said completely interrupting her. "Looks like she's just getting here."

Lexi whipped around to look at the front entrance, before turning back to Meg. "You know her?" she said, a mix of surprise and envy in her tone.

"Yeah, she helped me move in."

"Really?"

"I'm going to say hi. We have a few minutes, right? Before we head out?" Meg started over in Jesse's direction, without waiting for an answer.

Lexi watched, mouth agape, as Meg approached Jesse easily and chatted for several minutes before coming back.

"What happened?" Lexi asked, too anxiously to go unnoticed.

"Nothing. She was nice. She invited me over to her house for, like, a pre-party to that fall festival thing. Are you guys going to that?"

"What?" Lexi stammered. "Are you gonna go? I mean, to her house?"

"I don't know. I guess so, I said I would." Meg frowned. "It's not for a few weeks, though, right? Why? Is there something wrong with her?"

"Nothing's wrong with her, Meg." Sam fielded the question before Lexi had a chance. "Lexi's just jealous."

"Of what?" Meg furrowed her eyebrows.

"She's jealous because she basically picked a career just to get a sit-down with Jesse, and you just did it in two seconds." Sam laughed at her own joke as she slurred out her words.

"Shut up, Sam." Lexi shot an annoyed look at her friend, not as amused as she was by the turn of events.

"What do you mean?" Meg asked.

"Nothing. She means nothing," Lexi said sharply. "She's being a jerk. Come on, let's go. Julie and the other girls are waiting for us outside, her cousin's bus will be coming down Seventh in a few minutes."

There was little conversation between them on the short walk to the bus stop. As soon as the bus arrived, Sam and the blonde—whose name Lexi still hadn't learned—slid into a seat all the way in the back, not even trying to keep their hands off each other. Meg parked herself in the front and played with her phone, while Lexi and Julie flirted with each other a few rows back. When they reached Staten Island, Julie's cousin diverted from his regular route and carefully maneuvered the bus through the network of streets that made up Bay West in order to drop the girls off directly in front of the rental section of the condos. Sam and the blonde were out of sight in seconds.

"I guess they're not wasting any time." Julie smirked as she watched their path to the house. Then she turned her attention back to Lexi and said with unmistakable hope in her voice, "Do you want to come in?"

"It's pretty late, I should go home," Lexi answered, but she still flirted with her eyes.

"I'll walk you, then," Julie offered as Meg stood by awkwardly in the background.

Lexi refused the offer, explaining that she and Meg lived next door to each other. Julie didn't seem to be too put out. She gave Lexi a quick kiss on the cheek and waved to Meg before she scooted off toward her unit.

"Sorry about that," Meg said as they headed toward a cut-through path that led to the main section of the development.

"Please, don't even." Lexi waved her off. "It's not like I was going to make out with her outside my parents' house."

"She seemed nice, though. You guys seemed to hit it off."

"Yeah, she is nice. We actually made plans for Thursday. So we'll see." Lexi shrugged and smiled. "What about you, did you have fun tonight?"

"Yeah, I did," Meg answered truthfully.

"Listen, about before with Jesse."

"Yeah?"

"Sorry I was a weirdo. It's just that Jesse's kind of my boss right now."

"What do you mean?"

"I'm in law school, a 3L, and right now I'm interning at her law firm."

"Oh." Meg nodded, and Lexi was relieved she seemed to accept the explanation. "Well, that's pretty cool, right?"

"I guess. I don't know. I had, like, a meeting with her today, and I kind of blew it. So I think I just freaked out tonight when I saw her there. And then Sam just acts like a jerk, saying all that stuff."

"Listen, don't worry about it. Sam was drunk, people say dumb things when they're drunk. And I'm sure your meeting with Jesse was fine. You're probably overthinking it."

"You think?" Lexi was unconvinced.

"Sure." Meg smiled. "And if not, I'm totally going to get all the dirt at her fall festival pre-party." Meg bumped Lexi's shoulder and smiled, as they reached their houses. "Hey, I want all the details on your date Thursday," Meg said, opening her front door.

"I'm sure you do." Lexi trailed off laughing, as they entered their separate houses.

CHAPTER FIVE

Meg was seventeen slides into her presentation and about three inches from her computer screen when she was startled by the hollow sound of tapping at her back patio door. She nearly hit the ceiling at the noise as she turned around to see Lexi already through the sliders and halfway into the living room.

"Hey, stranger. Saw your light on. You should lock this door, you know." Lexi padded casually across the room toward the counter where Meg was sitting.

"You almost gave me a fucking heart attack."

"Whatcha doing?" Lexi glanced at the laptop screen.

"Work." Meg put her hand over her chest, feeling it thump. "Holy shit, my heart is still racing."

"Oh my God, calm down. You live in a lesbian community. Who'd you think it was? The neighborhood militia, storming in to see if you're recycling properly?" Lexi laughed at her own joke as she plopped herself on a stool across from Meg.

"Ha-ha. Very funny."

"Seriously, what have you been up to? I've barely seen you in the last few weeks. I was shocked when I noticed you were home."

"I've been working. Like crazy hours. Still working right now, actually." Meg nodded toward the computer screen.

"So what do you do that you're working all the time?" Lexi asked.

"I work for a management consulting firm."

"What does that mean?" Lexi folded her arms on the counter and rested her head on them as she waited for an answer.

"My company is hired by other companies to provide consultation on how they operate and manage their businesses. Then we offer solutions—how to cut costs, provide better management, increase profit margin, things like that."

"Sounds fancy," Lexi teased.

"Yeah, consulting firms are basically the middlemen for companies that want to either fire people or downsize. Instead of doing it themselves, they hire us to do an analysis. Then they can blame us when they let their people go."

"That doesn't sound fun," Lexi said seriously.

"No, it's not all bad. I'm just cranky." Meg saved her presentation and twisted on her stool, giving Lexi her full attention. "A lot of times you get the chance to find alternative solutions and save people's jobs just by thinking outside the box. Then it's pretty cool." Meg continued, "I'm just in a bad mood because I've been working at this project nonstop and I feel like I'm not getting anywhere."

"You want me to go?" Lexi made no move to leave.

"No way. I need a break. What's up with you? How's things with Julie?" Meg waited for Lexi to bring her up to speed on her fledgling romance. Two and a half weeks ago, on the Saturday morning after her first date with Julie, Lexi had come over to Meg's with bagels and coffee and dissected the entire evening with Meg. Since that day, Meg and Lexi had slipped into a quick friendship, but their schedules had kept them at cross-purposes for a true gabfest.

"I don't know. Things are good, I guess."

Apparently, Lexi needed some coaxing. "Come on, Lex. Give me a little more than that. My whole life right now is Sullivan and Son, Inc." Meg pointed a thumb at her presentation.

Lexi sighed. "What do you want to know?"

"Uh…everything," Meg said teasingly, although they both knew she wasn't kidding. "But let's start with the easy stuff. What does she do?"

"Julie? She works for a Web media company, doing research, some writing."

"How old?"

"Your age, twenty-six or twenty-seven."

"You're not sure how old I am?" Meg asked, mock-hurt.

"No." Lexi laughed, shaking her head.

"I'm twenty-six, by the way. Just so you know," Meg chided her. "What else, what else? How many times have you gone out with her or hung out?"

Lexi rolled her eyes upward, counting in her head. "Like…five, I think."

"Did she meet your parents yet?" Meg knew that they both knew the significance of the answer.

"No way!" Lexi practically screamed. "Are you crazy? We are so not there yet."

"Okay, okay. Just checking."

They were both laughing. Meg loved their revelry. In all the years she had spent with Becca's friends, she had never struck up a friendship as real as what she had developed with Lexi in just a few weeks. Truthfully, in her whole life, she really hadn't ever had a friend she felt so herself with. Only her longtime friend Tracy, who had moved out West after high school, even came close. Meg felt like she could ask Lexi anything, so she did.

"So, how's the sex?"

"Don't know. Haven't done it," Lexi answered promptly, looking directly at Meg.

"Really?" Meg paused and then continued without filtering, "Wait, you haven't done it with Julie, or ever?"

"I've had sex, Meg," Lexi answered, a hint of faux annoyance in her voice. "With girls *and* boys, thank you." She stopped and then added, "Not at the same time, just to clarify."

Meg held her hands up in surrender. "Sorry, sorry. I didn't mean to insult you or anything. I don't know, I just thought for a second there that maybe you were a girl-virgin." She dropped her hands back on the countertop. "You can't really blame me, you did give me this whole explanation about how you live here but, like, were never really part of the scene. Until now."

"I know. I didn't mean to jump down your throat."

"So what gives. Why haven't you and Julie slept together?"

Lexi shrugged her shoulders. "Just hasn't happened yet, I guess."

"But things are good, though, you like her?" Meg backed off a little.

"Yeah, I like her," Lexi said. Her small smile was enough to reveal the pronounced dimple in her left cheek.

"Sam must be psyched. The renter plan is working. What's going on with her and the girl from The Kitchen?" Meg asked, redirecting the conversation.

"Nothing, really. She's actually one of Julie's roommates. She's barely there, though—I mean, I still don't know her name, which is getting stupid. I think she has a girlfriend who lives in Jersey or something. Which is actually good, because Sam has been hanging out with me and Julie and Julie's *other* roommate."

"Wow, that's fast."

Lexi shook her head. "No, no, no. Not like that. They're just friends. All of us, it's nice. Which is why you have to hang with us this weekend. It's Fall Festival. We're all going to go to the fair together and then to the social that night. Are you in?"

Meg smiled. She was really excited about the Fall Festival fair and the social. As Lexi had explained in painstaking detail, there were three kinds of events at Bay West—socials, open houses, and closed parties. They were all held in the Bay West Commons, a two-story building in the center of the development. Socials were the biggest deal. They were massive parties that were thrown several times throughout the year by the Bay West board. Socials were open to everyone.

Meg was excited for her first big community event. "I'm definitely up for going. The only thing is, I'm going to this pre-party at Jesse's before."

"Oh, right, I forgot about that." Lexi's tone was unconvincing.

"But let's go to the fair together, then I'll go to her place and meet you guys over at the Commons. Sound like a plan?"

"Sounds good." Lexi nodded.

"Speaking of Jesse, how is your internship going?"

"It's fine. The lawyer I'm assigned to is kind of a bitch, but other than that, it's pretty uneventful."

"What about the whole Jesse situation? Is it weird working for her because she lives here and everything?" Meg asked.

"I haven't even seen her much since that one meeting. I guess I made a big deal over it for no reason."

"Well, that's good, right?"

"Yeah, sure."

Lexi fidgeted uncomfortably, avoiding eye contact. Her body language suggested there was way more to this story than she was giving up, and Meg was dying to find out what it was. But she could sense that tonight was not the night for it, so she let the conversation drift back to the previous topic.

"So, how crowded does this party get?"

"It'll be packed." Lexi seemed to be relieved to change the topic. "The board does a whole marketing push for it in the lesbian community."

"Yeah? Is it like all the same people that you see at The Kitchen and Cubby Hole?" Meg asked, referencing the two most popular girl bars in the city.

"I don't know. I've never been to any of the socials before. I never had anybody to go with. Friends, I mean." Lexi looked almost embarrassed to admit it.

"See, I knew there was a virgin in there somewhere." Meg laughed, reaching out and poking Lexi.

Swatting her hand away, Lexi shot back playfully, "How's your sex life, by the way?"

"Terrible. That's why I'm so interested in yours," Meg joked. "Seriously, it's like nonexistent." Meg paused and then felt the need to explain. "I just got out of a relationship. Before I moved here. So I'm kind of taking it easy on the dating front." She hoped that made it sound like a choice.

"What happened? With your girlfriend?" Lexi said, not letting her off the hook.

"Nothing really. I think that was the problem." Meg got up to get a glass of water. Talking about Becca still made her uncomfortable, mostly because she felt like the last one to realize that their relationship was a joke.

"Hmm?" Lexi prompted for more detail.

"We dated for two and a half years. Sort of," she mused, as her glass filled. "Maybe on and off is a more accurate description." She shut off the tap and leaned back against the sink. "I think, now, she really considered us friends that whole time. You know, friends who hook up." She shrugged, making light of it. "I guess that's what it was for her. Anyway, I thought it worked—I mean, I thought we were just taking our time. But at some point, like way after everyone else, I realized that it was never going to go any further." Meg sighed, looking straight through her glass to the floor.

"Not over her, huh?"

Meg shrugged and sipped her water.

"Well, I think it's time for you to get back out there." Lexi punctuated the statement with a nod for emphasis.

"I don't know. Maybe I should take it easy for a while. I have a lot on my plate. New job, new house."

Lexi shook her head. "Excuses. Meet up with us at the social. Julie's friends are coming in from New Jersey. Maybe you'll like one of them."

Meg couldn't help but smile at Lexi's determination. "All right. I'm in." There had never been any doubt that she was going, but it felt good to have a set plan, and a friend looking out for her.

Lexi slid off the stool and headed for the back door. "Back to your project. I'll let myself out. See you Saturday."

CHAPTER SIX

Meg was thankful she'd grabbed a zippered hoodie on the way out of her house. Sitting in Jesse's backyard, she could feel the breeze coming in off the water that lay just below the bluffs at the edge of the development. It had been gorgeous and warm during the afternoon festival, but since the sun had set, it was a little cold. At least the heat from the fire pit was helping warm her up.

She had gone to Jesse's pre-party completely unsure what to expect, and she found herself surprised by the intimacy of such a small gathering. Four other women sat in deck chairs carefully arranged around the fire—Rose and Teddy, who were a couple, and Betsy and Mia, who didn't appear to be. Right away Meg was intrigued by the makeup of this group. Rose and Teddy looked to be in their late forties, maybe even early fifties. Jesse and Betsy hovered in their thirties somewhere. But Mia, with her short platinum-blond hair and trendy tough-girl style, was right about Meg's age.

Taking one of the two empty chairs, Meg sat down as Jesse handed her a beer. She pushed against the backrest and clutched her drink as she tried not to appear too self-conscious. She was way too nervous to contribute to the conversation, so she simply sat back and absorbed it all, making a conscious effort to look relaxed and normal. As she listened, she learned that Mia was a young cop who had a story for everything; Betsy was a doctor, an obstetrician to be precise. This seemed to elicit endless ribbing from pretty much everyone.

She also found out that Rose and Teddy were what Bay West residents referred to as holdovers because they had both lived in the development when it was still simply a women's community, prior to becoming a place exclusively for lesbians. With Meg as a captive audience, Teddy explained how the Bay West development was built by Agnes Browne, a spinster who inherited the land from her childless uncle. Apparently her goal had been to create a place where women would feel safe, so she strategically set the units off from the main thoroughfare and planted the line of trees, which, to this day, outlined the enclave like a fortress.

Teddy took a final swig from her drink and looked into the empty bottle as she finished the lesson. "When old Agnes passed, she willed the land to her great-niece, who continued the all-women theme…she just tweaked it a little," she added with a brusque laugh.

"Mary Brown?" Meg piped up, remembering the fortysomething woman who'd accompanied her on her initial walk-through.

"Close. Kameron Browne," Teddy corrected her.

"They're a couple, right?" Meg knew the answer but asked anyway. Lexi had already told her that Aunt Kam and Aunt Mary, as she called them, were her godparents and her mothers' closest friends.

Rose answered, "Yeah. They actually have the same last name, like, originally. Except one's with an *e* and the other isn't. I can never remember which is which. Who's who, baby?" She patted Teddy's forearm.

"Mary is just Brown, like the color. No *e*," Jesse said quietly, without lifting her head, as she seemed to be studying the label of her beer bottle.

There was an exceptionally long pause.

"Anyway," Teddy continued in her lyrical voice, traces of her Dominican accent coming through on every word, "Kam has spent nearly the last thirty years making this place what it is today." She looked around for emphasis. "I mean, she may be a bitch on wheels, but she deserves some credit for what she's done." She laughed heartily again. "Pretty interesting, huh?"

"Definitely." Meg nodded as she said it. And it *was* interesting. But just as interesting to Meg was the fact that Mia had been checking her out through the whole story.

Now that Meg had engaged in the conversation, the floodgates opened. Right away the focus shifted to her. Rose and Teddy did most of the questioning, but the others chimed in too. Mostly they wanted to know where she was from and how she ended up at Bay West. They were all genuinely surprised to find out that she grew up in Staten Island but had never been to, or even heard of, Bay West before checking out her house as sort of a fluke.

"I know," she confessed. "Apparently I'm the only one. After I moved in, I was trying to explain it to my friend Tracy, who lives out in California now, but grew up on the Island. And I was giving all these particulars about where it is and doing a whole buildup until she was like, *Do you mean Bay West*?" Meg let out a laugh at herself and the other women laughed along with her. "I literally almost dropped the phone. She's been making fun of me since. She's even been to parties here." She took a quick swallow of her drink before adding, "Plus there's my Realtor, and I'm pretty sure she's not even gay. So really"— Meg pointed at herself mockingly—"the only one."

They all laughed again. They were an easy group to talk to. Feeling confident that for a change she hadn't said anything embarrassing, she walked over to the cooler to grab another drink and checked her phone at the same time. It was nine thirty and they were still in Jesse's yard.

Lexi had been texting for the last hour checking her status. With each message, she dropped more bait. The first text made a point of mentioning that several of Julie's Jersey friends were adorable. The most recent informed that they were all staying over: *Wink. Wink.* Meg smirked as she read it.

"What's funny?" Meg felt Mia's lanky presence as she sidled up to Meg's side and pretended to look over her shoulder at the phone.

"Nothing. My friend is just…making fun of me." Meg flashed a look up at Mia's cool blue eyes but couldn't hold the stare. She quickly checked out Mia's well-worn motorcycle boots, then reestablished eye contact, realizing only then that Mia was probably six feet tall.

"Oh yeah, why's that?" Mia bent down and grabbed two beers from the cooler, keeping her eyes locked on Meg the whole time. "Here." She twisted off the top and handed it to Meg.

"Thanks."

Meg stood there for a second not saying anything, until Mia pressed her again. "So, your friend? The texts? What's up?"

"Oh, right." Meg snapped out of her cloud. "She just wants to know when I'm getting to the social."

Mia nodded. "We'll probably head over in a few minutes. It

usually doesn't get crowded till after ten anyway. Jesse hates being there when it's too empty."

Meg was riveted by Mia's throaty voice. It sounded like she'd been smoking since the age of three. Meg hoped she never stopped. "Have you been to a lot of the parties here?" Meg knew from the intros that Mia didn't live at Bay West, but not much more than that.

"Yeah. A few. But I only go if someone invites me," she said with the slightest hint in her voice as she smiled. The way Mia half smiled and cocked her head to one side, Meg thought she was being flirted with—she was so out of practice, it was hard to be sure. But then Mia nodded her chin and added smoothly, "So, your friend. Are we talking friend-friend or *girl*friend?" There was no mistaking that.

"Just a friend." Meg used every fiber of her being to sound casual.

"How come?"

Meg was totally taken aback by Mia's boldness. She had no idea how to respond to the question, but luckily she was spared anyway. Mia looked past Meg before she could answer and said, "Yep, here comes the boss now. Guess we're getting ready to go. To be continued." Mia tossed her head back, downing her beer as Jesse approached them.

❖

They walked the short distance to the Commons in pairs. Rose and Teddy strolled hand in hand, while Betsy and Mia traipsed side by side a few feet behind them. Meg ended up bringing up the rear with Jesse, watching Mia strut a few feet in front of her.

Halfway down the block, Jesse interrupted Meg's stare. "So, everyone was nice to you, right?" Jesse asked as they walked through the crisp night.

"Your friends are great. Thanks for including me."

"Rose and Teddy gave you the third degree, huh? I should have warned you about that. Or I could have stopped them, I guess," Jesse added as an afterthought. "But, alas, I was curious about you too, so I just let them do the dirty work for me," she said with a smile.

"Typical lawyer."

"Ouch." Jesse covered her heart with both hands in mock pain. "Hey, how did you—"

"My friend—my next door neighbor, actually—works for you. Lexi Russo."

"Oh, right. Of course." There was an extended pause before Jesse added, "So you two are friends."

"Besides you, she's basically the only person I've met here. She'll be here tonight." There was another long silence. When Jesse didn't say anything, Meg went out on a limb. "Is that weird for you? You know, to be at this party with your coworker or intern or whatever?"

Jesse didn't answer right away, she just let out a sigh. Meg saw the cold breath as it hit the air. Jesse looked like she might say something more, but then changed her mind, simply shaking her head. "It's fine." But in the silence that hung between them, Meg felt like it was perhaps not fine at all. She was dying to know what the story was there but could tell by Jesse's tone that this topic was closed. Meg moved on.

"So, how long have Rose and Teddy been together?"

"A long time. Almost thirty years, I guess. They're gonna try to hook you up with Teddy's cousin."

"What?" Meg was astonished.

"I heard them conspiring when you were talking to Mia. They love playing matchmaker, those two." Jesse shook her head, a half grin spreading across her face. "I'm sure they'll mention it to you later. See that, I'm giving you a heads-up. Redeeming myself."

"Thank you for that." Meg nodded for effect. Then pointing her chin at Betsy and Mia who were still ahead of them, Meg tried for casual. "And what about those two, what's up with them?"

Jesse looked from Betsy and Mia to Meg, a question in her eyes. "Betsy and Mia?"

"They're not together, right?" Suave or subtle, Meg was neither.

"No. Definitely not. Mia's mother and Betsy's mother used to work together." Jesse shook her head. "Betsy's like a big sister for Mia. See, Mia came out to her mother in high school, and her mom totally freaked out about it." She waved her hand as she explained. "Not in the typical way. Her mom was actually fine with it, real supportive." She ran a hand through her disheveled short brown hair and Meg watched it fall perfectly in place. "It was more that her mom didn't know what to do. Her parents are divorced. I guess her dad was no help at all. Mia's mother was afraid she wouldn't do the right thing. Whatever that is." Jesse crunched a leaf under her foot as she walked. "Even though Betsy's only a few years older than Mia, her mom asked if Betsy would take Mia under her wing." She squinted a little as she reflected on it. "I think Betsy was the only gay person Mia's mom knew existed, and at the time, Mia was having a really hard time. Hard to believe, she's so cocky now."

"Oh." Meg hoped her excitement didn't show in her voice.

"Just be careful, Meg."

"What do you mean?" Meg said innocently.

Jesse tilted her head and raised her eyebrows giving Meg a knowing look. "Look, Mia's all right. But she's kind of a player. And you, Megan McTiernan, are not." Jesse's tone was light, but it was clear she meant it. "Hey, I mean that in a good way. You're a nice girl. I can tell. I just don't want you to get hurt." Jesse threw her arm around Meg's shoulders. "Just some friendly advice. Feel free to completely ignore it."

The line to get in was short, so Jesse and Meg waited with the rest of their party instead of cutting ahead as residents. They still had to show their ID cards—a formality Meg thought was especially odd since the door was being worked by Lexi's moms, Chris and Marnie, whom Meg saw in passing almost every day. After checking her card, Marnie pulled Meg aside and informed her that she was to come for Sunday dinner the next day, she wouldn't take no for an answer.

Kameron and Mary Brown(e) were also at the door checking resident cards and collecting the cover charge. The exchange between Kameron and Jesse was as tense as it had been on her front lawn weeks ago, only now Kam's animosity seemed to have spread to include Meg, as Kam snatched their money and ushered them in without a word.

As soon as they were inside, Jesse grabbed one of the last high-top tables, off to the side. There were only two tall stools at it, but it was perfect for putting their stuff down, and it gave them a rallying point for the rest of the night. It was right up against the wall next to the dance floor, and it was a great spot from which to see the whole room.

Meg had been in this building once before, the day she met with the condo board before officially moving in. Once it was clear that Meg had made the cut she was shown all the amenities, and Kam Browne had mentioned, almost in passing, that the development hosted community parties there a few times a year.

As Meg surveyed the room now, she realized that comment might have been the understatement of the year.

The place was completely transformed.

The overhead lights were turned down low, and the room was illuminated by strands of tiny white lights that edged the room and bordered each of the two full bars, giving the place a warm and festive feel. Tables of varying sizes littered the space and were filled to capacity. The DJ was set up on a small stage in the corner, cranking out music. Several people were already on the dance floor, breaking it down under the colorful strobes. This place was The Kitchen on steroids. Meg suddenly realized that she was in the biggest lesbian club in the city. In her own backyard.

She caught a glimpse of Lexi at a table across the room. She was about to walk over to her when she felt a hand on her lower back and heard Mia's unmistakable voice from behind her.

"I'm going to the bar. Want a drink?" Meg only had to turn slightly and Mia's face was inches from her own. Meg forcibly redirected her stare from Mia's lips to her eyes, which were really no less disconcerting.

"Yeah. Sure." She fished in her pocket for money, but was quickly waved off. "I'm just going to run over and say hi to my friends." Meg nodded in Lexi's general direction, trying desperately to sound indifferent.

"Okay. Meet you back here in a few." Annoyingly, Mia didn't even have to try.

After making her way through the thickening crowd, Meg slid onto the open chair between Lexi and Sam. "Is this seat taken?" she joked, nudging both girls with her elbows simultaneously.

"Hey, girl. I was just going to send out a search party." Lexi smiled, leaning over to give Meg a quick hug.

"I know. Sorry. I wanted to come sooner, but I couldn't really say anything, you know? Hey, I saw your parents at the door, by the way. They invited me for dinner tomorrow."

"Oh my God, they're obsessed with you. They talk about you incessantly."

"What?" Meg laughed out her response.

"Be prepared, they're going to ask you a million questions. Trust me, nothing is sacred. You have to promise not to hold it against me," Lexi joked.

"It'll be fine. They're sweet."

"Anyway, more importantly, I'm glad you're finally here. I want to introduce you to Julie's friends."

Meg sat back in her chair and spoke in a low voice trying not to seem too excited. "Actually, I kind of have some weird flirty thing going on with one of Jesse's friends. At least I think we're flirting—I mean, it could just be my imagination. I've never really been good at reading people. Take my entire last relationship, for example." She said it in an attempt at self-deprecation, but it came out sharp and bitter. And she knew it wasn't true. She was actually good at judging both people and situations. She had known long before it officially ended that her relationship with Becca was over. She just hadn't wanted to admit it.

"Which one is she? Point her out," Lexi asked as she and Sam both turned around to look. But the crowd was too dense to see more than a few feet in any direction.

"She's around here somewhere." Meg stretched her neck as she gripped the back of her chair. "Anyway, she's kind of hot, in that bad-girl sort of way. I should head back over there, she's grabbing drinks for us." Meg gestured toward Julie who was deftly maneuvering the crowd without spilling the drinks she was carrying. "Oh, perfect timing, here comes your girlfriend, she can have her seat back." She stood. "I'll be back in a little bit. Or come over to us. We're set up at one of the tall tables near the wall."

❖

Meg spent the entire night like this, shuttling between the two groups. Because of that, she never got into a real rhythm with either one. She tried a few times to get the groups to merge, but it never happened, and she never got to talk to any of Julie's friends, although she did meet two of them in passing. They *were* cute. But she was already preoccupied with Mia.

But that was the other problem. With all of the back and forth, she hardly saw Mia the rest of the night. It seemed like every time she came back from Lexi's group, Mia was either up at the bar, on the dance floor, or talking to other people. One thing was obvious—she was never alone.

As she made her way around the room throughout the night, she saw several people she recognized from her new neighborhood. She talked to Jesse quite a bit, and Meg found she had a real rapport with her. And she got to know Betsy a little too, who was a bit shy and guarded but from time to time came out with hilarious one-liners. She even allowed herself to be cornered by Rose and Teddy as they talked up Teddy's cousin. They were so endearing, it was hard to disappoint them, but Meg had a firm aversion to setups and this one was no different.

By one thirty the crowd was pretty thin. Even Lexi, Julie, and Sam had called it a night. Meg was actually enjoying the quiet, finishing up her drink in the brisk night air on the balcony as she watched the trees sway in the breeze to the muffled club music behind her. Out of the corner of her eye, something drew her attention. By the time she turned, Mia was already sauntering down the corridor toward her, smirking as she flicked the butt of a cigarette over the banister.

"Hey," Mia drawled out, as she leaned on the railing. Her voice was raspier than before, her crystal-blue eyes bloodshot and heavy.

"I thought you guys left."

"Without saying good-bye?" Mia nudged Meg's arm with her elbow.

"Well, I said good-bye to Jesse and the rest of them a little while ago," Meg offered as explanation.

"I came with Betsy. She's just in the bathroom and then we're going." Mia nodded slightly toward the building. "So it's pretty much fate that I happened to see you out here."

Meg raised an eyebrow, playfully suspicious. "I don't know about fate. We were in the same room all night."

"Yeah, but you were a busy bee. Flitting around. Running back to your *non*-girlfriend every five minutes. You had no time for me." Mia's tone was so coy there could be no mistaking her intention.

"You weren't chasing me down, either." Meg mirrored Mia's tone.

"How could I?" Mia said, feigning sincerity as she looked directly into Meg's eyes, doing a terrible job of concealing her smirk. "I didn't want to get you in trouble." She dropped her voice another octave as she continued the faux concern. Her crooked smile revealed a tiny scar on the top left side of her lip. Then she made a mockingly grand gesture of looking around before continuing through a wide grin. "So I guess your girl left then? Since you're finally willing to talk to me." Her voice oozed confidence.

Meg wasn't used to being hit on. Truthfully, she was usually the one doing the flirting, albeit badly. In her past relationships, and there hadn't been that many, she had been the pursuer. Usually she chased someone down, said all sorts of embarrassing things, and then crossed her fingers. Things either progressed from there, or more often than not, they didn't. This one conversation alone felt more like banter than anything Meg had ever initiated or been direct party to. So while she hardly knew Mia at all, and knew her compliments were hollow, Meg had to admit that this was fun, educational, and utterly refreshing.

So she flirted back. And did so with an ease typically foreign to her. "You know, all this talk about my *girlfriend*, you kind of sound a little jealous." She scrunched up her nose and crinkled her brow for effect, wondering who the hell she was, even as she did it.

"You think?" Mia raised one eyebrow as she pushed back from the railing, holding on to it with both hands.

Meg crossed her arms and turned around, so they were more or less face-to-face. "Listen, I'm just saying. You seem awfully concerned with someone that I've told you repeatedly is not in any way, shape, or form my girlfriend."

"Well, good. Then you won't have any explaining to do." Mia dipped her chin slightly and started to lean in.

Betsy interrupted them one nanosecond before their lips actually touched. "Wrap it up, Romeo. Some of us have work in the morning."

Mia threw her head back and laughed out loud, as she straightened up and pulled away. "Okay. I guess that moment's over." She laughed again at her own joke before she kissed Meg on the cheek, just at the corner of her mouth. "See you around, Meg." She whipped around and headed for the door, glancing over her shoulder once to flash Meg one more grin before leaving her alone on the balcony.

CHAPTER SEVEN

Meg busied herself with packing most of the day. Monday morning she was off to Sullivan & Son's London office for international orientation, a week-long drink-fest that passed as training. Because the London and New York offices often worked on international accounts together, it was tradition that the associates from each office made one initial visit overseas in their rookie year to meet the staff and be briefed on local laws and regulations that impacted their work, just in case they were needed on-site down the line. For years as part of the administrative crew, while earning her bachelor's degree and MBA, Meg had listened to the new hires tell crazy stories of wild nights with the London team.

While she picked out her clothes and packed her suitcase, she replayed the scene from last night over and over in her head. Initially she had been disappointed that she and Mia hadn't kissed, but as the hours went by, Meg was more and more convinced it was for the best. Mia, while smoking hot, was really not her type. And even though she had been flattered by the attention, she had to remind herself that she had seen Mia spreading her charm all over the room. Meg wasn't really into dating around, she had always been kind of a one-woman girl. Obviously Mia wasn't—even Jesse had warned her about that. Perhaps Betsy's untimely disruption had actually been a saving grace.

With her suitcase zipped up and ready to go, and her mind at ease with the rationalization she had provided to herself, Meg headed next door to Lexi's for dinner.

The smell of roasting garlic hit her the second she set foot in the house. Lexi was always talking about Marnie's outrageous meals, but her bragging didn't do it justice. Everything was so delicious, it almost made her homesick for her own mother's cooking. It was a good reminder that she owed her parents a call when she got home. The dinner table was loud and boisterous and lively. Lexi's college-age sister Andrea and two little brothers, Michael and Ethan, were there. They all referred to Marnie as Mom and Chris as Mush. Meg filed that detail away to ask Lexi about later.

As Lexi had warned, her parents did grill her some. But Meg happily answered their questions. She filled them in on how her parents moved to Florida right after she graduated from high school and that she had gone to college for a year down there, but missed New York too much. She told them how she moved back up here and lived with her sister for a while, before scoring her own place in Brooklyn while she balanced multiple jobs and went to school at night. Meg felt so comfortable with this family that she even explained all the details about how she turned a temp job at Sullivan & Son into permanent employment, spending the last four years as an administrative assistant until they bumped her up to consultant status.

"Does that happen a lot?" Chris asked, surprise clear in her voice.

"Not really." Meg looked down. She was always kind of embarrassed about being the center of attention.

"Wow, you must've really impressed them."

"I don't know. A lot of it was that I worked there so long on the admin side, I think they were just used to me." She let out a nervous laugh, still not entirely comfortable in her new position. She shrugged slightly continuing to downplay her promotion. "I would always stay late, so they knew I wasn't afraid to work. Eventually my boss, well, she knew I was taking business classes at night, so she started giving me little projects to work on. I'm actually pretty good with numbers, so it came naturally to me." Meg usually stopped at this point, but with this crowd she was relaxed enough to let her guard down. "You know, it's been kind of weird though, because for so long I was part of the support staff and now I'm an actual consultant, so I used to work *for* most of these people and now I work *with* them." She tried not to sound as bothered by it all as she actually was. "Let's just say the transition hasn't been super smooth."

"For them or for you?" Chris leaned forward.

"Both, I guess. The rest of the associates are mostly Ivy Leaguers.

I went to CUNY at night." Meg fiddled with the edge of her placemat. "Even the admin guys don't really know what to make of me now. So I don't really fit in anywhere at the moment."

Chris looked up, her soft brown eyes revealing the teddy bear underneath her handsome exterior, and Meg suddenly guessed the source of her nickname. "Hang in there, Meg. It'll work out." She said it with the confidence of someone who had been through it, combined with the concern of a doting parent.

Meg smiled, relaxed by the sentiment. Lexi's parents were awesome. Meg loved being in their company. They obviously adored each other. She hadn't realized quite how much Lexi resembled Chris, who was her biological mother. Perhaps it was because their styles were so dramatically different. Lexi was the very picture of femininity with her thick curly hair that hung almost to the middle of her back, while Chris was decidedly gruffer, her wavy dark hair cut short, accentuating her rugged good looks. But they both had a smooth tanned complexion, big chocolate brown eyes, and the same dimples that popped with every smile. The younger three kids, with their milky white skin and freckles, were all Marnie.

"Lexi said you're going to London tomorrow," Marnie said as she piled the dishes in the sink.

"Just for a week. For training."

"That's exciting."

"Yeah, it should be fun."

When the doorbell rang, Marnie turned to the boys, who were having a hard time sitting still at the table. "Get the door, guys, it's Aunt Kam and Aunt Mary. Then you can be excused to go play video games." She turned back to the table and directed her comments to Meg. "Of course you know Kam and Mary by now. They're practically family."

"Sure, yeah." Meg tensed up the second she saw them. She didn't know what it was but she couldn't warm to Kameron at all, and she got the distinct impression that the feeling was mutual. She watched as Lexi gave them both genuine hugs, and wondered if maybe she was being paranoid.

After just a few minutes, Meg and Lexi retreated to Lexi's room to talk, and Meg filled her in on everything that happened—and didn't— last night between her and Mia. Only by now, her enthusiasm had completely vanished. This whole evening, while amazing, had made her heart ache for all the things she wanted for herself that suddenly seemed so far out of reach. If she hadn't been sure before, this one family dinner alone was enough to convince her of what she absolutely wanted from life. She wanted to get married. She wanted kids. She longed for the future she had hoped to build with Becca, the one she certainly would not have with Mia.

Now that they were a safe distance from the grown-ups, as Meg and Lexi laughingly referred to them, Meg sought her friend's opinion on something else that was annoying her. "Do you think Kameron hates me or something?"

"What?" Lexi laughed out.

Meg frowned. "Don't even tell me you didn't notice her less-than-friendly greeting toward me before?"

"What are you talking about?" A baffled Lexi shook her head.

"Upstairs. I mean, when they came in, Mary came over and gave me a hug. Kameron barely nodded."

"That's just how Aunt Mary is, super bubbly. Very touchy-feely. Aunt Kam's just not like that. I wouldn't take it personally," Lexi offered in defense.

"If you say so. But this is like the third or fourth time it's happened. I'm starting to get a complex." Meg played with a loose thread on Lexi's bedspread. "I mean, last night she was actually kind of a dick to me at the door." She caught herself and tried to recover. "Sorry, I know they're like your family. I shouldn't say anything."

Lexi rolled her eyes. "Relax, Meg. I don't care. As for last night, you went to the social with Jesse, right?"

Meg nodded.

"Well, there's part of the problem, right there."

"What's the deal? They hate each other or something?" Meg had sensed the hostility between them, and she had entertained the possibility they could be exes—surely in a lesbian community there was more than one relationship turned sour—but, in her estimation, that didn't seem likely. For starters there was a pretty big age gap between them, but also their interaction was so frigid, Meg found it hard to believe it had ever been warm, much less intimate.

"It's a long story," Lexi started.

Meg waved her on with one hand, waiting to be filled in.

"They were all friends years ago. My moms, Aunt Kam, Aunt Mary, and Jesse. They had this big falling-out." Lexi shrugged. "Then they weren't anymore."

"Way to skip the good parts," Meg teased. "What happened?"

Exhaling deeply, Lexi continued. "I don't know really. Nobody talks about it, not even when I've asked. But from what I have gathered over the years, I guess Jesse was getting a little too close, or more accurately, trying to get close to Aunt Mary. You know Mary's a lot younger than Kam, probably closer in age to Jesse. So when the two of them started hanging out all the time, everybody freaked out. That's when it all fell apart."

"Did anything actually happen between Mary and Jesse?"

"No way. *That* I would know about." Lexi pulled at her long curls searching for split ends. "But the whole thing broke up the friendship. That was it, Jesse was out of the group for good."

Meg lifted an eyebrow. "And you work for her now. So you've gone over to the enemy." Meg squinted one eye, teasing. "Interesting."

"Yeah, well, my parents didn't think it was interesting. They were pretty mad." She twisted her full lips activating one dimple. "Actually that's not true. Mush was fine. But Mom, Marnie, she totally lost it at first. She tried to forbid me, if you can believe that. Finally she calmed down. I think part of the reason was she knew I wasn't going to listen. I mean, this is my career." She let go of the strands she was holding and pushed her hair behind her shoulders. "Anyway, she's over it now."

"Such drama, I love it," Meg said with a wicked grin. When Lexi didn't say anything, Meg asked, "So how is it going? With Jesse, I mean."

"It's fine. I hardly ever see her." Meg thought she heard disappointment in Lexi's voice but didn't have the opportunity to ask a follow-up. "Anyway, enough about that. You'll be back for the weekend?" Lexi tapped Meg on the forearm.

"Yep."

"Good. Let's go out. I'm thinking The Kitchen. Give us both something to look forward to."

"It's a plan."

❖

Meg's week of training in London turned into twelve days, and she missed the weekend altogether. For years as a staff assistant, Meg had heard stories about the London/New York exchange. It was party after party, pub after pub. There was little, if any, work involved. So when Meg was bombarded with projects the minute she stepped off the plane, she half wondered if it was some kind of practical joke. After a few days and nights of intense work on accounts she was completely unfamiliar with, Meg stopped looking for the hidden cameras. Instead she concentrated on actual problem solving for two high-profile clients.

She did get to know the London consultants, all of whom pitched in on the projects. The only person who was markedly absent was the one person Meg had been wanting to meet. Well, perhaps that was an overstatement. What she wanted was to get the meeting over with.

She and Sasha Michaels had started work at Sullivan & Son on exactly the same day. Although they were in different offices nearly three thousand miles apart, Meg got an earful regularly from pretty much everybody about how brilliant and innovative Sasha Michaels was. It had been mentioned on more than one occasion that she had gone to Oxford and graduated with honors.

Meg was certain Sasha had heard about her as well—they were the only two new hires in the last six months. But she was also pretty sure no one in London, or New York for that matter, was gushing about Meg's rise from being the girl who proofread their proposals to an associate consultant with clients of her own. The whole situation made her feel embarrassingly inadequate; she just wanted to get the fucking introduction over with and move on.

When, on the day she was getting ready to fly back to New York, Meg finally got the nerve to ask Nigel—seriously, there was a Nigel—where Sasha was, the nice young man just shrugged his shoulders. "Don't know, mate. Fucking weird though. Just took off last week. These are her projects we're doing."

It probably was weird, as Nigel said, but Meg just found it irritating. Knowing they were Sasha's clients made her feel more nervous than before. It was like she had some new standard to live up to. Plus, she was certain no one in New York was doing her work for her while she was gone, so she couldn't help but wonder why *she* was being forced to pick up superstar Sasha's slack.

Stressed out and annoyed, her only entertainment came in texting Lexi, using totally over-the-top British jargon. Today's message read: *Bollocks. Been here nearly a fortnight. Coworker still off on holiday. Blimey.* She laughed at her own joke as she wondered if Lexi found it remotely amusing at all.

CHAPTER EIGHT

Lexi smiled to herself as she read Meg's latest text. Sitting at the front desk in Stanton Ducane's main reception area, she inwardly chuckled at Meg's crazy wording and shot off a reply, telling Meg to meet her at the softball field in the morning for Julie and Sam's game.

Lexi was already looking ahead to tomorrow's plans because focusing on tonight was stressing her out. Julie had specifically set up one-on-one time for them and had been making a big deal about it all week. Lexi knew what the fuss was about. She and Julie had been dating exclusively for a few months now and things had yet to progress physically to the level Julie wanted them to be at.

Logistics were part of the problem, Lexi reasoned. They were rarely alone; someone was always around. Between Julie's roommates and Sam, who crashed on Julie's couch more often than not, Lexi felt like there was a constant audience outside the bedroom door. It made it difficult for her to relax and had provided a plausible excuse on more than one occasion. But tonight Julie had made a point of clearing the house so it would be just the two of them. The gesture was not lost on Lexi and it made her nervous in a way she couldn't explain.

It wasn't that she didn't want to do it. She was hardly a prude. Truthfully, on several occasions when they were alone together, Lexi had found herself so caught up in the moment that she'd almost given in to her urges. But something stopped her every time. She hated to admit it, but Julie's feelings were much more intense than hers and her instincts told her they always would be. The imbalance made her uncomfortable. Somehow, it felt like a lie.

She had been dwelling on this all day. Usually her days at Stanton

Ducane afforded her little, if any, spare time. The warnings about Allison Smith were true. She had high expectations and she wasn't overly friendly. But if her instructions were followed and timelines met, she wasn't the ogre she was made out to be.

As for Jesse Ducane, since her initial bombed meeting with the senior partner, Lexi'd seen her only in passing. There was never any kind of formal peace offering, but when they did see each other in the halls, their exchanges were cordial and professional. Usually it amounted to a head nod with a smile, sometimes even a quick good morning thrown in for good measure. In fact, just last week when they crossed paths in the ladies' room, Jesse had looked at Lexi in the mirror and said, "How's everything going?" as she soaped her hands in the sink. It was basically a rhetorical question, but her voice had sounded genuine enough. Lexi hoped this meant that despite their initial interaction, Jesse knew she wasn't a total idiot.

She was doing a good job, of that she was certain. She was always early, she never rushed to leave, and she never left a project unfinished. Once it had become clear who the two frontrunners were for the associate positions, most of the other interns worked harder to get over than actually put in an honest day's labor. Lexi had been bummed when she realized she had no shot, but Stanton Ducane was well respected in the legal community, and a good reference from a reputable firm could very well lead to lucrative employment elsewhere. So Lexi worked her ass off every time she stepped through the door, and for reasons that she knew were ridiculously desperate, she prayed that word of this made it to the top.

One thing was for sure, Allison noticed. Case in point, today she had given Lexi a break. While the rest of the interns were slogging through forty boxes of discovery material, Lexi had been assigned to cover the front desk after the receptionist called in sick. It was pretty much a day off and normally Lexi would have been grateful, but with so much idle time, her mind kept wandering to the night ahead with Julie.

At six twenty in the evening, as Lexi sat swiveling in the big leather chair counting down the last ten minutes to the weekend, the front desk phone rang. She answered, but before she could say anything, the woman on the other end of the phone spoke in a panicked whisper.

"I need to speak to Paul Harris. It's an emergency."

"Mr. Harris is not in today, can I take a message or offer you his voice mail?" Lexi said systematically. There was no immediate response, but Lexi sensed hesitation. "Are you okay?" she asked.

"Not really." The voice was a touch louder, but still barely audible. There was a short pause before the woman continued. "I need Paul. He's my lawyer. And I'm having a lawyer situation."

Lexi knew she needed more information to properly direct the call to one of the other lawyers. "What's wrong?"

"I…I'm at work and I have a problem. They want me to sign a letter of resignation and if I do that, it's over. My whole career. Over." Lexi heard a muffled sniffle. "I need some help here. Being a cop is all I've ever wanted to do. But they're telling me this is for my own good. If I just sign the papers and walk away, there won't be any charges, no internal. I don't know what to do. This is why I hired a goddamn lawyer." The woman was more or less talking to herself but Lexi could hear the fear and anger behind the words.

And Lexi realized she knew this case. This had to be the police shooting that Paul's intern, Beth, was talking about at lunch a few weeks ago. The cop who claimed she hadn't fired the shot in question. "Okay, so what's changed since the last time you spoke to Paul?"

"They just presented me with papers. Resignation papers. They said it's in my best interest to sign them. Because then my file will be clean. But I won't have a job either," she added flippantly.

Lexi practically cut her off. "Don't sign anything. Where are you now?"

"I told them I had to go to the bathroom. I'm hiding in the stairwell. You're a lawyer?"

"No. I'm an intern." Lexi felt as useless as that sounded. "But hold on. I'm going to get you some help. Just hold on for one second." Lexi knew most of the partners were gone for the day. She had said good-bye to Allison half an hour ago. Without wasting any time she started for Jesse's office immediately, only to turn around and come back to the reception desk. Picking up the receiver Lexi asked softly, "I'm really sorry, but what is your name?"

"Lucy Weston."

"Okay, hang on, Ms. Weston. I'll be right back."

Lexi virtually sprinted to Jesse's office and filled her in as quickly as she could. Almost before Lexi had finished speaking, Jesse picked up the call on speakerphone. "Ms. Weston. This is Jesse Ducane." She spoke with absolute authority. "I understand you have a situation. Here's what we're going to do. First of all, go back to your office. Do not sign anything, under any circumstances. Okay?"

"Okay."

"Okay. Tell whoever it is you are dealing with—Who are you dealing with?"

"My captain, a deputy inspector, and someone from legal."

"Okay. Tell them you have legal representation in this matter. Give them my name." Jesse provided her phone number and email, spelling it out slowly so there was no chance for error. "Tell them to send that letter over to me right now and I will look it over. Then leave. Come here right away. Do you know where we are?"

"Yeah, I've been there before." Lexi could hear the calm coming back into the voice on the other end of the phone.

"Great. Can you handle that?" Jesse asked.

"Yeah, I can do it. But what if they say I can't leave?"

"They won't. If they try to stop you, call me. Just, whatever you do, don't sign anything. Okay. We'll see you in a little while."

With that, Jesse disconnected the call and turned to Lexi. "Go into Paul's office and find the file. I'm going to try to get him on the phone. When you have the file, meet me in the conference room."

❖

Lexi sat in the conference room, reading the file. When she had completed the entire dossier and there was still no sign of Jesse, she checked the firm's electronic files to see whether Paul had made any additional notes on the case. There were a few entries, but nothing substantial. Lexi was about to text Julie that she might be a little late for dinner when Jesse entered the room, two coffees in hand.

"So, no luck with Paul. He's not answering. I did speak with Laney, but she's clueless. So we're basically going to have to start over." She put a cup of coffee in front of Lexi. "I didn't know how you take it, so I just got it regular. Hope that's okay."

Lexi nodded and took a sip. How weird was it that her boss was bringing her coffee? "Thanks. I read through the file and there are some notes in the system too. Here's what I can put together. Lucy Weston, detective, assigned to the Violent Crime Squad at the eighty-seventh precinct. Member of the police department for nine years. September eighteenth, at one forty-seven a.m., accidental discharge in the detective squad room. One officer wounded in the leg. Lucy's gun is the one that was fired. Lucy told Paul that she wasn't in the squad area when the accident happened." Lexi glanced up at Jesse who was leaning back in the chair taking it all in.

Lexi continued. "She left her service weapon in the top right desk drawer. She says she was in a different part of the precinct when it happened. And this is underlined in the file: *Billy said Tony is the shooter. It was a joke.*" Lexi looked up briefly, only long enough to make slight eye contact with Jesse, before she turned back to the file.

They sat together in relative silence, Jesse jotting notes while Lexi searched online for cases with similar facts. They both jumped when the office buzzer sounded.

Knowing her place, Lexi made her way to the reception area without being prompted.

While Lexi hadn't given much thought to what Lucy Weston would look like, she'd expected a hardier woman. Lucy was taller than she—but then, at five-two, most people were—but had a slight, almost fragile frame, capped by a mass of dirty-blond hair. Lexi approached the door and Lucy looked up, revealing soft gray eyes. She had a tough but feminine appeal. The word *weathered* popped into Lexi's mind. Lexi knew her age from her file, but standing just outside the door shifting nervously from one foot to the other, she seemed older than her thirty-one years.

When Lexi opened the door, Lucy formally reached out her hand. "Jesse?" Her voice held both anxiety and relief.

"No, I'm Lexi. The intern?" Lexi returned the woman's firm handshake. "Follow me, Jesse's in the conference room."

They took the brief walk to the conference room, passing empty offices as they went down the hall.

"Detective Weston. Jesse Ducane," Jesse said, extending her hand as they entered the room.

"Please, Lucy's fine."

"Have a seat, Lucy." As Jesse gestured to the chair across from her, Lexi realized Jesse had rearranged the chairs so she and Jesse were set up side by side. Lexi took her place next to her boss.

"First of all, let me apologize about Paul," Jesse started. "I'll be working with you going forward. Myself and Alexis Russo, my intern." She gestured toward Lexi. "You made it out okay?"

"It was like you said, I told them I needed to run it by my lawyer first before signing anything. They seemed so stunned, that I just walked out the door, no problem. It was kind of odd, considering they had just spent an hour trying to convince me to resign."

"If you resign, then the department has their scapegoat. The whole thing becomes your fault, but you're gone, so the department comes out looking good. Obviously we're not going to sign it." Jesse leaned forward. "But there's still a lot missing for us. We read through Paul's file but there's not a real clear picture of what went on that night. I hate to do this to you, but we're going to need you to go over it for us, step by step."

Lucy nodded and reiterated her story including scant more detail than Paul's file contained. Lexi could tell she was leaving details out and wondered why. But she sat silently and watched and listened.

Jesse dove right into the questions. "This incident happened at approximately two in the morning?"

"Yeah, around then."

"You work midnights?"

"No, I'm four by. Sorry, four to midnight."

"Were you on overtime?"

Lucy hesitated for a second. "No. Not really."

"What does that mean?"

There was a short pause before Lucy answered. "Look. It's complicated." Clearly she wasn't planning on elaborating, but Jesse won the waiting game. Lucy started and stopped several times before finally continuing her story.

"My squad, we see a lot of shit. And so a lot of times after a case is over or even after a rough night, we stay and hang out a bit. You know, to unwind." Lucy looked back and forth between Jesse and Lexi. Her smoky gray eyes revealed the stress she was trying very hard to conceal. "You do it so you don't bring it home with you. The job, I mean."

Jesse nodded in response. "This unwinding, does it involve alcohol?"

There was no immediate answer. Lucy looked down at her hands and then up to the ceiling as though the answer might be written somewhere around them. She let out a deep breath as she stretched her neck against the back of the large boardroom chair, clearly fighting the urge to talk.

Lexi had heard the expression *blue wall of silence*. Watching Lucy hem and haw over what she should and shouldn't say out loud, she supposed she was seeing it in action. It was painful to watch.

Finally, Lexi couldn't take it. She leaned forward, stretching her arms across the tabletop, almost touching Lucy to reassure her. She spoke with sincerity. "Lucy—Jesse is going to help you. She's the best. But you have to trust her. Tell her everything. She has to know what she's dealing with. It's the only way she can help you."

Lucy took another breath before meeting Lexi's gaze. "You don't understand. It's just part of the job. You see all this crazy, horrible stuff and you need to deal with it. Before you go home. Because the people in your real life, they don't understand. They don't get it. So it helps to be around the people who do. So yeah, after the tour, the bottles come out. And we sit back and have a few laughs and relax. It's never on duty. It's not like we're a bunch of drunks or anything. But yeah, to answer your question, yeah, I was drinking that night. We all were," she finished, looking directly at Jesse, an air of defiance in her voice.

"Okay." Jesse put her pen down and lightened her tone. "Just so there's no confusion later on. You didn't fire the gun, right?"

"No, I didn't fire the gun. I wasn't even there when it happened," Lucy snapped back.

"But it is your gun that went off. You are sure?"

"Yeah. It's mine. I left it in my drawer."

"So what happened?"

Lucy must have heard the concern in Jesse's voice, because her anger dissipated some. "It's this new kid. I guess he was trying to do some kind of practical joke." Lucy shook off a halfhearted laugh and rolled her eyes as she explained. "Tony Raymond. He shouldn't even be in the squad. The thing is, my squad, my team, it's a pretty elite spot. We work good cases, and we catch bad guys. Real bad guys. The people you want off the street. Rapists, pedophiles, real pieces of garbage, those are the guys we go after. And we're pretty successful. So it's a tough unit to get into. And because of that, we're all pretty tight with one another. But like six months ago, Tony gets assigned. He's only on the job a few years, but his uncle is some big shot, an inspector, I think, so he gets assigned to our unit. And it's bullshit, because it really doesn't happen that way on our squad. We all made our bones to get here. I swear to God, there's not one hook, until this fucking idiot gets assigned. The irony of it all is that he was a firearms instructor before he came to Violent Crime." Lucy snorted in disgust as she rocked back in her chair.

"Tony is the guy who actually fired the gun."

"Yep."

"And you know that because"—Jesse flipped open the file—"it says here…Billy told you."

"Not just Billy. Everybody. All the guys in the squad were talking about it when I got back. Tony even apologized to me. He was actually crying. Said he was just trying to play a joke. But that was all before IA got involved. As soon as that happened, everybody clammed up. All of a sudden, nobody remembers anything. Nobody was paying attention."

"Why?" Lexi interjected, disbelief apparent in her tone.

"Because of the uncle." Lucy's voice was calm and collected. "He has a lot of juice. Doesn't want the kid's name sullied. Or his own, for that matter."

Lexi pushed her laptop to the side. "Would it really be that bad? I mean, I know this is going to sound stupid but I Googled *accidental discharges* before you got here and they seem, well, not uncommon."

"I know." Lucy nodded. "Believe me, I've heard about them happening before too." Her tone indicated that she was clearly still trying to figure it out herself. "We all thought it would just be glossed over. That's basically what we were told initially, mostly because it involved Tony." Visibly annoyed, she cocked her head to the side. "But something changed. I wish I knew what," she said, nearly under her breath.

Lexi still couldn't wrap her head around it, but she worried she was talking too much—after all, she was only a student. She caught Jesse's eye, and Jesse's subtle nod gave her the go-ahead. She asked, "But would the repercussions really be that bad for the other detectives if they were just honest about what happened?"

"I don't know. They're scared. In a way, I don't even blame them.

They're afraid of retaliation. Like I said, it's a great unit. We all worked hard to be there. Nobody wants to lose their spot. So I guess they'll do what they're told."

Jesse picked up her pen. "When did the internal affairs unit get involved? You said it wasn't right away."

"I don't know exactly. In the beginning our captain told us all that the incident was being kept quiet. Nobody got hurt, not really—seriously, it was basically a scratch. The bullet tore through Will's pants and barely grazed his leg. I heard the department was working with him to make sure he was taken care of. He was getting ready to retire anyway. Now he'll actually get a better package." The corner of her mouth turned up a little at that realization. "Anyway, nobody wanted bad press and so we were told to keep our mouths shut. They told Tony that he would have to take a rip, like some kind of discipline for the incident. Then the Cap told me that because it was my gun, I might get a written reprimand for violating policy on securing your firearm properly." She pursed her lips in frustration. "Then something changed. It got all spun around. All of a sudden the whole thing is my fault. Because it was my gun and suddenly I'm the shooter. And I have to take the hit for everything. When I wasn't even there and everybody, I mean everybody, knows it."

"Where were you, again?" Jesse asked the question offhandedly, although Lucy had yet to mention her exact location at the time of the shooting.

Lucy broke the eye contact she had used to get her point across. She looked down at her fidgeting hands. "I was downstairs. In patrol. I went to see the lieutenant." The anger was gone from her voice, replaced by something decidedly different.

Jesse cocked her head to the side and crinkled her brow, effectively asking why without actually saying it.

"We're friends," Lucy offered in explanation, still unable to meet either woman's stare.

"Did other people see you there?"

Lucy shook her head and curled her mouth in a frown.

"How long were you there?"

"I don't know. Maybe forty-five minutes." She was visibly uncomfortable, picking at her short fingernails repeatedly. "We met up in the bunk room." Her neck was blotchy and her cheeks had reddened.

Her voice was just above a whisper. "Sometimes we go there for privacy. To talk. We're friends," she said again, guilty as sin.

"The lieutenant's name?"

"Calhoun. Danielle Calhoun."

Jesse noted the name on her pad, and as she wrote it out, she spoke casually. "So you and Lieutenant Calhoun are romantically involved?"

Lucy licked her lips and lowered her eyes, looking at the surface of the table as she thought about the answer. "I wouldn't say that exactly."

"But you are sleeping together?" Jesse asked it as though it was a perfunctory question, without judgment.

"Yes." Lucy had on a brave face, but her voice hitched in her throat, betraying her.

"So when your gun went off, were you two—"

"It's not—" Lucy started and then stopped abruptly. Shaking her head, she took a deep breath before starting again. "It's just, it's complicated."

Jesse stopped taking notes and gave Lucy her full attention. "I know this is hard. But it's important. I need to know what we're up against." Her tone held a surprising amount of sympathy.

Lucy looked up to the ceiling in a futile effort to keep the tears that had pooled up from spilling out. She nodded and in a second regained her composure, wiping the moisture from the corners of her eyes. "Yes." She breathed deeply again and fixed her steely eyes on the table in front of her. "The answer to your question. Yes. Dani, Lieutenant Calhoun I mean, and I were…together when it happened."

Lexi almost fell out of her chair at the direction this conversation had taken, but Jesse seemed unsurprised. Lucy was gay. Somehow or another she hadn't seen that coming at all. She was supposed to be taking notes and instead she was watching the interview unfold like it was a soap opera. She might as well have gotten a bowl of popcorn.

Jesse went right back to business. "Is she your supervisor?"

"No." Lucy looked totally ashamed.

"Who knows about your relationship?"

Collecting herself, Lucy arched forward in her chair and rubbed her thighs nervously. "I don't know. I don't talk about it or anything. But we are probably not as discreet as we should be." Wringing her hands, she leaned back in her chair again and exhaled deeply as she thought about it more. "People know." She sucked in her cheeks ,chewing at the inside of her mouth as she came clean. "Guys in my squad have made comments. Just teasing me and stuff, and I never answer them. But they're not idiots. They know."

Lexi focused on her computer and started typing, just to force herself to stop staring.

"This is obviously upsetting for you, I can see that, but it's actually good for your case. You said before that all the guys had a sudden case of amnesia. Couldn't remember if you were there or not. This is a solid alibi and that's good for you." Jesse's tone was not entirely optimistic but it held promise.

Elbows on the table, Lucy rested her head in her hands, holding back her blond hair and revealing darker roots at the base. "It won't work. She won't give me an alibi. I don't even want to ask her to."

Jesse looked over to Lexi as if checking if there was something she was missing. Lexi was too stupefied to make sense of any of it. Before either of them could ask, Lucy opened up.

"Dani and I, we have an understanding. God, I can't believe I'm saying this." Lucy breathed out, completely defeated. "What we have is just, it's just…" She looked around the room, struggling. "Honestly, I don't know what it is, I guess. But what I do know is that I have a girlfriend and Danielle has a wife, and this thing we have"—she balled her hands up on the table in front of her—"it isn't anything that either of us wants to be more than exactly what it is. My girlfriend would fucking die. I mean, she has no idea. This would kill her. Look, I know you both probably think I'm a total asshole, but I love my girlfriend. I would never hurt her, I don't want to break up with her. This, trust me, would destroy her." She took a shallow breath, almost hyperventilating. "Dani won't do it anyway. For the same reasons, I'm sure. And I won't ask her to." Lucy grew increasingly agitated as she spoke. She repeatedly clenched her fists but fell short of pounding the conference table. "Jesus Christ, I'm fucked."

Jesse scratched at her temple and mussed her hair. "Okay. Look, we'll figure something out. Let's call it a night. Go home, try to relax. I'm going to get in touch with the lawyer handling this for the police department and see what they're up to. It's obviously something because they don't have a solid case against you. They know you didn't do it, but they want you to take the fall. We're not going to let that happen. When are you supposed to work next?"

"Monday."

"We'll be in touch with you before then. Go home. It'll be okay." The reassurance in Jesse's voice convinced Lexi that it would be.

Lexi tried to echo Jesse's words as she walked Lucy to the door.

As the elevator opened, Lucy turned to her. "I'm sure you think I'm a jerk. I'm really not a bad person. I just wanted you to know that." Then she got in the elevator and was gone.

Lexi wasn't really sure what to think about any of it. She was still reeling from it all. But the fact that it mattered to Lucy what she and Jesse thought about her scored her at least a few points.

CHAPTER NINE

Glancing at her watch on the way back to the conference room, Lexi noticed the time. Seven minutes after nine. Shit. She was already two hours late for her date with Julie and she hadn't even called her. She grabbed her phone, but Jesse saw her and waved her into the conference room where she was finishing up a call, smiling into the receiver.

"Paul?" Lexi asked optimistically as she sat down across from Jesse.

It took Jesse a minute to register what Lexi was asking. "Uh, no." She cleared her throat and added awkwardly, "No, that was something else." She swiftly switched gears. "But I called the department lawyer listed in the file. No answer, so I left a message."

Lexi was sort of taken aback that her boss was updating her to this level but tried to cover it. "Okay. Should I put the file back in Paul's office?"

"No. It's our case now." Jesse sighed audibly. "And it's going to be messy."

"Why?" Lexi had a million questions she was dying to ask, mostly because Jesse had just referred to this case as something they would be working on together. She felt certain that was the wrong thing to focus on, so she opted for what seemed the most obvious question, even if it sounded naïve. "I know this is probably a stupid question. Obviously there are some issues, but if she didn't fire the gun, how bad can it be?"

Jesse rubbed her forehead and ran her hand through her unruly hair. "It's not a stupid question at all." Jesse had the kind of hair that really never looked bad. Shortish, wavy, and kind of wild, even after she messed around with it—something she did constantly—it always looked perfect. Lexi distractedly watched Jesse brush it with her hand as she spoke.

"You're right. It shouldn't be that big a deal. But it obviously is." Jesse hooked her thumbs under her chin and ran an index finger back and forth over her lips thinking out loud as she answered Lexi. "The department definitely wants her for the fall guy. And like she said, all of her colleagues are scared enough not to vouch for her. Plus there's the added problem that she was getting laid while it happened." Jesse raised an eyebrow. "And while that could actually help her in some ways, it has its own problems, not the least of which is that her personal relationship will likely suffer." Jesse put her hands down and drummed the table with her fingers. "Anyway, we'll figure something out."

Lexi was surprised by how positively sure Jesse sounded as she said it.

Then Jesse stood and started gathering up her stuff. "Come on, I'll drive you home."

She said it so resolutely that there could be no declining the offer, not that Lexi wanted to. But in an effort to not sound as absolutely thrilled by it as she was, she nodded and said simply, "Thanks, that'd be great."

In the few minutes she took to grab her coat and purse she texted Julie. A quick glance at her phone revealed several missed calls and texts. It was clear that she was going to have a lot of making up to do. She fired off a quick message. *Sorry, baby, caught at work. Long story will explain when I see you.* She cringed a little as she sent it. She'd never used any terms of endearment with Julie, so she knew *baby* was way over the top, but right now she needed all the help she could get.

❖

Sliding into the front passenger seat of Jesse's sleek, elegant car, Lexi was immediately hit with the aroma of the leather interior mixed with the latent scent of Jesse's musky perfume lingering everywhere. She snuck in one indulgent deep breath while Jesse arranged her stuff on the backseat, keeping her eyes open the whole time to make sure she didn't get caught. She reminded herself that this was just a ride home from her boss who happened to live across the street. A mere courtesy, nothing more. As they pulled out of the parking garage into the streets of downtown Manhattan, Lexi tried for a casual tone.

"So, I do have a question."

"What's up?" Jesse asked back informally, not taking her eyes off the road.

"I'm just wondering. How did you know? About Lucy. Weston. I mean, how did you know that something was up with her and the lieutenant?"

"I guess body language mostly," Jesse answered with a shrug. "She was obviously uncomfortable talking about it."

"I know, but how did you know she was gay? You seemed...well, not surprised by it at all. How'd you know?" It did not come out nearly as smoothly as Lexi hoped.

Jesse must have noticed too, because a slow smile spread across her face. She tilted her head to the side and made the briefest eye contact with Lexi. "I don't know." She was beaming from ear to ear as she shrugged her shoulders and put a palm up in the air almost grasping for the answer. "I guess just...how you know. You know?" She laughed as she said it.

Lexi laughed too and shook her head. "Uh, no. *I* didn't know. At all," she added with exasperation.

"I know." Jesse couldn't stop smiling as she wound through the maze of streets leading to the Brooklyn Bridge.

"Oh my God, was I that obvious?"

"Well, I was going to reach over and pick your jaw up from the floor, but I thought that'd be a bit much," Jesse teased.

Lexi tipped her head back against the headrest and groaned in embarrassment.

"I'm just kidding. It wasn't that bad. I'm sure she didn't even notice."

"You noticed."

"Come on, it's not that big a deal."

"For you. You acted like a normal person." Lexi was half laughing but there was disappointment underneath. "I can't believe I was so oblivious. And then so obviously surprised by it. I hate myself right now."

Jesse looked over at Lexi. "Stop beating yourself up." Jesse held the eye contact until she turned back to the road, a small grin starting again. "I happen to have excellent gaydar. Add to that the fact that I've seen just about everything by now." Her smile widened, revealing her perfect teeth. "I don't think there's anybody that's really going to surprise me."

Lexi saw the opportunity and took it before she had a chance to chicken out. "Really?" The lilt in her voice held just the slightest challenge.

Jesse nodded, pursing her lips slightly as she looked through the windshield.

"What about me?" It cost Lexi every drop of courage to ask. Was she flirting with her boss? "I'm gay. Does that surprise you?"

Jesse braked completely for a yellow light and waited as it turned red. She turned her whole body to face Lexi, giving her a quick once-over before she said through a devilish grin, "I don't think *surprised* would be the word I would use."

Lexi's heart was beating so hard she thought it might break through her chest. She was suddenly aware that her mouth hung slightly open in utter disbelief about where this conversation might be going.

But then the light changed, and with it the tone of the conversation, as Jesse drove on. "Sorry. Does that bother you? That I'm not surprised." When Jesse spoke, the undercurrent was gone from her voice, making Lexi question if it had been there at all.

Lexi collected herself quickly. "No, not at all." She shook her head, grounding herself as she continued. "It's just, usually people are surprised about me."

"Yeah, I can see that. But I'm not just anybody." The playfulness from a moment ago was back in Jesse's voice. "You know, we do work together. And you live across the street from me." Jesse glanced over, gauging Lexi's reaction. "So I do have some insight that the average person wouldn't have. Like, for example, I've seen you and your little friend, the one you've been hanging around with forever." Jesse paused and waited for Lexi to fill in the name.

"Sam?" Lexi said with a half smile.

"Yeah, Sam." Jesse nodded. "Sam is clearly a lesbian. And I know you're friends with Meg. Also gay. Not that you can't be straight and have gay friends or anything, particularly growing up in Bay West," she said, providing the counter to her own argument. "But I did see you at Fall Festival. And you were sitting on some girl's lap, and you looked kind of cozy, so I did the math." She looked over at Lexi and wrinkled her nose, a frisky smile evident all the way up to her gorgeous eyes.

"Ah, so you spied on me. I'm not really sure that you can pass that off as having good insight, as you say," Lexi answered back, matching Jesse's light tone.

"It was hardly spying. You were in a public forum." Jesse leaned over, raising her eyebrows for effect as she added in a husky whisper, "And you could barely keep your hands off each other."

Lexi could feel her face redden and was thankful it was so dark. "I don't know what you are talking about," she responded impishly. Of course, she knew exactly what Jesse was talking about. There hadn't been that many times she and Julie had displayed any kind of public affection. Lexi was at once mortified and completely turned on at the thought that Jesse had witnessed it.

As they made the turn into the development, Lexi could feel the energy change again and had to fight back her disappointment.

"On a serious note, Lexi, I didn't say it before, but you did a really phenomenal job today." Jesse looked right at her as she said it and Lexi wasn't sure how many more times tonight she could look into those dark-rimmed, pale sage eyes before she jumped clear across the center console. Unable to form any words at all, Lexi just nodded.

"I'm serious. I know it may sound trite, but that is why we do this. To help people. And today it was you. You know, most people would have dumped that call into voice mail. You saved Lucy Weston today. I hope you realize how important that is."

Just like that, they were back to being the attorney and the law intern, Lexi thought. Despite their spirited conversation and one tense moment that Lexi wasn't sure happened other than in her imagination, that's all they ever were, Lexi realized, swallowing her disappointment.

"Thanks," Lexi said, quickly hopping out of the car, not giving Jesse a chance to read the emotion she was sure was all over her face. She hurried down the street toward the path to the rental section, stopping once she was through the clearing to collect herself. She had a lot of work ahead of her to make amends with her actual girlfriend.

CHAPTER TEN

M eg filled a travel mug with coffee as she got ready to head over to the softball field. She stepped out of her house and inhaled the salty breeze coming off the water, studying the brightly colored treetops that lined the path as she walked. She couldn't help the smile on her face. She was happy to be home and meeting up with her friends at the softball game on such a beautifully crisp Saturday morning. Her only regret as she strode across the Bay West campus to the edge of the property where the field lay was that she had not been brave enough to sign up for the Bay West softball league herself. Maybe next year.

She was just cutting through the auxiliary parking lot when she noticed an unmistakable lanky blonde emerging from a shiny red pickup just ahead. Mia saw her right away. "Hey, Meg." Mia squinted a little as the sun behind Meg beat down on her face. "Coming to watch my game?" A lopsided, arrogant smile stretched across her face as she reached into the truck bed, grabbing a bat and glove.

"You wish," Meg teased back. "My friends are playing. I guess they're up against you." Meg slowed to wait by the rear of the car as Mia got her gear together.

"Here we go with the friends excuses again." Mia smirked, accentuating the scar on her lip that Meg had almost forgotten about. "We're not gonna go through that whole routine again, are we?"

In spite of herself, Meg laughed at Mia's playful interpretation of their previous interaction. She found that she was both entertained and enthralled by Mia's quick wit and effortless charm. She could learn a thing or two from her, she thought offhandedly. Giving up on even attempting a clever retort, Meg shrugged. "I can't help it. It's the truth. I didn't even know that you were in the league." She tried to cover her smile as she brought the coffee cup to her lips.

Mia leaned down and said, "Yeah, but now that you know I'm playing, you are *so* going to be watching me." With a wink, she trotted off to the far dugout and greeted her teammates. As Meg climbed up the bleachers to where Lexi and Sam were seated, she thought Mia was probably right.

Meg's butt hadn't even hit the cold aluminum before Lexi pulled her in for a hug.

"Thank God you're back. I want to hear all about London, blah-blah. But first, who was that you were just talking to?"

"That's Mia."

"Mia-from-Fall-Festival Mia?"

Meg nodded, sipping her drink.

"She's cute, Meg." Lexi didn't even try to conceal her enthusiasm. "How did you two…" Lexi motioned back and forth with her hands.

"I just ran into her in the parking lot. I guess she's playing you guys, Sam."

Sam glanced over toward where Mia's team was warming up.

"Where's Julie, by the way? Wasn't last night your big date or whatever? I figured you stayed at her place. That's why I didn't call before I headed over." Meg looked around for the obviously absent Julie.

"My date didn't really happen. Long story." Lexi rolled her eyes and shook Meg off with a pointed look that Meg understood to mean that Lexi would fill her in later. "Anyway, she's on her way now. She'll be here in a few minutes. But don't change the subject. What's up with you and Mia? What did you guys talk about?"

"Nothing really. We just…we basically just flirt. It's actually kind of fun," Meg answered honestly.

"So do you like her?"

"I don't think so." She was a little surprised by how quickly that answer came to her. "Not really. I mean, I don't really know her, but she's totally cocky. That's not really my thing."

Sam huffed and shook her head as she stood and grabbed her glove to head toward the rest of the team slowly gathering on the infield.

"What, Sam?" Meg's tone didn't hide her annoyance. In Meg's

opinion, Sam thought she knew the answer to pretty much everything. Usually she let it go, but today Meg wasn't in the mood.

Eyebrows raised in judgment, Sam just stared at the ground and shook her head again. "Nothing." It was so smug Meg couldn't let it pass.

"Then why are you shaking your head?"

Sam hopped down to the ground and took a few steps toward the field. But then she stopped short and turned to face Meg and Lexi where they sat in the third row. "You know, you guys. You're both so… uptight. Everything has to be fucking perfect. It's all about The One." Sam stopped talking to throw air quotes around the term. She must have seen the look of shock on their faces because she looked at the ground and pushed around a rock with her cleat before continuing in a much calmer voice. "I just think you both need to relax a little. They can't all be the one, you know. That's why we go out. To get some experience and have some fun. Before you say anything"—she held up her hand to stop Lexi, who was about to interject—"I'm not saying you should be like me, exactly. Believe me, I know I have my own issues," she said as she covered the center of her chest with her palm. "I just mean…" She tugged the brim of her cap as she spoke. "I guess what I'm trying to say is how will you know *the one* unless you ever date the ones who aren't the one? Meg, you've been hung up on your ex-girlfriend since you got here. Look around." Sam gestured openly with both arms. "You live in a goddamn lesbian mecca. And now, here's this hot girl who repeatedly flirts with you and you're not interested because, what, she's probably not the be all and end all. You just said yourself that talking to her was fun. Here's a newsflash—it's supposed to be." She looked back and forth between Meg and Lexi. "You're in your twenties, for Christ's sake. Live a little." With that, Sam turned on her heel and jogged off to the field, leaving them both gaping after her in stunned silence.

A few seconds passed before Meg broke the quiet. "Well, that was weird."

"Kinda."

"What's weirder is that I maybe think Sam is a genius."

"Well, she's never been afraid to say exactly what she feels." Lexi rolled her eyes in annoyance.

"Thing is, I get what she was saying about me, but why is she picking on you? I wasn't gone for that long. What'd I miss?"

Lexi folded her arms and hunched forward, leaning on her knees. "It's this whole Julie saga. Sam basically thinks I'm a terrible girlfriend. She thinks I'm not trying hard enough."

"Why?"

"Well, there's the thing with dinner last night. Julie wanted to do something special because we never really do anything alone. You know, there's always the bunch of us hanging out together. So I guess she kicked her roommates out and cooked and everything."

"Okay."

"Yeah, well. I kind of missed dinner."

"What?" Meg's jaw dropped.

"Just listen before you say anything." Lexi told Meg about the emergency case, and how she got stuck in the office, and how she couldn't break to call or text.

"So Julie's pissed, huh?"

"Yeah, she was pretty annoyed. But when I finally got to her place last night, I explained the situation. We fought about it a little, but ultimately she did understand where I was coming from, and that I had no control over it. She was mad, and hurt, I guess, but she forgave me. And I did end up staying there last night. Although not quite in the way she wanted, but still." She looked down sheepishly, biting her full lower lip as she considered her words. "Honestly, Sam is the one giving me the hardest time about it. She basically told me that I should have gotten up and left my office. Like I'm supposed to turn to my boss in the middle of a work crisis and tell her that I have to go because my girlfriend of two months is making me a romantic dinner? Give me a break." Lexi blew out a long breath and tucked her hair behind her ears. "Sam would never do that. This is all because it involves Jesse. She's trying to make it out like I picked Jesse over Julie, and it wasn't like that."

"Okay." Meg could hear the defensiveness in Lexi's voice and wondered how much of it was justified.

"I know, I'm totally tense right now. Sorry for dumping all of this on you. I'm just, I'm just really glad you're back." She leaned in and nudged Meg's shoulder with her own.

"Me too." As she nudged Lexi back, Meg caught a glimpse of Julie navigating her way through the other spectators to where they were seated.

"Hey, Jules." Meg hoped she wasn't in the way as Julie reached them.

"Meg. Welcome back." Julie patted Meg lightly on the shoulder and then used it as a support as she leaned in toward Lexi. "Morning, babe." She kissed Lexi sweetly on the cheek and settled down in the row in front of them, scooching back between Lexi's knees as she laced up her cleats. Lexi inched forward and put her arms around her girlfriend. Obviously whatever had gone down between them last night was history.

Meg averted her eyes, trying to give them a little privacy, and found herself scanning the field for a gangly blonde. She found her in left field, close enough that Mia's piercing blue eyes were visible from the bleachers. Having been caught, Meg did an unusually uncharacteristic thing. She simply wiggled her fingers in a wave, smiled, and shrugged, and continued to stare. Mia mouthed *I knew it* and smiled into her glove.

When the game ended, Meg continued her run of courage, inspired solely by Sam's soapbox speech. She walked right up to where Mia was packing up her equipment.

"Nice game."

"Oh, you saw some of the game?" Mia said not wasting any opportunity to tease. "I thought you were just watching me."

Meg rolled her eyes. "Anyway, my friends and I are going to The Kitchen tonight. I came over to see if you wanted to meet up."

Mia scrunched up her nose and puckered her lips. "I have to work later. I'm on until midnight." She paused for a second, then added with a hint of hope in her voice, "But I'll come by after. Will you stick around?"

"If nothing better comes along," Meg said jovially, seizing the opportunity to take the upper hand.

"As if." Mia was all adorable arrogance.

❖

The night started full of potential. Meg, Lexi, Sam, and Julie got an early ferry into the city and grabbed dinner at a cute little burger joint before making their way to The Kitchen. They were becoming a regular foursome. At The Kitchen, Meg was having a great time throwing back drinks with her friends while she eagerly awaited Mia's arrival. She tried not to look at her watch every five minutes and did a halfway decent job until after midnight, when Sam caught her in the act.

"Seriously, you should at least attempt to look less desperate." Sam's voice was disproportionately loud in Meg's ear.

It annoyed Meg that Sam thought she had the right to give her any unsolicited advice. At the same time though, she knew she should listen. Sam had natural talent when it came to girls. If she noticed Meg's eagerness, then Mia would too, and Meg really wanted to come off calm and relaxed, neither of which were appropriate adjectives to describe her inner state. She nodded at the tip and noticed Sam wobble a little before leaning up against the wall to regain her balance.

"You okay?" Meg asked, genuinely concerned as she saw the glazed-over look in Sam's eyes. When the other girl didn't respond right away, Meg lightly punched her arm to snap her out of her stupor. Instead of coming back into the conversation, Sam's eyes rolled back and she started to collapse before Meg caught her and shook her awake. They began to draw some attention and thankfully Lexi and Julie rushed over to see what was going on.

Between the three of them, they were able to guide Sam outside. The brisk night air roused her some, but only enough to keep her awake as she threw up on the curb.

"How much did you drink, Sam?" Lexi said as she helped her friend. Sam didn't respond, so Lexi looked over to Meg as though she might have an explanation.

Meg shrugged back, before adding, "We've been going up to the bar together. She's only had as many as I have, maybe three vodka-sodas."

"Plus the two beers at dinner."

"Still, she shouldn't be like this, something's wrong." Meg looked at her watch. Twelve twenty. She shook her head. "You know, some weird girl was chatting her up pretty hard about a half hour ago. She was fine up to that point. You think the girl could've slipped her something?"

"I don't know. But we've got to get her out of here." Lexi directed Julie to get them a cab. "Meg, stay here and wait for Mia. She'll probably be here any minute," Lexi said with authority. "Julie and I will take care of her."

Meg shook her leg nervously, considering the options. As much as she wanted to do exactly that, she knew she couldn't. The right thing to do was to make sure Sam was okay. She shook Lexi off. "No way. I'm coming with you guys."

As luck would have it, Meg caught sight of Mia sauntering down the street just as she was about to get into the cab. Mia saw her too and spread her arms out to her sides, palms up in playful disbelief.

"Ducking out on me already?" Mia asked good-naturedly as she approached.

Meg shook her head and hurriedly provided what she knew sounded like a lame excuse. "One of my friends is really sick. I'm sorry." She wanted to say more, but glancing into the backseat of the cab, she regretted there wasn't time. "Sorry, I gotta go," she muttered as she slipped into the taxi and pulled the door closed behind her. Stealing a look through the rear windshield, she watched as Mia walked into The Kitchen without her.

They brought Sam back to Meg's house and the three girls took care of her together through the night. By morning it was clear that Sam was out of the woods, and although they never determined for sure what had happened, they all agreed that the important thing was that she was okay. Meg was glad that Sam was fine, of course. But she couldn't help feeling a little sorry for herself over her aborted rendezvous with Mia. Even Sam's genuine apology for ruining her night didn't perk her up. Meg simply couldn't shake the feeling that she had missed her moment, that what had happened at The Kitchen was probably a sign that she and Mia were not meant to be. The problem was she already knew that. So repeating it to herself did nothing to comfort her. In her mind, the beauty of what could have been with Mia was that Meg *wasn't* in love with her. She *wasn't* the one. She was supposed to be a fling, a casual hookup. No deep feelings, no broken hearts.

But instead, Meg was alone as usual, flitting back and forth between work in London and work in New York with no romantic prospects on either continent. The winter holidays were approaching fast and Meg was in the exact same rut she had been in since her breakup with Becca. These days she thought of Becca often—remembering only the good stuff, quite a feat considering that Becca could hardly be described as a good girlfriend. She was selfish and demanding, but she could also be funny and charming, and that was the side of her that Meg focused on now as she gazed out the tiny oblong window as her plane got in line for takeoff heading back to New York, where no one in particular awaited her arrival.

Meg knew deep down that she didn't actually miss the person Becca was or their ill-fated relationship. What she missed was the idea of Becca. This was a big part of the reason she was so bummed about not connecting with Mia. With the Christmas season would come family gatherings, and she'd prefer to be dating someone—or at least hooking up with someone—when she spent time with her family. Not so she could bring her to meet the family—she probably wouldn't even mention her—but Meg felt better on the inside knowing there was someone out there who thought she was interesting enough to spend time with, be intimate with, even. It gave her the confidence she needed to get through her Aunt Ginny's probing questions. *Are you seeing anyone?* she would ask, her voice and eyes full of doubtful hope. At least she would ask. The rest of her extended family struggled at general small talk. They clearly suspected she spent her nights in some back-alley bar donning the trademark purple handkerchief and exchanging code words with the other sexual deviants.

Her own generation of relatives was different. Her sister and brother-in-law were amazing on a daily basis. They never treated her like a mutant. And most of her cousins had issued their moral support over the years, but still she sensed their pity—not because she was gay, but because she was single and alone, reminders of the fact that she was universally undesirable.

There really was nothing quite like being by yourself at Christmastime in New York City to make you feel like a frigging loser.

CHAPTER ELEVEN

The days at Stanton Ducane passed entirely too quickly for Lexi's liking. While she was still technically assigned to Allison, most of her time was spent on Lucy Weston's case, which meant hours of direct contact with Jesse. She assisted Jesse during the witness interviews, each of whom had a department attorney present, and none of whom admitted to having witnessed anything. She had even accompanied Jesse to Lieutenant Danielle Calhoun's home, where Jesse practically begged her through the closed front door to speak to them. Lexi thought for sure that Jesse would persuade her, but they'd left defeated.

Plus, she did tons of research, something she thrived on. She reveled in digging up obscure cases and dissecting policy. She had to admit that she was good at it too. She'd already found several similar cases from departments around the country, and she had pointed out a number of divergent directives within police department policies. Jesse agreed there was precedent for Lucy Weston to keep her job.

Unfortunately, Lucy was not convinced. She had been placed on restricted duty until the completion of the internal affairs investigation. This meant she was forced to turn in her firearm and was essentially chained to a desk, allowed only to perform administrative tasks. It was destroying Lucy, and Lexi could hear it chipping away at her spirit each time they spoke on the phone.

Jesse had set up a full schedule for them today. The first item on the agenda was a meeting at the police department. This was to be followed by another meeting on an entirely separate case—some kind of divorce mediation Jesse was handling. Jesse had said she thought it would be good for Lexi to come along, just for the experience of something different. The appointments were scheduled pretty much back to back. Rather than trek separately into the city, Jesse had suggested they drive in together so they could brainstorm in Jesse's truck as they fought traffic.

Perfect, Lexi thought. It was a Friday and she had no classes. Plus the Bay West Christmas Extravaganza was tonight. Since she was just going in for a few meetings, she'd be home in plenty of time to go to the party with her friends as planned.

As had been the case in the past, the meeting with the police department legal department was a waste of time. Every time they met, there was a new lead attorney assigned, and the process started from square one. As they climbed back into Jesse's Range Rover to head to their next appointment, Jesse said, "Something about this whole thing is just not sitting right with me." Jesse turned the engine over. She drummed the steering wheel for a second. "All the research you did indicates that they can't fire her. Not based on this one incident. Certainly not without a countersuit from Lucy based on gender discrimination or sexual harassment—all things that are way worse than the negligent discharge of a weapon. And aside from this, her service record is impeccable. What is their game, Lex?" She kept both hands on the wheel as she looked at Lexi.

Lexi just shook her head. "I don't know," she replied honestly.

Jesse snapped her fingers and reached for her phone. "I have an idea." She tapped the screen a few times and held it to her ear. "Nick, it's Jess. I need your help with something. It's sort of unusual. Involves the police department actually. I'm on my way to my two o'clock now, but give me a call if you can meet up later." She pressed the end button on her phone and placed it on the armrest between them.

"So, my friend Nick is a private investigator. I use his services a lot on"—she waved her hand in the air while she thought about the right description—"all sorts of cases, really. He's a great guy, has tons of excellent contacts. He can get the score on anything. But"—she pointed an index finger for dramatic effect—"he was a sergeant in the NYPD before he left to start his own business." She looked over at Lexi, the signature gleam back in her eyes. "I bet he still has some hooks in there and can get us the scoop on what's really going on. I can't believe I didn't think of this until now."

Lexi smiled, enjoying Jesse's confidence in her new strategy as she shifted into drive and they headed uptown to their next meeting.

Lexi endured the divorce mediation, although she had a hard time concentrating on the content. It was all finger-pointing. She found it boring and sad, with no real resolution, just another meeting set up down the line. She entertained herself throughout by stealing glances at her boss, watching her lick her lips and ruffle her hair as she hammered out details.

Walking back to their parking space, Jesse checked her phone. "Fabulous. Nick can meet at five o'clock." She glanced at her watch. "It's four twenty-five now. So that'll work. I'm going to text him back. Is that okay? I mean are you in a rush to get back or anything?"

"Nope. It's fine." Lexi was thrilled to extend her time with Jesse. "Where are we meeting him?"

"The Banana Warehouse."

"The boy bar?" Lexi did not expect to hear that.

Jesse smiled and rolled her eyes. "Yes, Lexi. Nick is gay, just like us." She laughed as she pressed the button to unlock the car doors. Climbing into the truck, Jesse was half laughing to herself. "So a few things about Nick Decker. He and I have known each other for about fifteen years. He abuses me relentlessly. He's gay but very straight looking and straight acting. I'm telling you this so you don't get confused—I remember the whole jaw-dropping incident with Lucy Weston," Jesse teased.

"Never gonna let me live it down, huh?"

"Never." Jesse shook her head, smiling from ear to ear.

❖

Jesse filled Nick in on Lucy Weston's case. He nodded as she spoke, interrupting her only once to tell her that he knew of Dani Calhoun from his days in vice. He added that she was kind of a rising star, no-nonsense and very well liked by the guys, clarifying that to mean the guys she supervised. It was well known that she was a lesbian, not that that deterred too many from giving it the old college try.

Nick assured them both that he would reach out to his buddies and see what he could find out. Then the conversation turned social as the three of them sat together at the bar. Jesse and Nick teased each other ruthlessly about everything from age to work to relationships. Just as they were getting ready to go, Jesse took one last opportunity to call Nick out.

"Really, Nick, when are you going to settle down with one of these lucky guys?" Jesse gestured openly toward the bar, which was starting to fill.

"In a few hours, probably." He laughed at his own joke. "What about you? You with anybody?"

Jesse took a sip of her drink, and as she swallowed, she squinted one eye, cocking her head to the side, and shrugged a little. It was such a non-answer that even Nick seemed uncertain. He subtly shifted his eyes toward Lexi, asking if it was her. Jesse answered with a furrow of her brow and a brief shake of her head. She hoped Lexi didn't pick up the exchange. "Anyway, we should probably get going." Jesse finished her drink and clapped Nick on the shoulder. Looking around she added, "Clear the path for the circling sharks."

Lexi excused herself for a minute to use the ladies' room, and as she walked away, Nick watched Jesse's eyes follow her the entire length of the bar. He interrupted her stare as soon as Lexi was out of sight.

"Seriously, you're not hitting that?"

Jesse rolled her eyes at him. "Nick, she's my intern," she responded as if that were a full explanation.

"Even better. Sexy and transient. Sounds right up your alley."

Jesse shook him off. "It's different. She's different. Amazing, actually." She heard how she sounded, and she tried to keep her voice even. "You know, smart, hardworking, eager to learn."

"Terrible qualities," he teased.

"She's just—" She swallowed the end of her sentence trying to regroup. "She has a lot of potential."

"She's also young and pretty, with fantastic tits."

"Since when do you care about girls' chests?" Jesse joked, but her tone was off and Nick noticed.

"I don't," he quipped. "But I think the better question is, since when don't you?" His square jaw hung open a little as he waited for an answer.

"Look, she's sweet and beautiful, yes." Jesse peered into her beer hoping for one last sip. "And, well you've met her, she's completely unaffected and intelligent. And adorable." She shrugged dismissively attempting to make light of her words.

Nick called her bluff. "Nice try, honey." He spoke directly to her even as he scanned the crowd over her shoulder. "Sorry, Jess, but I've known you a long time. This is exactly the type of girl you try to nail all the time. Usually do, if I'm not mistaken."

"Not this girl." She turned to see what young stud had caught his attention as she continued. "This isn't the girl you nail. This is the girl you marry."

She turned back and looked up at Nick finding him wide-eyed, mouth open. He puffed his chest out and put his hands up dramatically. In the most flamboyant voice he could muster, he said, "Holy. Shit." With one finger he poked Jesse in the chest, emphasizing each word. "You fucking love her." He smiled. "Don't even deny it, girl."

Jesse was about to talk, but Nick moved his finger, strategically placing it over her mouth as Lexi rejoined them. Jesse turned to her. "Ready to go?" she asked quickly, but it was more of a statement than a question, so Lexi just nodded.

"Okay. I'll let you know what I come up with on that other thing," Nick said. "It was nice meeting you, Lexi the intern." He hugged Jesse and said in her ear, "That's an idea. An intern. Maybe I'll get myself an intern. I'm going to start interviewing right now."

Jesse bit her bottom lip as she punched his biceps, and she wondered if Lexi could see that her boss was blushing.

As they headed back to the car, their heads down against the crisp wind, Jesse spoke first. "You going to the party tonight?"

"Yeah. You?"

Jesse nodded a yes as her breath escaped in a cloud, visible against the cold. She glanced at her phone. "Wow. I didn't realize how late it was. No wonder I'm starving."

"I know, me too," Lexi responded, if only to keep the conversation going.

"Oh my God, I didn't even let you eat today. Come on, I'll buy you dinner before the party. There's a cute little Italian place three blocks over." Jesse's tone was so enthusiastic that it almost seemed like

Lexi didn't have a choice, not that she wanted to say no. But as she was about to respond, Jesse cut her off. "Sorry. I didn't mean to assume. You probably have plans with your friends or your, uh, girlfriend." She sounded flustered. It was adorable.

"No, it's fine. Let's eat." Lexi's mind was made up the minute the offer had been made. It was still early, and if she was starting to cut it close, she would simply text Julie and the girls that she was running late.

Half an hour later, warmed up at a cozy table for two by the fire, they sipped red wine and rehashed the day together. Lexi had been nervous that they would run out of things to talk about, but the conversation flowed easily between work and non-work topics. When the waiter set down their entrees, Jesse swirled the linguine around her fork and asked breezily, as though they were old acquaintances, "So, Lex, what's on the agenda for Christmas?"

Lexi took it in stride. "Well, Christmas Eve, we go to my grandparents' in Brooklyn. My aunts and uncles and cousins will all be there, so it's pretty big. We do the whole Italian fish thing. And then on Christmas Day, we'll just stay home. Have a big breakfast, open presents."

"Sounds nice."

"Yeah, it's pretty great. What about you?" Lexi looked down, mixing her Caesar salad around.

"I'm going up to Cape Cod. My family has a house out there, so we do Christmas there every year. I was toying with heading up there tonight. Sometimes I like to get there ahead of everyone. Enjoy the quiet before the storm, so to speak."

"So, you're going?"

"Nah, too late. I'll stop by the party for a bit and then head out in the morning. Christmas isn't for a few more days. My brothers won't be there until Christmas Eve anyway. I'll have some down time still."

"Do you have a big family?" Lexi asked between bites.

"Three brothers. And my parents, of course. So that's kind of big, I guess, by today's standards."

"Same as mine." Lexi took a sip of her wine.

Jesse paused. "Sure, yeah. Four kids. I guess it is sort of the same." She raised her eyebrows. "Except I don't have any sisters. And my parents aren't gay." She squinted one eye closed. "At least, I seriously doubt it."

Lexi laughed. "What are they like?"

"Who, my parents?" Jesse seemed taken aback by Lexi's curiosity.

Lexi hoped she wasn't crossing the line, but the way their back and forth was so seamless, it felt like a natural thing to ask. "Yeah. Your parents, your brothers. Tell me about them."

If Jesse was put off, she didn't show it. "Okay." She thought about it for one second before continuing. "I'm closest with my youngest brother, Justin. He and I talk all the time. I see him a lot when I go up there." She fiddled with a crust of bread on her plate as she continued. "Which I do a lot." She reflected on it for a moment like she was unsure what to say next. "I grew up right outside of Boston. They all still live there. It was like I defected when I moved down here after law school. Now when I go back, I mostly just go to the house at the Cape. I love it there."

"They were mad when you moved to New York?"

"I think more disappointed than anything. See, my dad is a real-estate developer. He has a pretty successful business, and I think he always figured that I would use my degree to join his company. I don't know why he thought that," Jesse stated definitively. "I was always very clear about what kind of law I wanted to practice." She shook her head. "But my older brother, John, joined the company right after he finished school, so I guess my dad thought I would do the same." She leaned back in her chair. "A few years ago my middle brother, Jake, he's also an attorney, he finally joined the business too, so Dad relaxed after that."

Lexi took a long blink, then held up one hand, signaling to Jesse to stop her narrative. "Hold on a second. Do all of your names begin with *J*?"

Jesse looked down and laughed her deep, sexy laugh. "Yes, they do." She rolled her eyes. "Not my mom. But the rest of us. All *J*s. So cheesy." She finished with a smile, adding, "One more Ducane tradition I will not be subjecting my own children to."

Lexi coughed to cover her surprise that Jesse had just mentioned having kids, then swished her hand and apologized for the interruption. "Sorry. You may continue," she said, giving the floor back to Jesse.

"That's okay. I actually have a question for you, since we're talking about names."

"Yeah?"

"How come you're Lexi Russo and not Russo-Markowski or the other way around?"

Lexi was impressed that Jesse remembered Marnie's last name. "Good question. Really, it's just because Chris had me, I mean actually gave birth to me, and that's what they put on the birth certificate. Marnie had my sister and my brothers, so they're all Markowskis. My moms always said a name is just a name. Doesn't make you family. Thank God, though. Russo-Markowski, that's definitely not fitting on any forms."

Jesse smiled at Lexi's response. Smiling back, Lexi spoke again. "So, back to you. How come you didn't want to work with your dad?" Lexi was halfway through her wine and she could feel it relaxing her nerves, giving her the confidence to ask the questions she was dying to know the answers to.

"It's not that I didn't want to work with him. I just had my own ideas of what I wanted to do."

"Moving to New York, you mean?"

"Well, that's part of it."

"And the other parts?" Lexi pressed her lightly.

"Look at you, trying to get my life story in one night," Jesse teased. "You're not writing my unauthorized biography, are you?"

Lexi was immediately embarrassed. "I'm sorry. I didn't mean to overstep."

"I'm just kidding, Lex." Jesse reached out and momentarily laid her hand on top of Lexi's reassuringly before withdrawing it just as quickly. "I met Laney when we were at Wellesley. Even though she's two years ahead of me, we hit it off right away. Ultimately, I followed her to Harvard for law school. Somewhere along the way, we hatched the idea for Stanton Ducane. She's from New York anyway, and by then I had heard about Bay West. I was sold before ever stepping foot inside the grounds."

"You started the firm right away?" Lexi had always been impressed by Jesse's easy success, even more so now, as she was struggling to line up her own interviews.

"Not right away." Jesse shook her head. "Laney got a job with the district attorney's office, then she got me in there too, when I finished school. We had a five-year plan. Stay with the DA's office, get some real experience, then branch out on our own." She twirled some pasta on her fork and lifted it to her lips, slightly smiling as she swallowed. "After a year, I was ready. I couldn't wait anymore. Too impatient, I guess."

Lexi took a risk. She looked at her salad and speared a hunk of romaine. "I guess when you want something, you just go for it." She looked up to see Jesse nearly choke on her wine. Fearing she had gone overboard, she attempted to reel it back in. "It worked out though, look how successful you are now."

Jesse finished coughing into her napkin and cleared her throat. "Yes, well. It wasn't all smooth sailing. We had a lot of help from Laney's dad—he threw a ton of business our way early on, and still it was tough. Tons of work. Terrible hours. Laney had always wanted to stay with the original plan, but I kept pushing. It very nearly destroyed us."

"You and Laney were a couple?" Lexi was dumbfounded.

Jesse almost choked again. "God, no." She wiped her mouth. "I didn't realize it sounded like that. Not at all. Laney's been with her wife since we were in college. But all of it was super hard." She leaned forward and placed her wrinkled cloth napkin next to her plate. "Laney's relationship with Mira, her wife, was seriously strained in those early days. Probably some of that was my fault because I wasn't willing to slow down at all. It put a lot of pressure on our friendship, our business, everything."

"It did work out, in the end, though." Lexi popped a crouton in her mouth and crunched it over her self-satisfaction at the obvious truth of the statement.

"It did." Jesse smiled back.

"Being in New York, do you miss seeing your family?"

Jesse shrugged off the answer. "I see them a lot. So, not really." With a soft chuckle she added, "Hopefully that doesn't sound too callous. Anyway, I'll see them all in a few days."

"They'll all come out to the Cape?"

Jesse nodded. "Yep. John and his family, he's got three kids. Jake and his wife and their two girls. My Aunt Cynthia will be there too. Plus, I hear that Justin is bringing his new girlfriend. So that should be interesting." She took a long drink.

Finishing the last of her wine and feeling its effects, Lexi went for it. "What about you? Do you bring your girlfriend with you?"

Jesse's laugh was raspy and sexy as hell. "So, what? The wine just unleashes your inner detective or are you really writing my biography?" she asked playfully, her light eyes peering out from under long dark lashes.

Lexi felt the blood rush to her cheeks. There was no turning back now. She fingered the base of her wineglass and teased, "I saw you duck the question with Nick earlier. We're not at work now." She tilted her head. "Figured this is as good a time as any to get the inside story." She teased her lower lip with her teeth, a trait she knew drove Julie wild.

Lexi saw Jesse focus on her mouth and immediately look away at having been caught. She took the smallest moment to regain her composure, briefly running a hand through her hair before meeting Lexi's eyes. "Well, I have to say, this is a line of questioning I did not expect at all." She could not stop a grin from spreading ear to ear. "I'm definitely getting you another glass of wine when the waiter comes back." She took a sip from her own glass. "To answer your question, no, I'm not bringing my girlfriend."

Lexi knew she was way out of bounds, but if she wasn't mistaken, Jesse seemed to be enjoying their tête-à-tête. Jesse was clearly about to offer more information, but in a lull between the carols playing on the restaurant's sound system, they both heard Lexi's cell phone ringing in her purse.

"Do you need to get that?" Jesse nodded at the oversized bag hanging off the back of Lexi's chair.

"No, it's okay." Lexi pulled out her phone and silenced Julie's call, noticing as she did so that she had four other missed calls. She was going to have a lot of explaining to do. She continued to hit the ignore button on her phone and placed it to the side of her wineglass before reaching for another sip, forgetting momentarily that she had finished it.

"So why aren't you bringing your girlfriend to Christmas?" Lexi asked.

Jesse swirled the wine around in her glass, a smile still playing at the corners of her mouth. "Well, Detective, that would be because I'm not dating anyone right now. Or at least anyone that I would consider my girlfriend."

"Ooh. What does that mean?"

"It means exactly what you think it means." Jesse's voice was surprisingly playful. "So how come you get to ask all the questions?"

"You can ask me anything you want. I'm an open book." Lexi smiled, intentionally showing off her signature dimples. "But I'm not done yet." She waved her hand at Jesse's growing smirk. "We were just talking about how you have several different girlfriends."

"I wouldn't call any of them girlfriends, actually."

"Come on, what about that lady with the long black hair, I see her leaving your house all the time. And I've seen her at the office too. Or the blonde with the Lexus, she's also a frequent visitor. Are they aware that you don't consider them girlfriend material?"

"What's with the surveillance?" Jesse said, laughing. "You're not stalking me, right?"

"It's a small development. We work together. I can't help it if I'm observant."

"Hmm…I don't know if I believe you." Jesse crinkled her brow a little, clearly enjoying the banter. "But, since you're keeping tabs on my visitors, I'll indulge you. The blonde with the Lexus, as you call her, is my best friend Betsy. There is nothing going on there. The other one, with the dark hair, that's Sara. She and I have an understanding. One that she is fully aware of." She licked her lips and wagged a finger at Lexi. "And perhaps you should spend a bit less time looking out your window," she chided.

Before Jesse could razz Lexi more, the waiter stopped by to ask if they needed anything else.

"She'll have another glass of cabernet," Jesse stated matter-of-factly. Lexi tried to object, but Jesse held up her hand in protest before she could even get a word out.

"And for you, miss?"

"I'm fine for the moment," Jesse stated, inspecting her glass, which was still half-full.

"Jess, you didn't have to do that." Lexi was a bit surprised by her own informality.

"Why, you don't want one?"

"No, I do. I just, I don't know, I feel bad."

"Well, don't. It's Christmas. We're going to a party, which I'm pretty sure you're already in trouble for being late to. So you might as well enjoy yourself. Besides, it's my turn to ask the questions." She smiled her killer smile and nonchalantly slid a last forkful of linguine into her mouth.

The waiter had barely set Lexi's drink on the table, before Jesse nodded at it. "Drink up." Then she sipped her own drink and rested her chin on one hand as she met Lexi's eyes dead-on. "So, what's the deal with your girlfriend? How long have you been dating, where'd you meet, and what do your parents have to say about it?" She wiggled her eyebrows. "Start talking, girl."

Lexi smiled and felt herself blush at the same time. "Her name is Julie. I met her at The Kitchen, but she lives in the development, in the rental section. We've only been dating for a few months. It's still pretty new."

"A renter, that's nice." Jesse smirked.

"What does that mean?" Lexi asked defensively.

"Nothing. Just that it's nice. Close, you know. Are you guys doing Christmas together?"

Lexi shook her head, playing around with the remnants of her salad. "Her family is in New Jersey, so she's going there."

"Your parents like her?"

"Yeah."

Jesse turned to the side in her chair, leaning her back up against the wall. "They must be so excited that you're gay." She shook her head, sounding almost wistful.

"I guess they are, now," Lexi acknowledged. "They weren't always, though. Marnie was tough in the beginning. I basically came out to them when I was in high school. Chris was fine, but Marnie didn't believe me. She thought that I was just trying to make them happy or something. Or going through a phase, like I just wanted to fit in. Funny, right?" She paused, assessing Jesse's reaction. "And then I dated a few guys over the years, so that threw her off too. I guess I wanted to be sure. Or maybe I was just experimenting, but with guys, you know, the way some girls do with other girls when they're in college. When I told them that I knew for sure, she was pretty much just happy for me. They both were."

"Always the drama queen, Marnie," Jesse said with more than a touch of venom before quickly backpedaling. "Sorry, that was uncalled for. Your moms are great. You're lucky to have them." Although she was going for sincere, it sounded more like annoyance as she breathed out the last line.

"What happened with you guys anyway?" Lexi asked, taking full advantage of both her liquor-infused boldness and the path the conversation had taken.

Jesse opened her mouth to answer but stopped, her eyes narrowing as a look of confusion came over her face.

Lexi's phone vibrated on the table, momentarily stealing her attention. She quickly scanned over the text message from Meg warning her that both Sam and Julie were starting to get pretty pissed about her absence. Lexi frowned as she read it.

Jesse pushed her plate toward the center of the table. "I guess I should get you back. I don't want your girlfriend to think I kidnapped you."

"No, it's okay. That was actually just Meg. I texted them before to say I'd be a little late. Meg's just keeping me updated."

"Ah, Meg. She's the best."

"Yeah, she's pretty great." Lexi watched as Jesse signaled the waiter for the check.

When it came, Lexi wasn't sure if she should offer Jesse money. She knew it would be awkward to do that, but she also didn't want to look rude. She figured she could at least suggest paying for her half. But as she reached for her purse, Jesse stopped her and explained that this was basically a working dinner.

Lexi couldn't help feeling a little deflated as she realized that for Jesse, this was really still work, while for a few minutes she had allowed herself to believe that it was way more than that.

CHAPTER TWELVE

According to Lexi, the Bay West Christmas Extravaganza was the biggest party of the year. All week, the plan had been to head over to the Commons around eight so they could stake out a good spot. Meg spent the entire day secretly wondering if she might run into Mia tonight, because since they'd almost met up at The Kitchen over a month ago, Meg hadn't seen or heard from the girl. She had bumped into Jesse yesterday morning and knew Jesse planned on going, but Meg hadn't the nerve to ask about Mia. Anyway, she figured the odds were pretty good, it being a social and all.

Meg had just made her third and final outfit change when she heard her phone beep. She read the text from Lexi which said simply, *Stuck at work. Don't wait for me. Meet you there*. Meg looked at her watch. Seven forty. She figured that the message was sent to Sam and Julie as well, a fact that was confirmed one minute later by Sam's text to Meg informing her that they would swing by her place in fifteen minutes.

The three of them arrived at the Commons promptly at eight as planned, and it was just in time to score a perfect table on the far side of the room, situated nicely between the bar, the dance floor, and an exit to the balcony. Looking around, Meg saw that the room was softly lit just like the Fall Festival a few months ago, but there were Christmas decorations everywhere. Colored lights adorned the tables and glass balls hung from the ceiling, making the place beautiful and festive.

As the minutes ticked by, Meg busied herself talking to Sam and Julie, but she couldn't stop scanning the room for Mia. She was also anxious for Lexi to get there already because she could tell Sam and

Julie were getting annoyed. They had just started running through the possibilities of what Lexi could be doing at work. Truthfully, Meg was kind of wondering too, but the thought shot completely out of her head at the sight at the entrance to the room.

Standing in the main doorway were two uniformed police officers. Meg would have recognized that wiry frame anywhere. She tuned out her friends and watched as Mia conversed with Kameron Browne for several minutes before turning to her partner, a petite brunette who looked like a teenager dressed up for Halloween. Mia pointed around giving the other girl some kind of instructions. Her partner nodded before turning and exiting to the outdoor balcony. Mia walked through the party, staying close to the wall before disappearing down the back staircase to the first floor. Meg knew that the first-floor common area was off-limits during all the Commons parties. But she couldn't resist. She was dying to know what was going on and—okay, mostly—to get a closer look at Mia in that uniform. Barely saying a word, she got up from the table and slipped down the back staircase.

The stairs were dark, so she treaded slowly and held on to the railing. At least the first floor was slightly illuminated by the ambient light from street lamps glowing in through the windows. Right away, she spotted Mia in the main area, flashlight out, walking casually as she pointed her light around the room. Meg paused in the open doorway. The last thing she wanted to do was sneak up on a cop in a dark room.

She leaned up against the door frame and knocked on the wall. "Looking for something, Officer?"

Mia spun on her heel and shined her light right at Meg. "You know, sneaking up on an armed person in a dark, supposedly unoccupied space is a really bad idea." Her tone was as playful as ever.

"I had to get your attention somehow. Nice outfit, by the way."

"You like it?" Mia said with a knowing grin. Meg could only imagine the number of girls who melted on a daily basis at the sight of the tall blonde in the dark blue uniform.

"You don't look terrible in it."

Mia rolled her eyes and shook her head, smiling.

Meg moved from the doorway toward Mia. As she walked alongside the pool table, she ran her hand across the smooth felt top. "So, really, what are you and your twelve-year-old partner doing here?" Meg asked.

"Just checking things out. Making sure there are no unwanted guests, haters, pervs, etcetera."

"Seriously?"

"Yeah."

"Has that ever happened?" Meg raised her eyebrows, lighthearted mockery in her tone. "You know, someone lurking in the rec room waiting to pounce on an unsuspecting lesbian?"

"You mean not counting right now?" Mia countered.

Meg swallowed a laugh. "Listen, I'm just trying to figure out what my Bay West association fees are going to. Now I know." Meg gestured at Mia.

"Well, I don't know about your fees, but this is a courtesy drive-by. My boss is friends with Kam Browne," Mia said, as though that explained everything. "So part of our assignment for the night is just to come by, show our faces, and do a cursory search."

Meg grinned, nodding her head. "Convenient."

Mia chuckled, moving over to where Meg had stopped by the end of the pool table. "What does that mean?"

"Oh, nothing," Meg chided her. "Let me just put on my police uniform and head into a room full of dykes, no big deal."

"Hey, I'm just following orders. Doing my job." She held up her hands and looked around the dark room. "Speaking of which, in this situation, normally it would be procedure for me to do a complete pat down of anybody I come across under suspicious circumstances."

Meg huffed out a laugh at Mia's quick wit. Almost before she registered what was happening, she felt Mia's hand on the side of her neck. Mia kissed Meg softly on the lips—once, twice—until even through her absolute shock at this turn of events, Meg was kissing her back.

Things got hot fast. Meg reached up to the back of Mia's head, running her hands through the short, perfectly sculpted hair. She stood on tiptoe in an effort to get a better angle, but Mia lifted her up onto the pool table and pressed herself between Meg's legs. Meg ran her hands down the front of Mia's shirt. Feeling an unexpected stiffness underneath, she pushed at it uncertainly.

"Vest," Mia explained in a word, uttering it into Meg's mouth. Then she resumed their make-out session, moving her hands to Meg's lower back and pulling them closer together. They continued like this for several minutes, kissing each other hard and hungrily, capitalizing on the buildup of multiple missed opportunities over the last few months.

They might have continued even longer, if not for the voice that interrupted them through Mia's shoulder mic.

Riggs, what's your twenty?

Mia pulled back and hesitated only for a second before pressing the mic down. "Interior is clear. I'm just finishing up. Start the car. I'll be out in a second."

Ten-four.

Meg looked at Mia, question in her eyes. "Riggs?"

"Nickname." She pointed to the nameplate where the name *Riglio* was etched just below the silver shield on her uniform.

"So, Riggs. What now?"

"I have to work. I'm on till midnight."

"And then?"

"Meet you back here?"

"That could work." Meg nodded, grinning as she scooted herself off the felt tabletop.

"All right, then. I gotta go." Walking backward toward the door, Mia adjusted her uniform, methodically checking to make sure all of her gear was in place. Smirking from ear to ear, she wagged one finger at Meg and teased, "Now, Meg, try not to skip out on me this time."

❖

Meg reentered the party easily. It seemed like nobody had even realized she was gone. A quick glance at her watch revealed it was just after nine—and a quick glance around the room, that Lexi was still missing in action. Even she was beginning to get curious about Lexi's whereabouts.

When she got back to her table armed with a fresh round of drinks, it was clear that she was not the only one wondering about Lexi. Sam and Julie were in full-blown conspiracy theory mode. Jumping right back into the conversation as though she had never left, Meg quickly ran to Lexi's defense, giving both girls an impromptu lecture on work and internships. She laid it on super thick that Lexi obviously had no control over her situation right now and they could all be a little more understanding—of course Lexi would rather be at the party than at work, she had been talking about it all week, for God's sake. But while Meg was delivering her missive, she shot off a quick text to Lexi, under the table.

Beware: Natives getting restless. Keeping them at bay best I can. Where the f are u btw!

Meg's diatribe seemed to resonate a little with Sam and Julie, because both girls calmed down considerably. For a while the three of them made harmless small talk about their Christmas plans, until Julie's roommates arrived with their girlfriends in tow, filling up the table and turning the conversation to new topics.

A half hour later, when Meg saw Lexi enter the party with Jesse at her side, she actually thought no one else noticed. That is, until Sam flew from her chair and was at the entrance in no time flat, corralling Lexi toward the table as she leaned down and barked in her ear. Meg could tell by Sam's sneer and Lexi's facial expression that this lecture did not involve the kind words and understanding that Meg's had.

Meg decided to get out of the way and let Lexi and Julie have a minute of privacy to work things out. She started across the room toward Jesse, but after clearing a small crowd, she saw that Jesse was already surrounded by a group of women Meg had never seen before. Too shy to approach, she opted to stay more or less where she was and redirected herself to the bar. With nothing else to do, she watched the scene at her table unfold as she sipped her drink. It was more interesting than she expected.

Lexi approached Julie's chair from behind, placing her chin on Julie's shoulder as she wrapped her arms around Julie. Meg could see Lexi's full lips pucker and pout as she whispered what had to be an apology in the other girl's ear. Then she gave Julie a chaste kiss on the cheek, which garnered no response, before changing tactics completely. In a second, she swung around and positioned herself squarely in Julie's lap. She leaned in closer than she had before, brushing her lips against Julie's face and neck while she continued to whisper in her ear. Clearly this method was working because Meg saw Julie's sullen expression turn to one of pure lust as she placed her hand at the back of Lexi's head and pulled her in for a kiss so intense and so long that Meg actually had to look away.

She had yet to look back when Lexi appeared next to her at the bar.

"Hey."

"Hey, yourself." Meg looked Lexi up and down with a smile. "Need a glass of water?" Meg laughed thumbing in the general direction of their table. "That was some display. For a second, I thought she was going to throw you down on the table and go for it right there."

"Yeah, well." Lexi averted her eyes and ordered herself a glass of wine. "I guess I have some making up to do," she muttered under her breath.

"You okay?"

Lexi nodded. "Thank you for the texts. And for, you know, everything." She took a long sip of her drink. "Julie was pissed, huh?"

"Eh. Not pissed, really. I think maybe disappointed is a better word. But from the looks of things, I think she's going to forgive you."

Lexi raised her eyebrows and nodded into her wine.

Meg bent down a little to catch Lexi's eye. "Can I ask you a question?"

"Mmm-hmm." She took another long swallow of her drink.

"Is there something going on?" With her head Meg gestured toward the other side of the room. "You know, with you and Jesse?"

Lexi jutted her jaw out in complete annoyance. "You too?" she said, barely concealing the irritation in her voice.

"Whoa." Meg put her hands up defensively. "Whoa. I'm on your side here. I was just asking. Calm down."

"Sorry."

"It's okay. Look, I'm just glad you're here. Let's relax and have some fun. Okay?"

"Okay." Lexi clinked her glass to Meg's beer bottle.

Meg put an arm around Lexi and gave her a half hug as they looked back at their table together. "We should get back there. By the way, have I got a story for you."

❖

Meg finally made it over to Jesse close to midnight, which was where she still was, engaged in easy conversation, when Mia strolled into the party. From her vantage point, Meg noticed her immediately and felt all her muscles stiffen the second she spotted her. Jesse's back was to the door so she didn't see Mia enter, but she witnessed Meg's entire body language change. Right away Jesse looked over her shoulder to follow Meg's line of sight.

"Mmm-hmm," she said with a lilt, one eyebrow up as she turned back to Meg for an explanation.

"It's not what you think." Meg wasn't sure why she was lying. "She just was here earlier. Working. And she asked if anyone would be around if she came back after work. I said we would."

As comfortable as she was with Jesse, Meg wasn't about to tell her what had happened earlier. It didn't matter—Jesse saw right through her anyway.

"Please. It is so on." Jesse shook her head with a knowing look. "Well, don't stand here talking to me. Go get her. She's looking for you."

Sure enough, when Meg glanced over, she saw Mia scanning the crowd. When she spotted Meg, one corner of her mouth turned up in the slightest smile.

Meg turned back to Jesse and watched her scan the room. When her gaze stopped abruptly, Meg followed her line of sight and saw where Jesse had stopped: on Lexi, who was gently rubbing Julie's back as they chatted with the other girls at their table. Meg was just about to comment when Jesse cut her off. "All right, kid. I'm out of here. Merry Christmas." She put her empty drink down and gave Meg a quick hug, shaking her head with exaggerated disapproval. "Have fun tonight."

Meg crossed the room to Mia, trying to keep her cool as she indulged in her very own dirty little secret. Right now only three people in the room knew what had happened earlier between them—Meg, Mia, and of course Lexi, who had delighted in each juicy detail. Only, as she got closer, Meg realized that there might be one other person in the know. Standing next to Mia was the baby-faced cop who was with Mia earlier. Dressed in regular clothes, she looked even younger.

Mia greeted Meg unexpectedly with a kiss right on the lips.

"Hey. This is Amanda, my partner," Mia said by way of introduction.

"Hi." Meg shook the girl's hand and realized she was actually kind of adorable. "Come on, my friends are over this way."

They stopped at the bar before reaching the table. As Mia's partner purchased a round of drinks for the three of them, Mia laced her fingers through Meg's and leaned in.

"So, listen. Amanda's single and kind of shy. Think we can maybe find her a playmate for the evening?" Mia asked, eyebrows raised.

Meg didn't even have to think about it. "I know just the girl."

Meg and Mia spent the night flirting shamelessly. Meg didn't care who knew they were totally into each other. And her intuition had been on the money—Sam and cute little Amanda were hitting it off nicely too.

At one thirty Meg announced from her perch on Mia's lap that they were moving the party to her house. Right away, Sam and Amanda said they were in.

Meg turned to Lexi and Julie. "What about you guys? My house. Drinks. Keep the party going?"

Lexi whispered in Julie's ear before answering. "Not tonight, Meg. I think we're just gonna go home."

Meg saw the look of acknowledgment on Julie's face and was genuinely happy for her. Because while Meg had a pretty good idea about the direction her own night was headed, and she saw the probability for Sam and Amanda too, she was absolutely certain what lay in store for Julie.

❖

At ten thirty the next morning, as Meg lay alone in bed gratuitously replaying the events of the previous evening in her head, her phone vibrated with a text from Lexi.

I have bagels. You alone?

Yep. Except for Sam sleeping in the guest room, she typed back.

K. Be there in 5.

Pushing the covers back, Meg got up and grabbed a sweatshirt and pajama pants to throw on over the T-shirt and underwear she had slept in. She barely had the coffee going before she heard Lexi open the front door.

"You really never lock any of your doors, huh?"

"I do. Mia must've left it open when she left."

"Can't wait to hear the whole story," Lexi said as she placed the brown paper bag full of bagels on the table.

"I want to hear it too!" Sam's muffled yell came from the top of the stairs. "Where's a sweatshirt I can borrow, Meg?"

"In my closet, top shelf," Meg hollered back.

Meg grabbed some stuff from the fridge as Lexi set out plates and mugs in preparation for their debriefing breakfast, which was how Meg had come to think of these sessions that were quickly becoming part of their morning-after ritual. She noticed that the top of Lexi's head was still wet, but the rest of her hair had begun to curl up at the ends where it was drying, proving that she had showered a while ago. She was dressed in fresh clothes, rather than a reboot of last night's outfit. Meg figured she must have actually gone home prior to coming over. She was just about to ask when Sam shuffled down the stairs.

"Who went to Wharton?" Sam held out the bottom of the sweatshirt as she read the bold letters printed across the middle of the shirt.

"I did." Meg met the very surprised looks of her two friends with a smirk.

"Really?" Lexi's jaw literally fell open.

"I thought you went to a city college at night," Sam added, although she clearly was not impressed the way Lexi was. Meg knew she wasn't being judgmental. Sam simply didn't believe in name-brand anything. It was one of the few things she and Meg actually had in common.

Meg walked over to the table, carrying butter and cream cheese in one hand and a full carafe of coffee in the other. "I did undergrad at night. I got my MBA at Wharton," she responded nonchalantly, tossing a look back at Lexi as she depressed the plunger on the French press and watched the coffee grounds sink to the bottom. "You don't have to look so completely surprised, you know," she teased.

Lexi shook her head, grabbing a bagel. "Please, I don't mean anything by it and you know it. You just never mentioned it. Caught me off guard." She generously applied butter to her sesame bagel. "Anyway, your academic career is not what I came here to discuss." She paused for dramatic effect, making eye contact with both Meg and

Sam. "So ladies, how was *your* after-party?" Lexi's emphasis on the word *after-party* more than implied that she knew exactly how it was.

For a second, no one spoke. Meg and Sam exchanged a glance before Meg said simply, "Good." Sam nodded in agreement.

"You're both going to have to do better than that."

"Not much of a party. We basically had one drink and then went to bed. It was pretty late." Meg took a gulp of coffee, shielding her smile.

Sam pointed at Meg with her bagel as she fished around for a knife. "Seriously, you two were all over each other. I was shocked that you even made it through your drinks before disappearing into the bedroom."

Meg swallowed a laugh and shook her head before Lexi added, "Well, Jesus, it had been going on all night. It was like extended foreplay. They must have been dying. It was going on since what, eight o'clock, Meg?"

Sam was still in the dark about the early evening events and she looked blankly between her friends. Although Meg hadn't planned on sharing that particular part of the story, it felt rude to leave Sam out of the loop, so she rehashed how she and Mia had initially kissed downstairs in the Commons.

Sam's interest was piqued. "Everything is coming together now. Amanda mentioned something last night but I had no idea what she was talking about. Now I get it." She nodded her chin. "It sounds kind of hot."

"It really was." Meg grinned, her mind drifting back there for the moment.

The three of them were quiet for a second before Lexi noisily stirred some milk into her coffee, clinking along the sides of the cup. "Well, girls. I think a toast is in order." She raised her mug in the air. "To the three of us. All getting lucky on the same night. Merry Christmas."

Meg choked down a bite of her bagel, trying hard to get some words out. She swallowed hard, waving her hand in the air. "I didn't have sex." She cleared her throat. "I mean, don't get me wrong, we hooked up. But it was strictly PG." She paused, cocking her head to the side as she thought about it. "Well, maybe R. I don't think I really know where that line is," Meg added as an afterthought. "But definitely no sex."

Lexi turned to Sam, coffee cup still slightly aloft. "To us, then."

"Don't look at me." Sam shook her head.

"Really?" Lexi and Meg uttered in surprised unison.

"What, do you guys think I sleep with everybody?"

The answer to her question lay in the silence it was met with, before the three of them broke into laughter.

"Look at that. I get no love, no respect," Sam joked as she wolfed down her bagel. "Anyway, I'm with Meg. We hooked up, fooled around a little. No sex." Sam shook her head, smiling as she reached for her own coffee. "I say we toast to Lexi and Julie. Finally."

Meg joined her, tapping their cups together before taking a swig. "So how was it, Lex? Give us the details."

Lexi obliged but gave them only the bare-bones basics. She fielded a few questions from Meg but gave mostly bland answers.

As soon as Lexi finished, Sam swallowed the last of her coffee and sprang up from the table. "Sorry to break this up, girls, but I gotta go. Haven't been home since before work yesterday. Meg I'll get your shirt back to you next time, 'kay?" Barely waiting for a response, she threw on her jacket and headed for the door.

Meg waited until she heard the latch of the outer screen door catch before turning to Lexi. "So, are you ever going to tell me what you and Jesse were doing until nine thirty last night?" Meg said without looking up as she poured more coffee for both of them.

"Working."

"Until nine thirty? The night of the biggest party of the year?"

"We went to dinner."

Meg nodded in acknowledgment. "Yeah? How was that? All work, right?" Meg said skeptically, answering her own question.

"No, actually." Lexi's voice softened as she drew lazy circles with her middle finger on the ceramic cup. "It was nice. She's nice."

"She is," Meg agreed with a lilt in her voice.

Lexi's big brown eyes pleaded with Meg. "Don't. It's not like that."

"Are you sure?" Meg matched Lexi's serious tone.

"Yes," Lexi said emphatically, staring squarely at Meg. Seeing that Meg was not convinced, she broke eye contact and pushed around the crumbs on her plate. "Look. You obviously know that I think Jesse is hot, and yes, I guess I have, like, a fantasy crush on her or whatever.

But nothing is going on. She's my boss and I'm working on a case with her. That's it. I swear."

"Okay." Meg finished her coffee. "Just one question, Lex. What are you doing with Julie?"

"What do you mean?"

"Come on."

Lexi pulled her knees up to her chest and wrapped her arms around her legs. She rested her head on the back of the chair as she searched the ceiling for an answer. "I don't know. I like her."

Meg could hear the defensiveness in Lexi's voice and decided to press her a little. "Yeah?"

Lexi methodically wiped her hands with a paper napkin. "Yes. I do. She's sweet and nice and obviously patient," she said, rolling her eyes. "Plus my parents like her. She's good for me."

"Sounds like you're trying to convince yourself," Meg responded, not sold.

"I thought you would be happy for me this morning," Lexi implored.

Meg shook her head. "I am happy for you, if you're happy. I'm just not sure you are." Lexi just looked down at the table and didn't say anything, so Meg continued. "Thing is, Lex, you don't really seem that happy. I mean, you waited three months to sleep with your girlfriend, which is nice and noble and everything. But I would think if it was important enough to wait that long, you would be ecstatic about it. Unless of course…" Meg stopped, tilting her head as she entertained a thought.

"Unless what, Meg?" Lexi bit, some levity creeping back into her tone.

"Unless you slept with Julie out of guilt."

Lexi crinkled her brow.

"You know, because you feel bad that you *totally* want to fuck your boss," Meg finished with a devilishly knowing grin.

"You're a jerk." Lexi laughed and threw her wadded-up napkin at Meg.

"I know. But I'm right, aren't I?" Meg nodded, proud of herself for uncovering what she believed to be the absolute truth.

Lexi huffed out a small laugh. "Look. I can fantasize about Jesse all I want, and I'm not saying I do—"

"You *so* do."

"Whatever. Either way, there's nothing going on. Julie is my girlfriend and she's the girlfriend that it makes sense for me to have."

Even though that statement made no sense at all to Meg, she let it go. She had made her feelings known even if she had made light of it. Lexi had let her get away with saying some pretty bold things, but Meg didn't want to push it further.

"So what's the deal with you and Mia now?"

Meg laced her fingers behind her head and shrugged. "Don't know really." Frowning, she added, "I think it's like a whatever kind of a thing. Whatever that means."

"And you're okay with that?"

"Yep," she said with a nod.

"Well, good for you. I didn't really think that was your thing."

"It's not." Meg kicked back in her chair. "But the relationship route hasn't really panned out for me, so what have I got to lose?" She rose from the table, walked to the sink, and filled a glass with water. "The way I figure it is this. What I was doing before wasn't working, so maybe I just need a change. Shake things up a bit. Have some fun, like Sam said a few months back. That really stuck with me. And, you know, Mia's hot, she's nice. And she was fun to hook up with. Truthfully, I don't care if she goes out tonight and hooks up with someone else. There's no pressure, no commitment. And therefore, no chance of getting hurt." Taking a long drink, Meg let out a big sigh of relief.

Lexi opened her eyes wide and raised her eyebrows. "Well, this has disaster written all over it."

About to take another sip, Meg laughed into her water, spraying it all over. "As opposed to your rock-solid plan. What was it you said, *Julie is the sensible girlfriend.* Yeah, that's gonna end well."

Lexi doubled over in laughter. "I think we're both screwed."

Meg toasted with her water. "Well at least we'll have each other."

"Thank God for that."

CHAPTER THIRTEEN

In January alone, Meg traveled to London three separate times. It was beginning to feel like her primary office. Sometimes she absolutely hated it—living out of a suitcase and doing double work was getting to her. Yet at the same time, Sullivan, London, had its perks. For starters, when she was there, she wasn't constantly worried about proving herself to everyone. There wasn't time. Practically every time she landed at Heathrow, she was whisked directly to the office to deal with some emergent crisis with one of Sasha's clients. It was annoying. But if she was being honest, all the extra time and work did have its benefits. Meg realized that she had done more in the last six months than any new associate she had ever seen come through the doors at Sullivan, New York. She probably owed a debt of gratitude to Sasha Michaels for being solely responsible for accelerating her learning curve.

What little she knew of Sasha's situation was she was dealing with some kind of family problem, whatever that meant. No more details were given to her, and Meg didn't ask any questions. She had been part of the Sullivan team long enough to know that the company really was a kind of family. For Meg, that had always been part of the allure of Sullivan, not that she'd really had a choice. Unlike her peers, Meg hadn't been recruited out of college. Solely based on her years working as an administrative assistant, Sullivan & Son had covered her tuition to business school, and for that she owed them the next five years of her career. But from being around the business and dealing with other consulting firms, Meg had learned that in the other big agencies, an associate at her level was just a number, but at Sullivan, the principals and partners knew you, they knew your spouse, your kids. So it made sense that if Sasha was having a family issue, Meg and the rest of the staff should and would pick up her slack. It was just how things worked around here.

The only thing that really bothered her about being away so much was the timing of it all. At home she was finally in a groove—she had new friends and even some romance action happening. Since Christmas, Lexi and Julie had been in a kind of honeymoon phase, which meant they were constantly up for hanging out, having parties at Julie's, and going out in the city. Being overseas, Meg lost out on entire weeks of socializing. Just as importantly, she missed possible hookups with Mia.

Meg had seen Mia exactly twice since the Christmas party. They had first crossed paths at The Kitchen the weekend after New Year's. At the time they had deliberately not coordinated their plans, although each had known that the other was going to be there. Meg was trying to appear cool and aloof while acknowledging Mia actually *was* cool and aloof. Meg was still trying to wrap her head around this kind of spontaneous relationship. She wasn't really sure of the ground rules and she didn't want to screw it up by being, well, herself.

But since that uncoordinated meet-up, Mia had been texting Meg regularly. Meg loved getting Mia's messages. Whenever she saw her name pop up on her phone, she felt a little spark of excitement shoot through her. True, not all the texts were bawdy—much of the time they were just normal messages any friends might exchange—but a number of them were. The best part was the timing. Mia typically worked late shifts and had taken to texting Meg on her way home from work. Meg had been in London most of the month, so with the time difference, most mornings the texts served as a wake-up call in her hotel room.

It was a remarkably pleasant way to start the day—playfully flirting back and forth with Mia as she got ready to go into the office.

Then on a random Wednesday night in mid-January, when Meg was supposed to have been in London, she received one of those very texts from Mia wishing her *Good morning across the pond.* When she responded that she was actually home, unpacking and doing laundry, Mia spontaneously asked if she felt like having company.

Exactly twenty-two minutes later, Mia was inside Meg's house, laughing and talking easily like no time had passed at all since they had frantically groped each other in the cab of Mia's truck, two weeks earlier. Mia sat on the couch and watched Meg fold her clothes, teasing her as she offered to help with the underwear only. When Meg swatted at her with a shirt, Mia caught the end of it and used it to pull Meg down onto her lap. They moved quickly from kissing on Meg's couch to complete nakedness in her bed. There were no questions from either of them asking if this or that was okay or if any of it was going too fast. After all, Mia had invited herself over at twelve thirty in the morning. Meg had welcomed her in. There could be little confusion over where the night was headed.

Afterward, they were as relaxed with each other as before.

Meg stretched out on her side propped up on one elbow, studying Mia's face as she listened to Mia vent about work. Interrupting her midsentence, Meg gently rubbed Mia's upper lip with her thumb.

"What is this scar from?"

Mia let out a small laugh. "I should probably tell you some story about how I arrested this huge guy and that he fought back until I used my mad skills to take him down." As she spoke, Mia had shifted her weight and grabbed Meg's wrist, flipping her over onto her back and landing on top of her with a smile. "But that would be a lie," Mia said dropping a kiss on Meg's lips.

"So, the real story…" Meg drawled out.

Mia shook her head and hung her chin for a second before answering. As she started she let out a small breath through her gleaming white grin. "Honestly? It was my third week out of the academy. My training officer and I had just stopped at Dunkin Donuts. No jokes please," Mia instructed through her devilish smile. Meg obeyed, tightly tucking her lips in exaggeration. "Anyway we got our first big call over the radio. *My* first big call, I should say. Robbery in progress, like two blocks away. I was so excited, so nervous." She laughed a little as she continued. "I opened the car door too fast and stepped forward at the same time. Split my lip. Got four stitches. Total rookie move."

"Love it." Meg couldn't keep the smile from breaking through.

"Which? The scar or the story?"

"Both, actually."

Mia rolled off onto her back. "Oh my God. I don't even feel like moving."

Without thinking, Meg answered casually, "Don't. Stay here."

Mia arched her eyebrows. "Are you sure?"

"Absolutely."

In less than five minutes, they were curled around one another in comfortable silence before falling fast asleep.

❖

Looking at the calendar distractedly, Meg realized that her night with Mia had unfolded exactly one week ago today. It felt like longer than that. Probably because she'd been in London, trapped in back-to-back meetings, since she'd woken up the morning after to an email informing her that she was already booked on an afternoon flight.

Scanning through Sasha's notes in the double-wide cubicle that passed as her workspace in London, Meg allowed her mind to drift back to that event, indulging in the memory. She nodded to herself as she acknowledged that it had been surprisingly sweet for a booty call—she felt no need to sugarcoat it. Eight thirty p.m. She was supposed to be back home already, but instead she'd been at the office for fourteen and a half hours trying to calm down her—correction—*Sasha's* most needy client. She idly wondered if she would have the courage, if she were at home, to text Mia right now and suggest she stop by again after work tonight. As though they were on the same wavelength, her phone buzzed on the desk with a text from Mia.

Up for company tonight? I get off at 12.

Before she could even write a response, a second text came through.

Which means you could be getting off by 12:30...

Meg laughed out loud. Sadly she typed back her regrets, explaining that there was a change in her schedule and she was in London until the end of the week.

Mia answered simply with a sad-face emoticon.

She was about to type back when Nigel came up behind her.

"Meg, have you got the numbers sheets for the warehouse staff?"

Snapping right back into work mode, Meg answered him in a cranky tone. "The breakout sheets, you mean? No, I didn't do them."

Looking up from the stack of papers he was carrying, Nigel responded. "I know. Sash did them before she left. They should have been in the file."

"Well, they're not." Meg was annoyed. Another chore added to the list.

"Can you check her office? I'm positive she did them."

With a huff, Meg got up and trudged into Sasha's office. Of course the file cabinet was locked, adding to her frustration. It irritated Meg that this girl consistently dumped all her work on them and then didn't even have the courtesy to leave them free access to her resources. Now she had to find the goddamn file key too. She wondered if this situation could possibly get any more annoying.

That question was answered with a resounding yes one millisecond later as Meg opened Sasha's top desk drawer. There she found a single file-cabinet key and next to it a copy of Sasha Michaels's most recent pay stub. Her mouth went slack and her eyes nearly fell out of her head when she saw the numerals on Sasha's paycheck. Quickly doing the calculations in her head, Meg discovered that Sasha was making exactly 31 percent more than she was. They had the same job title, had been employed for the exact same length of time, and Meg was handling all of her projects for far less money. Life was not fucking fair.

Shaking her head, she shoved the drawer shut and opened the file cabinet. The folder she was looking for was right in front. She plucked it out, turned around, and took a good look at Sasha's office. On the surface she let herself believe that she was searching for clues to gain a better understanding of this girl who was still such a mystery to her. But deep down she knew that a part of her was hoping to find more concrete evidence that Sasha was a complete slacker.

Meg gave a full eye roll when she noticed Sasha's diploma from Oxford University perfectly framed and hung on the far wall. She spied a small potted plant in the corner of the L-shaped desk and snidely wondered if watering it was a task expected of her as well. Then she was drawn to a silver double-hinged picture frame containing two photographs. Meg had never met Sasha but she had looked her up on Sullivan's internal website. She knew what Sasha looked like—dark hair, pasty complexion—completely average. As Meg studied this picture she chuckled inwardly, wondering who Sasha had pissed off in HR because the girl in *this* picture was breathtaking. Placing the file on the desk, Meg picked up the frame to sneak a closer look.

The photo on the left was a close-up of Sasha on graduation day with a woman who could only be her mother. She was still in her cap and gown, long straight dark hair flowing past her shoulders. She had deep sapphire-blue eyes framed by the kind of lashes people paid good money to replicate. Her broad smile showed perfectly straight teeth and accented the high cheekbones that gave her face an almost heart-like shape. In the opposite photo, she stood on the street in downtown London her arms wrapped around some guy's neck, undoubtedly her boyfriend. He was equally gorgeous, with the same creamy skin and dark hair. In this picture Sasha's hair was full of wavy curls. It figured that she would be one of those girls who could wear their hair straight or curly and look just as beautiful. Her smile matched the first photo. Meg noticed how happy Sasha looked in both. And why shouldn't she be, Meg thought with a sigh. She was fucking beautiful, had a hot boyfriend, was making a shitload of money, and never had to be at work.

Meg was so engrossed that she didn't even notice Nigel in the doorway until he spoke.

"She's a looker, eh?"

"Huh? Uh, yeah." Meg shook her head and put the frame back in its place on the desk, embarrassed at having been caught. "I don't know what I'm doing. I found the sheets. I just got distracted for a sec."

Nigel laughed. "Don't worry, you're not the first."

Meg crinkled her brow. "What do you mean?"

"Nothing. Just that Sasha is beautiful. Kind of objectively beautiful, you know? Everyone fancies her. Men, women. She turns all of their heads. Plus she's darling. The genuine article, you might say. Not like one of those cold ice queens."

Meg wondered if Sasha was just allowed free rein to do whatever she wanted because she happened to be blessed with good looks. She clearly had everyone in the London office securely wrapped around her finger.

Grabbing the file, she went out on a limb. "So what's going on with her? She barely works. What's the deal, anyway?" There was no mistaking the annoyance in her voice.

Nigel nodded toward the photo that Meg had put down a moment earlier. "Her mum is sick. She has cancer. Sasha has been going home to see her, take care of her. I think it's not going well." He looked at the floor and seemed genuinely affected. "I gather she may not make it."

Meg dropped her shoulders and sighed, disappointed in herself for her typically untimely comment. "Well, now I feel like a jerk."

Nigel met her gaze. "Nah. Someone should have told you. You are doing all of her work."

Meg started toward the door. "Come on. Let's finish up and get out of here."

Nigel took the folder from Meg as she reached him. "I'm meeting up with some of my mates after. Come have a drink with us."

Meg didn't even have to think about it. "Nigel, I think it's entirely likely that I will have several." She smiled back at him.

CHAPTER FOURTEEN

Looking in the mirror, Lexi used one finger to blend the classic red lipstick onto her full bottom lip, wiping the excess on a piece of her sister's junk mail piled on the dresser. She futzed with her hair as she waited for Julie to pick her up. She was truly looking forward to tonight. This was the first time she'd ever had a girlfriend on Valentine's Day and she wanted everything to be perfect.

Julie had made reservations in a nice local restaurant. It wasn't too extravagant but it was quaint and cozy. To Lexi, it seemed just right for them. Its overall vibe matched their relationship—not too intense, but certainly serious. In the past, Julie had sometimes had the tendency to go overboard, but this seemed right on cue. The past month had proved that they were finally on even footing. Inwardly, Lexi scolded herself for doubting that they would get here.

When her phone rang, she was so sure it was Julie calling to say she'd be there in a few minutes that she didn't even look at the caller ID before tapping the answer button. Her heart dropped as she saw the name *Jesse* illuminated on the screen.

"Hello?" She clenched her eyes closed knowing her voice revealed her surprise.

"Hey, Lexi, it's Jesse."

"Hi." Lexi was trying but she couldn't mask the elation in her voice.

"Sorry to bother you. There's been some development in Lucy Weston's case. I wanted to update you. Are you busy right now?"

Lexi wanted to lie, but she knew she would get caught. Any minute now, her doorbell was going to ring and her parents would yell for her. "I'm just getting ready to go out."

There was a noticeable pause before Jesse spoke. "Ah, right. Valentine's Day. Well, this will only take a second."

Lexi wondered if Jesse was still at work or if she was calling from across the street. In the background she heard Marnie open the front door for Julie, who had just arrived.

"I just got off the phone with my buddy, Nick. You remember him, right? The PI?"

"Mm-hmm," Lexi answered, trying to focus on two conversations at once.

"Well, he gave me a lot of information about what's really going on in Lucy's IA."

"Oh, yeah?" Lexi managed. She was distracted listening to Marnie and Julie chat away in the hall. Lexi's parents had both been smitten with Julie since the moment they met her.

"Yeah," Jesse said with a heavy sigh. "So I want to bring Lucy in tomorrow to discuss her options. I know it's not a regular day for you, but I'd really like it if you could be there."

"Okay."

"I know you have class, but we'll work around your schedule," Jesse offered.

"Sure. I'm finished with class tomorrow by eleven thirty."

"Great. I'll set it up." There was a short silence. "All right, then—"

Lexi was suddenly overcome with anticipation. "Wait. You never told me what it was. What did Nick tell you?"

Another long sigh escaped Jesse. "It's a long story. Not all of which centers on Lucy." She paused. "I'll fill you in on everything tomorrow."

As Jesse was about to end the call again, Lexi stopped her. Again. "Uh, Jesse?" Hearing herself say her name out loud sounded funny and it caught her off guard even though it had come out of her mouth.

"Yeah?" Jesse answered in her effortlessly sexy voice.

"Did you want me to do it? Call Lucy, I mean, to set up the meeting. I know that's sort of my job."

"That's okay. I'll do it. You go have fun on your date." Jesse let out a silky laugh. "But, Lexi…" Jesse drawled her name, and her lyrical tone was sultry and playful at the same time. "You know what they say, don't do anything I wouldn't do."

"Hmmph. What does that leave?" Lexi bantered back to her own surprise.

"Not much, honey. Not much."

Lexi heard Jesse's throaty chuckle fade in the distance as she hung up. She looked in the mirror, still holding the phone, and watched as her cheeks filled with color at the thought of Jesse's implication.

❖

Lexi swirled the wine in her glass as she desperately tried to concentrate on Julie's conversation. She kept replaying the call with Jesse over and over in her head. Before walking out of her bedroom to greet Julie, Lexi had made sure to thoroughly collect herself. She had forcibly blocked out the last part of the phone call. It kept creeping back in though. Over the last few months there had been moments with Jesse, times she hadn't been quite sure if she heard some intent or inflection in Jesse's tone or if it was all in her head. Tonight she was sure.

"You okay, Lex? You seem distracted." Julie pushed around the remainder of her entree with her fork.

Lexi placed her hand on top of Julie's, stilling her fidgeting, something Lexi knew Julie did when she was anxious. "Nope. I'm fine." She ran her hand up Julie's forearm, rubbing it gently for emphasis.

"So, what do you think?" Julie was waiting for a response to a question she'd obviously missed. Damn.

"About what?"

Julie flipped her hand and took Lexi's hand in hers as she spoke sincerely. "Vacation this summer. Just me and you." Squinting, she looked mildly disappointed as she added, "Were you even listening?"

"Yes. Sorry, I am a little distracted. You want to go away this summer. But I'm taking the bar this summer, so I'm not sure how that's going to work," Lexi answered skeptically.

"I know. That's why I said August. The bar is in July, I thought." Julie shifted in her seat. "You really weren't listening." She dropped Lexi's hand entirely.

"I just have some stuff on my mind. Work stuff," Lexi added. Julie could not have looked less interested. "I have a big meeting tomorrow and I guess I'm trying to mentally prepare for it." It was partially true, she rationalized to herself.

Julie jumped all over her excuse. "Tomorrow? Tomorrow's Thursday. You don't even have your internship on Thursdays."

Lexi could feel the knot forming in her stomach as she realized that her impending explanation was going to cause confrontation. Cringing, she began anyway. "I know, but Jess called me before." She heard her own voice catch as she abbreviated Jesse's name, and she knew Julie caught it too. "She asked if I could come in for this meeting."

"Jess?" The disdain in Julie's tone was unmistakable. "You call her Jess now? How cute," she said, pointedly making fun of Lexi.

Lexi just looked down at her plate in front of her and pleaded, "Please don't, Julie."

But Julie was already off and running. "Don't what? Don't be annoyed?" She let out an angry huff. "Right. I'm supposed to be just fine with the fact that your predator of a boss calls you up on Valentine's Day with some scam about how she needs you to come in. Please." She grabbed for her drink, spilling a little on the tablecloth. "You know what, Lex? I think I'm pretty justified in being annoyed at that. I mean, look at you now." She gestured. "Whatever she said, it worked, because you haven't paid attention to me all night."

Lexi rubbed her forehead, trying to keep her composure. She could feel the color drain from her face when she realized what she was about to do. She shook her head and didn't lift her eyes from her plate.

"This isn't going to work." Lexi said it in so even a tone, it was as though she was informing herself for the first time at this very moment.

"What?" Julie responded with such sharpness that it jolted Lexi, directing her attention to Julie.

She reached out and tried to touch Julie but Julie recoiled. Lexi's voice filled with emotion as she attempted an explanation. "I think maybe we're just not on the same path right now."

"Are you kidding me?" Julie's voice was a mix of pain and anger.

Lexi pressed on, holding Julie's stare. "Look. You're talking about taking a vacation six months from now. All I want to do is talk about tomorrow. I listen to you talk about work all the time. Well, tomorrow is important to me. I'm nervous and excited. I'm working on a huge case and it's a big deal for me to even be involved. And you know, I think I may get offered a position at this firm, which I'm not sure I even want because I don't really think this is the kind of law I'm interested in. But it would be a job and it's not like I have anything else lined up. So I'm confused and I want to talk to you about it." Lexi broke eye contact but continued to talk. "I mean, these are the things I should be able to talk to my girlfriend about. But every time I mention my job or say Jesse's name—who is my boss, by the way—you totally freak out or roll your eyes. You totally dismiss me."

There was dead silence between them for a minute before Lexi spoke again.

"I know we never talk about it, but this is what's going on for me right now. I think I'm just—" Lexi shook her head again almost in disbelief at her own words. "I'm done."

"Excuse me?" Julie's voice was so bitter that it was clear that any sadness she might have previously been feeling had been completely taken over by anger.

Lexi tried to keep the tears from falling. She swallowed hard past the soreness in her throat and spoke softly. "We both know that we're not in the same place right now. I'm sorry. I'm just done pretending that we are." The tears spilled out. She wiped them away, knowing her makeup was probably a mess. "I'm sorry, Jules. I swear I didn't mean for this to happen tonight." The fact that she was certain she was doing the right thing made it no less upsetting, and Lexi was having a hard time holding it together. She knew that any minute she would completely break down sobbing. "I am so sorry. Will you please just take me home."

"Are you fucking for real?" Julie was fuming. "You're actually breaking up with me on Valentine's Day." She shook her head in utter disbelief. "You know what, Lexi?" She spit out the words as she threw a wad of cash on the table. "Find your own fucking way home." Sliding her chair back from the table, she stomped out of the restaurant.

Lexi grabbed her purse and hurried out. The place had been crowded enough that no one noticed their argument. Once Julie made her dramatic exit, leaving Lexi alone crying at the table, people started to stare.

Now that she was outside, though, she really didn't know what to do. The restaurant was only about a mile and a half from the development, but it was freezing and Lexi had five-inch heels on. She dreaded calling her parents and facing their sympathy just yet. She'd rather freeze than listen to a lecture from Sam right now. Quickly she dialed Meg's number and hoped she was alone.

"Can you pick me up at Lombardo's?" Lexi asked, her teeth chattering into the phone.

Meg didn't ask any questions. "I'll be there in five minutes."

❖

Lexi was thankful that Meg had the heat on full blast as she shivered into the passenger seat. "Thank you, thank you, thank you. You are a godsend right now." Lexi held both of her hands up to the vents. "I am so sorry. I hope I didn't screw up your Wednesday night thing with Mia."

Meg laughed a little at the comment. "Not at all. First of all, she never shows up before midnight, and it's not every Wednesday anyway. It's only when I'm home, which is, like, never lately. Plus, I guarantee that I won't even hear from her tonight. Trust me, Valentine's Day is way too committal for Mia," she said with a shrug. "Who cares anyway?" Meg looked over at Lexi. "What happened?"

Lexi filled her in during the short drive back to Bay West. As Meg pulled in to her driveway, Lexi leaned back against the headrest. "I really don't want to go home yet." She was mostly just thinking out loud, but Meg took her at her word.

"Come on then. We're going to my house." Meg cut the engine. "There's cheesy movies on every channel. I've mostly been flipping between *The Notebook* and *Titanic* all night."

"That sounds depressing."

Meg curled her lower lip. "I guess. But Rachel McAdams and Kate Winslet," she said optimistically. "We could do worse."

Lexi nodded in agreement as she reached for the handle. She relaxed for the first time all night as she followed Meg into her house.

A half hour later, wearing borrowed pajama pants and an old sweatshirt, Lexi texted her parents from Meg's couch. She told them where she was and about the breakup. Somehow it was easier to write it out than to actually have a conversation about it.

Meg and Lexi were about a third of the way through *50 First Dates* when a knock at the back door startled them both. They looked at each other without moving and Lexi mouthed to Meg, "Mia?"

Meg shook her off completely and responded, "Julie?"

Lexi shook her head doubtfully as Meg crossed to the door. When she pulled back the blinds, Lexi saw her mother standing on the other side of the glass, one hand in her pocket, the other holding a plate.

Meg slid the door open. "Hey, Chris."

"Hey, girls." She stepped inside. "Mom sent me over with these for you guys." She handed the plate of homemade brownies to Meg. She looked over at Lexi, concern etched deeply in her forehead, "You okay, kiddo?"

Lexi nodded as she rose from the couch and threw her arms around her mother. "Thank you, Mush," she whispered. She knew she didn't have to explain anything.

CHAPTER FIFTEEN

"So Nick's guys told him that this whole thing, Lucy's entire Internal Affairs investigation, is all being driven by the inspector." Lexi listened carefully as she sat in one of the chairs opposite Jesse's cherrywood desk, as her boss explained how she had spent the better part of last night on the phone with Lucy Weston, laying out the options for her.

Lexi's mind kept drifting back to her own conversation with Jesse from the night before, wondering how much, if any, influence it had on her breakup with Julie. She tried to shake it off, forcing herself to focus on the case as Jesse continued.

"In addition to being the actual shooter's uncle, the inspector absolutely despises Dani Calhoun. Once he found out she was involved, however remotely, his goal has been to expose her. Nick explained that on the night of the shooting, Calhoun was the tour commander, so to leave your post, it's a pretty big deal." Jesse paced back and forth behind her desk, going over the details for Lexi's benefit—but it also seemed she was still trying to make sense of them herself. "Nick said if it came out that Dani was not where she should have been, there would be definite repercussions. She might not get fired, but at the very least she would face discipline, and I'm sure in this case what she was actually doing would become public, leading to the obvious embarrassment."

She sat in her high-backed leather chair. "Plus she's married, so probably some problems at home too. It would likely bring her career to a complete standstill. So this inspector has been trying to get someone to go on record to jam her up, to use Nick's words. But nobody will do it because she's actually very well liked. Bottom line is he's dragging this whole thing out trying to force Lucy's hand. He's hoping that Lucy will give her up to save herself."

"Wow. That seems vindictive. So what now?"

Jesse leaned back and ran her hands through her hair, lacing her fingers together behind her head. "Well, I think we have two choices, really. One, we challenge them. Tell them we know the whole IA is nonsense. We're aware of the ploy to get Lieutenant Calhoun. Completely turn the tables on them. Demand the reinstatement of Lucy Weston, with the back pay owed her. When they laugh at us—which they will—we threaten suit, citing discrimination on the grounds of gender and sexual preference. We'll mention that we will be seeking damages for lost pay, plus mental anguish, pain, and suffering and we say that our plan is to go to the press, full boat. Regular media in addition to all the LGBT outlets, women's groups, etcetera."

Lexi loved listening to Jesse talk about anything. Her smooth voice, the way she licked her lips constantly. Nothing beat it when she was fired up, which she very clearly was at the moment. "Option two?"

"Option two." Jesse leaned forward on her desk. "Much less aggressive approach. Take the punishment for not securing the weapon. Nick says that Lucy could get demoted, but more likely she'll just get transferred out of her squad. She'll have to admit to where she was, that she was with the lieutenant, because that takes her out of the shooting itself. Let Dani speak for herself."

She rose from her chair, grabbed a bottle of water, and offered one to Lexi. Lexi shook her off and watched, mesmerized, as Jesse twisted the cap and drained half the bottle, before continuing. "The problem is that everybody knows that the inspector's nephew did it, but no one will admit seeing it. Likewise, they all know that Lucy wasn't there. They all know where she was, but everyone is keeping quiet about that too, because nobody wants to screw her up either."

"What do you think she should do?"

"I don't know. Normally, my instinct is to be as aggressive as possible." She moved behind her desk and glanced over her shoulder out the large window before turning back to Lexi. "It pisses me off that they're using Lucy as a pawn. And I do think ultimately we would win, but it will be dragged out for God knows how long. It'll be vicious and dirty and it means taking some serious risks, ultimately just to protect Dani Calhoun." She took another sip of her water. "We all know that the good lieutenant would not do the same for Lucy," she added, rolling the plastic cap between her thumb and forefinger. "I told Lucy that last night on the phone when I laid all of this out for her."

"And?"

"She didn't really say much. She knows that either way she has to own up to being with Calhoun. She cannot pretend that she fired the gun. She would basically be saying that she shot someone. She can't do that—it would be used against her forever. That seemed to resonate."

"Sounds like it was a pretty interesting night."

Jesse bent over her desk to straighten a stack of papers that hadn't seemed disorderly at all, and Lexi's eyes were drawn to the black strap of Jesse's bra visible where her shirt gaped open. "Speaking of, how was your date?"

Lexi hoped she hadn't been caught. She was surprised by Jesse's question and embarrassed by her answer. "It was pretty bad, actually."

"Wait. I thought you were going out with your girlfriend."

"I was. I did." Lexi swallowed hard, still not ready to talk about it. "We broke up. At dinner."

"Last night?"

When Lexi simply nodded, Jesse's confused look morphed into something like irritation. "Wow. That's brutal. Breaking up with your girlfriend on Valentine's Day?" She shook her head in sympathetic disgust. "Who does that, anyway?"

In a low voice Lexi admitted, "Me, I guess."

"Huh? Oh, shit." Flustered, Jesse said, "Sorry, I didn't realize. I thought...crap. I suck at this." She continued to straighten her already pristine desk, as she stammered around trying to recover. The office phone rang loud and shrill, saving her. She picked it up quickly and listened before replacing the receiver. "Lucy's here."

Lexi stood up to go retrieve her, but Jesse stopped her by coming around her desk and placing a hand on her shoulder. "It's okay. Roe is going to bring her back." Keeping her hand in place, she looked Lexi in the eye. "For what it's worth, I'm sure you did the right thing." She gave her shoulder a gentle rub and slid her hand all the way down Lexi's back and away as Lucy appeared in the doorway.

❖

The conversation with Lucy was fairly straightforward. Jesse reviewed the options again in as much detail as she had the previous night.

Lucy didn't ask any questions. She just waited for Jesse to finish and nodded. There was a long silence before she spoke.

"I've been up thinking about this all night. For months, really."

"So what do you think?" Lexi's voice was warm and comforting.

Lucy looked from Lexi to Jesse. "I thought about what you said. My choices." Her gaze drifted past them to the skyscrapers out the window. "I can't do it."

Lucy continued to stare out the window as she spoke evenly. "The options, they all involve screwing Dani over." She looked back and forth between Jesse and Lexi. "Just hear me out. It's not what you think." Lucy leaned forward on the sofa. "I told my girlfriend about Dani, when all of this happened. I knew it would come out and she deserved to hear it from me. She's amazing, my girlfriend. She's been completely supportive this whole time. We're working through our issues. It's not that."

"What, then?" Lexi asked earnestly.

"Dani is a good person. She's a good cop. She got where she is because she's smart and fair and she knows what she's doing. And like you said, Jesse, I'm sure there's a ton of people, like the inspector, who would love to see her fail because she's a woman or a dyke or whatever." She sank back into the cushion, shaking her head. "I can't be part of that. Her career shouldn't be ruined because of a stupid, selfish mistake."

Jesse was calm but firm. "Lucy, you need to think about your career right now."

"That's just it." Lucy half laughed. "My career is already over."

"But you—" Jesse started.

"You don't understand. Since I've been on modified duty, it's been a nightmare. Nobody looks at me. Nobody talks to me. The trust, the relationships that it took me years to build up—it's all gone. I'll never get them back. I've seen it before. This thing will follow me around forever. It will never be over."

Lexi crossed her legs and leaned her elbows against her knee. "So what do you want to do, then?"

Lucy let out a heavy breath, sounding almost relieved as she answered. "I'm going to sign the letter of resignation."

"Lucy?"

"Are you serious?"

Lexi and Jesse spoke at once. Lucy shook her head slowly, silencing them both.

"I know you've both done a lot of work for me and I appreciate it, I do. But I've made my decision. I'm leaving the police department." She said it resolutely, bravely, as though she was trying to convince everyone in the room, herself included, that it was the best move.

"Are you sure?" Jesse asked, but she knew the answer. When Lucy nodded, Jesse spoke again. "Well, I think we should at least try to get you some kind of deal." When she was met with confused stares from both Lucy and Lexi, Jesse explained. "Look, they wanted you to just sign and go away, but now we know all this other information about what was really going on in the IA. Let's turn the tables a little, get the department to make you an offer to leave. If you're sure it's what you want."

"It is."

"Understand it's not going to be enough to live off of or anything."

"Okay."

Jesse stood up. "If you'll excuse me for a second."

❖

Lexi was uncertain if Jesse had left to immediately contact the police department. That didn't seem likely but she still couldn't explain where her boss had run off to. She filled the silence with an obvious question. "So what will you do now?"

"I have no idea." The corner of Lucy's mouth tweaked nervously as she fingered a loose fray at the knee of her jeans.

"Are you scared?"

"A little. I don't really think it's sunk in yet."

Lexi tried to be optimistic. "At least things worked out with your girlfriend. That's good."

"Yeah, I guess so. She's pretty amazing. I'm lucky."

Lexi forced a smile and checked the door, hoping Jesse would be back soon. She was running out of fodder.

Lucy followed Lexi's eyes to the office door. "What about you two? How long have you been together?"

"Me and Jesse?" Lexi felt her face flood with color. She shook her head and attempted to laugh it off. "Oh no, we're not together."

"Oh, sorry," Lucy deadpanned, although it was clear that she wasn't. "It's just that you guys always seem so cozy. Even when I got here before, it looked like you were having a moment."

Lexi had thought the same thing at the time, but she denied it anyway. "No, no. It was nothing like that."

"My bad." Lucy smirked slyly, and they both turned toward the door when Jesse opened it.

Jesse went over some rudimentary details of how the settlement offer would likely play out before Lucy left with the promise that they would contact her as soon as they had any information. When they were alone in the office, Jesse turned to Lexi.

"What did you talk about when I left?"

"Nothing really."

"No?" Jesse seemed disappointed. "I was hoping you might be able to talk some sense into her. Get her to come around. I figured if I left you two alone she might relax a little. She's way more comfortable with you than me."

"I'm pretty sure her mind's made up." Dropping her eyes to her skirt, Lexi pulled it down where it had ridden up a little. "So what now? Like, how long until it's over?" She tried to sound casual, but Lexi could feel her whole body tense up. Her internship had ended over a month ago, and the only thing keeping her at Stanton Ducane was Lucy Weston's case. Now it was slated to end, one way or the other.

"It'll be quick, I bet. The department wanted this to go away from the start. They won't want to give her the chance to change her mind."

Jesse outlined possible variations of the settlement. Lexi pretended to listen, but she already had the only answer that mattered. Her days with Jesse Ducane were numbered.

CHAPTER SIXTEEN

"Tell me again why you need to go in at the ass crack of dawn," Mia called out from the bed, covers hanging around her waist just below one of her many tattoos.

Meg had already explained that she had an early morning conference call with the people from Davis Pruitt, her biggest and most exasperating London client, but she answered anyway.

"Because I have to be on a call at seven," Meg answered from the bathroom. "It's with the CEO and he's a pain in the ass. It took me forever to convince him to push the call back. At first he insisted on doing it at nine a.m. their time, which is four o'clock in the fucking morning here." She sighed, prattling on mostly to herself. "He's going to ask me a ton of questions, all of which he has the answers to already. But he's a nervous guy and he needs me to hold his hand a little." Meg shrugged as she looked at herself in the mirror. "I want to be in by six thirty just to get set up and everything."

Meg turned her head from side to side, watching the wispy ends of her hair touch her jawbone as she moved. She pulled each side back and tested out what she might look like if she cut it all off, a notion she toyed with from time to time but had never had the courage to actually pull the trigger on. She looked over at Mia sprawled in her bed, deeply involved in her phone, and studied her short blond coif. Such a bold look; she'd probably never be brave enough to do anything even remotely like it.

Now that Mia had been promoted out of uniformed patrol into a plainclothes squad, her hours were constantly changing. It was harder in some ways for them to get together. With Mia's rotating schedule and Meg always running off to London, neither one of them had a set routine. On the up side though, when they did manage to keep their Wednesday-night arrangement, like tonight, they were able to hook up at a normal hour and hang out a little, which made it all feel less tawdry.

About to hop in the shower, Meg paused and wrapped her robe around her body. She stepped back through the bathroom doorway to the bedroom and cautiously broached a subject that had been itching at her for the last week or so.

"Hey, Mi, are you doing the whole Save Tabitha's thing?"

Mia looked up from her phone. "Not sure. That's the thing up in P-town?" She yawned, stretching her long arms above her head. "Betsy mentioned something about it and I saw a flyer the other day at The Kitchen, but it didn't really say much. What is it anyway?"

Meg grabbed her iPad from its charger and scooched Mia over as she sat next to her. "It's this fundraiser thing for some famous bar there—Tabitha's. Apparently the bar, the owner, really, is having serious money problems. So The Kitchen and some bar in Boston along with Bay West joined forces to promote this weekend in April to raise money and help keep the bar afloat. Here, check out this email that the Bay West board sent out, it has all the details." Meg clicked open the message as Mia read it over her shoulder.

"Yeah. Looks cool, I guess," Mia said as she finished reading. "April eighth and ninth," she pondered aloud. "I'm pretty sure I'm actually off too. I should call Betsy tomorrow and let her know that I'm in." Looking at Meg she added, "Why, what's up?" noticing Meg's sullen expression.

"Nothing, I was just curious." Meg folded the flap of her iPad closed.

"Are you going?" Mia asked.

Meg turned on the mattress and faced Mia, answering as honestly as she could. "I want to, but I don't know."

"Why?"

Taking a deep breath, Meg reached over and gingerly placed the tablet back on her dresser. "I totally want to go," she said optimistically. "I've actually never been to P-town," she added with a little smile, "but, truthfully, things are sort of fucked up with my friends right now. So I don't know if I will."

"What do you mean?"

"Well, since Lexi and Julie broke up, things are really…" She paused, searching for the right word. "Tense, I guess. I mean they're trying to be friends, but it's touch and go. Julie obviously still has feelings for her, despite the way things ended." Meg had filled Mia in on the whole drama when it happened but hadn't really updated her since then. "They kind of made up, as friends, I mean. Basically they both apologized for the fucked up things they did—Julie for leaving Lexi at the restaurant and Lexi for having the worst timing ever and breaking up with her on Valentine's Day. Since then we've all hung out a few times. But it's weird. Sam has actually become pretty tight with Julie, so she's sort of holding the group together right now." Meg shifted a little. "Initially Lexi was going to go, and we were all going to rent a house together for the weekend, but Lexi pretty much told me the other day that she's going to bail. Which I totally get. It's just, I don't know." She retreated into her own thoughts before continuing. "Sometimes I feel weird around Sam and Julie without Lexi there. It almost feels like I'm in the way or something." She shook her head. "I'm probably imagining it. And Julie's roommates and their girlfriends will be there too, so I'm sure it'll be fine." She shrugged. "I'll figure it out. I just wanted to see if I'd know anyone else there."

Mia's light blue eyes filled with defiance. "Do not let some fucked-up girlfriend, ex-girlfriend, friends-taking-sides bullshit ruin your chance to experience P-town. It is fucking awesome, and you should absolutely go." Mia leaned up and gave Meg a small kiss. "And if your friends act like assholes then you can come crash with me at Betsy's. Deal?"

"Shit." Meg leaped off the mattress and immediately started to pace the room. She held both her hands up to her temples and clenched her jaw.

"What now?" Mia said with a half laugh as she leaned back into the pillows.

"Nothing. It's just something you said." Meg quickened her step, turning sharply on her heels. She looked up at Mia, who was waiting for Meg's implosion to blow over. "My ex-girlfriend. Becca. I guarantee you she's going to be there. This is exactly the kind of thing she would go to."

"So?"

Meg shook her head frantically. "Fuck." She paused, considering for a second. "Nope. I can't go. There's no way."

"Hey." Mia sat up and patted a spot in front of her. "Stop freaking out and sit down." Meg did as she was told. Mia hooked Meg's hair behind her ear. "This girl, Becca, this is the one that you're still hung up on?" Without waiting for an answer she plunged into her next question. "I've never seen you like this. Seriously, what did she do to you?"

The question wasn't rhetorical. Mia raised her eyebrows waiting for an explanation. That was the problem, though. The answer was kind of lame. Becca really hadn't done anything that bad. She hadn't cheated. She hadn't even lied, really. She'd told Meg straight off that she didn't think they were right for each other. That they continued to hook up for the following two years wasn't Becca's fault alone. Logically, Meg knew that. Still, she blamed her. Meg had spent twenty-seven months wearing her heart on her sleeve, believing that Becca would ultimately come around. Becca had known how Meg felt, it wasn't a secret. She just hadn't cared. She'd used Meg as a place keeper, waiting for something better to come along.

Meg wished the truth was more dramatic, something that matched her visceral reaction at the thought of seeing Becca again.

Even though it made her feel foolish, and vulnerable, and completely exposed, she gave Mia the real version of events. Finishing up her saga, Meg's voice cracked. "It's stupid, I know. But I just don't want…I'm not ready to see her yet." Meg pulled her knees up under her chin and wrapped her arms tightly around her shins.

"I don't know why," Mia responded sarcastically. "She sounds like a real gem. Stringing you along for two years and all."

"It's not even that. She's not all bad," Meg offered in defense. An old habit, not easily broken.

"They never are. Exes." Mia hung her head in exaggerated frustration. "They have these annoyingly irresistible qualities. Usually the things that hooked us in the first place."

Meg breathed out a sigh in agreement, feeling relief that Mia was so easy to talk to. She knew it was weird that she would choose to confide in Mia about Becca given the nature of their relationship, but Mia always made her feel comfortable and relaxed, and tonight was no different. Mia sensed Meg's stress over the situation and turned it around immediately.

Tipping Meg's freckled chin up with her thumb, she forced eye contact, revealing a devilishly sinister gleam as she pitched her idea. "Here's what you're gonna do. You're going to P-town, because it's fucking awesome. You're going to Save Tabitha's because you are a good lesbian and Tabitha's needs you." Mia nodded affirming her declaration. "And if you see her there, you see her. Your friends will be there and I'll be there too. We'll get you through it."

Meg gave a small smile. She appreciated Mia's understanding and she loved that they were able to talk like this. Still, she wasn't sure she was ready to see Becca. "I guess," she muttered.

"All I'm saying is, you are going to run into her sooner or later." Mia continued to try to win her over. "I'm sort of surprised it hasn't happened yet."

She said it offhandedly but it hit Meg like a ton of bricks. "Fucking A. Of course." Meg flopped back on the bed and covered her face with part of the crumpled up comforter. "She totally has a girlfriend," she groaned into the blanket.

Mia leaned down on top of her, pulling the blanket away. "You don't know that," she said lightheartedly. "You are completely jumping to conclusions."

"It makes sense though," Meg responded. "You're right. I haven't seen her in months. She's never at The Kitchen. And, believe me, she loves it there."

"So who cares if she does?" Mia shrugged, inches from Meg's face. "You just finished telling me you don't want to be with her."

"I know." Meg sulked. "I just wanted to have a girlfriend first. Or at least by the time I saw her." She shut her eyes. "I know it's stupid. I wanted to prove I was over her. I wanted to have actually moved on."

Mia moved closer and brushed Meg's cheek. "I have a solution for that." She kissed the spot just below Meg's ear and continued down her neck, reaching down and undoing the bathrobe's sash. "I say"—she pushed the robe to each side of Meg's body—"that we go to P-town"—Mia went on, taking Meg's legs, one at a time, and wrapping them around her back—"and if we see your ex, well then"—she kissed

Meg's chest—"I'll just have to pretend to be your girlfriend." She reached up and kissed Meg slowly, seductively on the mouth.

"That's the plan?" Meg asked distractedly.

"Yeah," Mia breathed out. Her entire demeanor changed as she moved between Meg's legs. "Right now though, I think we should probably practice," she added with a naughty grin.

"If you insist." Meg smiled back as she pushed Mia's shoulders down, guiding the way.

❖

As she and Mia walked toward Mia's pickup, Meg was disproportionately sublime for five thirty in the morning. Her mind relaxed and her body refreshed, she was enjoying the predawn quiet when she heard Jesse's husky voice a few feet away.

"What are you two hooligans up to at this ungodly hour?" Jesse stood by the rear passenger door of her SUV in sweats as she hung her work clothes from the hook in the backseat.

Mia nodded a hello. She really wasn't a morning person. Meg answered for both of them. "Morning, Jess. I'm going in to work. Mia was just going to drop me off at the ferry. You?"

"I'm on my way in too. Headed to the gym before work." She gestured toward her truck. "Hop in. I'll give you a lift."

"Great." A ride all the way into the city was way better than taking the ferry. Once she grabbed a subway from downtown, Meg would be at her office in minutes, giving her extra time to prep for her meeting. She awkwardly kissed Mia good-bye, steering clear of Jesse's judging gaze as she climbed into the passenger seat.

Backing out of the driveway, Jesse didn't waste any time. "So, Mia? That's still happening, huh?" She looked over at Meg as she shifted into drive.

"Give me a break, okay," Meg defended herself. "She was super sweet to me last night," she added.

"I'm sure." Jesse nodded. "And I'm sure she'll be super sweet to whoever she's with tonight. And whoever she happens to be with tomorrow night too." She raised her eyebrows and pursed her lips at the same time.

Meg laughed. "So what?" She shrugged her shoulders. "It's not serious. We're not exclusive. I know that." She chuckled. "Trust me, I'm fine with it. Honestly."

Jesse shook her head and looked out the window. Meg caught her and called her on it. "Why do you hate her so much anyway?"

"I don't hate Mia." Jesse looked right at Meg. "I actually count her as one of my friends."

"So?" Palms up, Meg asked, "What, then?"

Jesse took her time. "I don't want you to get hurt." She hunched forward a little in the cool morning air as she waited at the traffic light before the entrance to the bridge. She turned and looked directly at Meg. "Girls like Mia"—she breathed out heavily—"they crush girls like you."

"Well, I'm a big girl. I know what I'm doing. So I appreciate the concern, but it's not necessary," Meg responded, totally put off.

Her irritation did not go unnoticed. "Hey, don't get all pissy. I realize that it's none of my business, but...look, if I had a younger sister who happened to be gay, I wouldn't let her near Mia. But I don't. I do, however, have you. So I feel like it's my responsibility to warn you off her. So I'm sorry if that annoys you, but as your *slightly* older and wiser lesbian mentor, that's my job." It was delivered with the perfect amount of concern and levity that Meg couldn't stay mad for a minute.

"Duly noted, gay Yoda."

Jesse smiled. "Just looking out for you, kid."

"*Slightly older*, by the way? That's a stretch, don't you think?" Meg teased, leaning into the door to avoid Jesse's inevitable punch. Jesse was exactly nine years older, almost to the day, a fact that Meg never let her forget.

"Careful, or you'll be walking," Jesse joked back.

Meg looked ahead at the clear highway ahead of them. It was amazing the difference a few hours made. At this rate she would be at work by six fifteen. "So, what's your story?"

"Hmm?" Jesse grunted, confused by the question.

"Well, you've just declared yourself my lesbian mentor. As your protégé, I'm inquiring as to what your current romantic status is. I mean, how am I going to learn, if not by example?" Meg was half joking but genuinely curious.

Jesse let out a small laugh. "I'm not sure you should follow my example. I'm trying to help you avoid making mistakes."

"That sounds interesting."

"Look, I just haven't historically made the best choices." Although the statement was given as some kind of warning regarding her past transgressions, Meg took note that Jesse's tone sounded more nostalgic than remorseful.

Meg let it go, and pressed on. "Seriously, though, you're seeing somebody, right? You're never around lately. Something's up."

As they entered the tunnel connecting Brooklyn and Manhattan, the rising sun disappeared and was replaced by the dim safety lights that hid Jesse's facial expressions.

"Yeah, I guess I am. But not for much longer, to be honest."

"Talk to me." Meg rubbed her hands together in delicious anticipation of some good gossip.

Jesse gripped the steering wheel with her left hand and messed her hair with her right. "There's not really much to say. I opened a door that's been closed for a long time." Jesse paused considering for a moment. "Sometimes I think we should never have dated at all. Should have just stayed friends, you know?" She placed both hands back on the wheel definitively. "Suffice it to say, the second time around's not going any better than the first."

"Who is it?"

"Just an old girlfriend. No one you know."

"So how did you and the mystery woman end up back together?"

"Well, we're not technically back together." They emerged from the tunnel and Meg could see Jesse's face again. She looked more than unsettled as she spoke. "I saw her around the holidays. In a way, it was easy. Familiar. You know how it goes." She sighed. "Anyway, not a good idea."

"Why?"

"For starters, the problems that we had years ago—still there." She glanced out the window looking both ways before turning into the oncoming traffic. "And, to be honest, my motives were questionable at best."

"What do you mean?" Meg pressed her, genuinely interested in the details.

Jesse shrugged. "I don't know, it was Christmas. I was…" She sighed. "Lonely, I guess."

Meg let the last comment drop. "Betsy?" she asked, taking a stab at the identity of Jesse's secret girlfriend.

"No, Meg. It's not Betsy."

Meg believed her. "What's the deal with you two? Were you guys ever together?" She'd been wondering about that.

"Me and Betsy? Nah."

Meg nodded.

"You're surprised, right?" Jesse looked over and Meg knew she could see the answer written all over her face. "I know. People never believe me when I tell them that. But it's the truth." Without prompting, she went on. "I met Betsy when I was going through a really rough time. She was totally there for me and has been ever since. I know most people find their best friend in high school or college, some even earlier, but for me it didn't happen until I met Bets in my twenties." She shot a quick glance at Meg. "Which brings me to an interesting idea."

Meg was pretty sure where this was going but she waited for Jesse to continue anyway.

"What about you two?"

"What about us two?" Meg played dumb.

"You and Betsy. You guys would be cute together."

The controlled way Jesse played it off made Meg certain that this was not the first time this pairing had occurred to her. Meg didn't say anything she simply squinted and wrinkled her nose.

"What, you're not into her?"

"It's not that. She's very pretty, obviously." Betsy was tall and blond with eyes that ran the spectrum from sea-foam green to aqua, dependent on the light and the color of her shirt. Meg doubted there were too many people that didn't find her attractive. "It's just that I'm not into setups. I feel like if it's gonna work, then it should work on its own."

Jesse had pulled up right next to the 4/5 subway stop. As Meg stepped out of the truck, Jesse's sarcasm followed her. "Well, maybe it would happen on its own. If you quit spending all your free time with Mia."

Free time. Meg harrumphed to herself as she swiped her Metrocard through the turnstile. She wished she had any free time. Lately it seemed that every minute was split six different ways. In New York she worked on her local projects and fielded calls all hours of the day and night from her UK clients. In London the same thing happened in reverse. On more than one occasion Meg had gotten up in the middle of the night, showered, and dressed before she realized her internal clock was set to the wrong time zone.

It seemed everything had fallen by the wayside. Her house was still completely unfinished. Only the master bedroom and the living room had undergone any kind of decorating at all. She'd intended to make one of the spare bedrooms into an office, but currently it still housed the remainder of her unpacked boxes. Not that it mattered—she was never home long enough to work there anyway. And she still had to fully remodel the guest bedroom. Right now it was solely occupied by her old futon with its ripped and tattered cover, battle scars from the doorways and staircases of her previous apartments. She had plans for that room. She wanted it to be a real guest room, inviting and cozy. Her sister had even promised to help her with the color scheme.

Her sister, that was a whole other story. Since Meg had moved to Staten Island, she had barely seen Shannon and Matt or her adorable niece. Come to think of it, she had actually seen her sister and brother-in-law more when she lived in Brooklyn. That was going to change. All of it was, she promised herself.

❖

Toward the end of March, things almost started to fall into place. Meg closed out two major London projects and Nigel was made the project manager on a third, which left Meg the lead associate on only one. Allegedly the remaining project would be turned over to Sasha Michaels by the end of the month. Rumor had spread through the London office that Sasha's mother's health had stabilized, and the phantom herself would be returning to work full-time. Meg couldn't help keeping her fingers crossed that it was true.

It couldn't happen soon enough anyway, Meg thought as she sat in the airport on April 1, waiting in JFK for her flight to board, like some cruel April Fool's prank, a precious few days before she was to leave for Provincetown. Unfortunately, the eternally needy team at Davis Pruitt had insisted that she be present at the new prospectus rollout. Meg was certain it was something she could do by video—a battle she'd lost before it even started. Meg had made it clear to all the players that she absolutely had to be back home by the weekend.

Mia had been right, seeing Becca was inevitable. Meg had made her peace with it and was determined to have a good time in P-town. Lexi had told her about all her favorite places to eat and Meg was excited to check some of them out. She had bookmarked the house she had rented with Sam, Julie, and Julie's roommates and had visited the site at least a hundred times. The house was small, but it would certainly do. Since Julie's roommates were both bringing their girlfriends, the three single girls—Meg, Sam, and Julie—were expected to share a room. No big deal, since she thoroughly expected to spend at least one night with Mia at Betsy's anyway.

❖

From her dining room window, Lexi watched as Meg dashed toward Sam's Jeep Wrangler, duffel bag slung over her shoulder as she climbed into the backseat behind Julie.

Lexi was jealous. She loved Provincetown, and she hadn't been there in years. Meg would fill her in on every last detail when she returned, which would no doubt add to her envy. But she knew in her heart that staying back had been the right thing to do. Sharing a house with Julie, even for a weekend, was a bad idea. They were slowly, painstakingly trying to be friends. A weekend in a shared house with tons of alcohol was ill advised.

Although she hadn't had the courage to ask Meg, she was certain Jesse would be there. She did have a house at the Cape, after all. Her presence at such a huge weekend was pretty much a no-brainer. Lexi could almost see her breezing in to Tabitha's, commanding attention with her subtle charisma.

Lexi hadn't seen Jesse in weeks, since the day Lucy had come in to sign the settlement agreement. Lexi had been nervous because it would be her last day at Stanton Ducane and she didn't feel ready to be done yet. It all happened so fast. Lucy had brought her prim girlfriend along, who'd sat ramrod straight by her side the entire time, never speaking a word. Jesse had taken the time to go over each component of the contract, making sure Lucy understood its weight. Lucy had been anxious but unwavering. She'd fully comprehended that her signature meant accepting responsibility for the accident and that she would never be a police officer again. She hadn't even bothered to ask questions. She listened. She nodded. When the time came, she signed. Then she left.

That was it. It was over.

Lexi and Jesse hadn't moved from the conference room. They'd remained there, talking about the wording of the agreement, the settlement amount, how it would be dispersed to Lucy, and a myriad of other banal details regarding the arrangement. None of what they had discussed was particularly important or worthy of the conversation, really. It had occurred to Lexi that they were both stalling, neither of them quite sure how to end it. Then they were robbed of a farewell entirely when Laney and Allison had burst in, declaring that they were taking Lexi to lunch. Jesse passed on the invite, citing a client meeting later in the day. Lexi kept a brave face and forced herself to smile, although she was sure the disappointment showed in her eyes. She had known Jesse's calendar was clear. She'd blocked the entire afternoon for Lucy Weston, just in case.

Lunch had been fine, nice even. But she had left her internship feeling completely unfinished where Jesse was concerned.

Later that afternoon, when the sun was starting to set on the deserted street, Lexi stared out the window at Jesse's empty driveway and cursed herself. Screw Julie and their stupid drama. She should have gone to P-town and tracked Jesse down. Then she would have had the opportunity to thank her boss for her time, for her mentoring…fuck, who was she kidding? She just wanted to see her.

She turned from the window and started to set up her laptop and class notes at the dining room table. With a deep breath she washed away her thoughts of Jesse and Julie, of P-town, Meg, and Sam and willed herself to do some work. She planted her butt firmly in the hard-backed chair and attempted to focus. One way or the other, she was going to get something out of this weekend.

CHAPTER SEVENTEEN

Saturday afternoon, Lexi took a break from her books and walked Butter through the nearly vacant rental section. She was enjoying the feel of the late-day sun on her face and, for once, she didn't have to rush through this area. The rental section had always been her favorite part of the development because of its proximity to the ridge. Just beyond a thicket of trees lay a steep drop-off to the beach below and a breathtaking view of the New York City skyline. Since her breakup with Julie, Lexi rarely headed over this way. She'd hoped Butter would comply today and allow her a glimpse of the scene. Instead, the old dog pulled on his leash, eager to get back inside where he could sprawl out on the cool kitchen tile.

It was unseasonably warm for this time of year, the temperature reaching into the low eighties by the middle of the day. Lexi took pity on the dog and cut the walk shorter than she wanted. Scooting down the path that led to her block, Lexi was surprised not to see more people outside enjoying the summer preview. More people had gone to Save Tabitha's than she thought. But she couldn't hide her ear-to-ear smile as she came upon Jesse lying flat on her back in the middle of her lawn.

"You okay?" Lexi ventured jovially.

Jesse breathed out audibly as she propped herself up on her elbows, her face completely flushed and dripping with sweat. "Long run," she said by way of explanation.

"Yeah, how many miles? Or do you run for time?" Lexi stopped directly in front of her, seizing the opportunity to make any kind of idle chatter.

Jesse squinted one eye closed and bobbled her head back and forth. "Neither really. I'm working on some stuff for a new case and I just needed to get out of my head a little." She leaned forward and a floppy brown curl fell to her forehead. "I guess I did around five miles or so, but I didn't realize how hot it was."

"This weather is crazy, huh?"

"I love it though. Give me the heat. I'm a summer girl," Jesse said with a shift of her eyebrows. "It probably helped the whole Save Tabitha's effort. This place is a ghost town. I guess everyone's up there."

"I know." Lexi nodded and looked around as though she was checking the validity of Jesse's statement.

"I'm actually surprised you're here. How come you didn't go with Meg and those guys?"

Lexi tried not to give too much weight to the fact that Jesse had considered her plans. "A bunch of reasons, really," Lexi started, and then decided that Jesse didn't really need to know all of them. Providing a partial truth she stated, "My family went to Vermont to see my grandmother this weekend. I have finals to get ready for." She wound the leash around her wrist reflexively. "I would have felt bad not going to see my Nan, but then going to P-town instead. So I decided to stay home, do some schoolwork. Take care of old Butter here." She patted the dog's side, hoping that her answer sufficed. "What about you? What's your excuse?"

"Work."

Jesse leaned forward and began to stand up, brushing off the blades of grass stuck to her shins. It occurred to Lexi that she should move on at this point, continue to her house since their conversation was clearly winding down.

"What are you doing for dinner?" Jesse asked.

Lexi froze, completely blindsided by the invitation.

If she noticed Lexi's shock, Jesse didn't show it. "Why don't you come over? We'll order a pizza. Give you a break from your studies. I'll take a break from my briefs. Since it seems we're the only ones here, we might as well hang out together." Jesse casually lifted up the bottom of her shirt and wiped the sweat from her forehead with it, revealing glistening washboard abs.

Lexi maintained her composure, just barely. She forcibly tore her eyes from Jesse's bare stomach, willed her gaping mouth to close, and answered as calmly and nonchalantly as she could. "Yeah, okay. I could do that."

"Great. Come by around seven. That'll give me a chance to get some work done and obviously take a shower." She fanned over her body with one hand as she said the last part as if she was not the perfect specimen that Lexi had been drooling over her entire life. As she backed away toward her front door, Lexi thought she saw Jesse wink as she said, "See you in a little while."

Three hours later, Lexi stood on Jesse's doorstep, dressed in cutoffs and a T-shirt, her hands stuffed into the pockets of her unzipped hoodie. She had fussed over her appearance for the last 180 minutes, primarily concerned with what to wear. The night was still warm, so she figured she could pull off shorts and flip-flops, a look she knew worked for her. Even though she was short, she had nicely defined legs from years of running. Plus the weather had been awesome lately, so she even had a slight tan going on. With it she'd paired a distinctly weathered tee that hugged her in all the right places, highlighting her curves. She hoped it reinforced the irresistible-without-even-trying look she was going for. After all, this was just a break in their respective busy schedules. Not quite a work dinner, but certainly not a date. She reminded herself of that a thousand times. Gathering up all her courage and resolve with one last deep breath, she knocked on the door.

Jesse held the door open and Lexi deliberately avoided looking at Jesse's exposed collarbone, which protruded from the V-neck of her perfectly broken-in T-shirt. She did a quick scan of the house as she followed Jesse into the kitchen and couldn't help but notice how different this place was from both Meg's and Julie's. Of course the layout was the same, but in its decor and its design it was light years ahead of the other two. It was modernly decorated, not overdone, but with quality furnishings. In contrast, Julie's place always felt like a frat house while Meg's didn't quite have the lived-in feel yet. But this was a home. Adult. Modern. Tasteful. Refined. Very, very Jesse.

Seeing that Jesse was already halfway through a Sierra Nevada, Lexi accepted her offer of one without hesitation. Jesse popped the top off and handed it over. "Have you heard from Lucy Weston at all?"

From her seat at the table Lexi crinkled her brow and shook her head, taking a quick sip of the cold beverage. "No, why?"

"No reason. I just thought…I don't know. You two seemed to connect. I thought she might reach out to you." Jesse's voice trailed, kind of dismissing her own comments, but then she continued. "I think about her a lot. Worry about her, I guess. She seemed kind of lost, you know? I hope she's okay."

It wasn't that Lexi thought that Jesse was unfeeling or cold. But still she was touched to hear Jesse's continued concern for someone who was simply a client—a past client at that. "Well, if anything, you helped her get the best deal from a pretty terrible situation."

"I guess." Jesse shrugged. "But money isn't everything, and she didn't get that much anyway. She'll need to figure out what she's going to do. She'll never be a cop again. I think that sort of defined her. Plus, you saw her with her girlfriend the day she came in to sign." She raised her eyebrows dramatically. "Things are not good there." Jesse took a long swig from her drink and leaned back against the granite counter, placing the empty bottle next to her.

"I know. You're right about that," Lexi agreed. They hadn't discussed it at the time, but Lexi had sensed it too. "But maybe it's for the best. You know, we don't really know what their relationship was like. Obviously there were problems—I mean, Lucy was cheating. Maybe they just aren't meant to be. Who knows, maybe this is what needed to happen for them to see that."

Jesse's smile reached all the way up to her eyes. "That's what I like about you, Lex. Smart, savvy lawyer one minute. Complete romantic the next. It's adorable." Jesse locked eyes with Lexi for so long that Lexi felt her heart bottom out completely.

Somehow she found her voice. "Hey, it's not just me. Apparently you're up nights worrying about her."

"Not really. I just hope she lands on her feet."

"Me too. She will though." Lexi absolutely believed it.

"See what I mean, ever the optimist." Jesse grabbed two more beers and opened them, passing one to Lexi as she took the seat across from her.

"Listen, I'm not always so upbeat. I basically didn't go up for Save Tabitha's because I felt like I would ruin the weekend for everybody. And I was pretty much dying to go. I love P-town and I haven't been there in forever, and I've never been to the bars there or anything because I've always gone with my family. But I was so nervous that my going would make everything uncomfortable that I stayed home."

"What are you talking about?"

"Meg and Sam, my best friend from—"

"I know who Sam is." Jesse cut her off, a look of concern growing on her gorgeous face.

"Well, they rented a house with my ex-girlfriend and some of her friends. Originally I was planning on going too. See Julie, my ex, and I are trying to be friends." Lexi half wondered why she was talking about this, but continued anyway. "But it's hard. I knew something messed-up would happen if I went. Even though I can't think of anything more fun than P-town with Meg and Sam." She puckered her lips and gave a flippant sigh. "So I didn't really bring my glorious optimism to that situation." Lexi took a sip of her drink. She still wasn't sure why she was telling Jesse all this, but it felt good to get it out. And strangely not uncomfortable at all.

"What do you think would have happened if you went? With you and Julie—would you fight, hook up? Both?" Jesse asked, curiosity steeped in her raspy voice.

Lexi huffed into her drink. "Definitely not hook up." She ran her middle finger up and down the side of her beer, flattening the drops of moisture as they beaded up on the bottle. "I think that's the problem. We had been getting along fine. But the past few weeks, we'll be talking or joking about something and it's all normal. At least I think it is." Lexi worried her bottom lip. "But then I'll look at her and she has this look." She shook her head. "I don't know. I can't describe it." She worried that she was talking too much, but Jesse seemed not to mind. "I guess I'm just afraid she's still holding out hope for us, and I'm not. I just want to be friends. That's it." Lexi paused for a second and then added, "I hope you don't think that I'm obnoxious or totally vain or anything. I realize how I must sound."

Jesse lowered her brow and looked at Lexi with sincerity. "Not at all. First of all, I know you. I know you're not vain or obnoxious. I pretty much just finished telling you how sweet I think you are."

Lexi breezed past the comment, primarily because she didn't have the time to deconstruct what it could mean. She pressed on with her story. "The thing is, after she gives me the look and I don't respond, she totally turns on me. She can be pretty nasty when she's drinking. Then we end up fighting. It becomes a whole scene, just kind of takes over everything." She took a sip of her beer, licking her lips. "And for some reason I can't understand at all, Sam totally sides with Julie every time we argue. And Meg will be with Mia, so I didn't want to get in the way of that."

Jesse hung her head in mock disgust. "Don't get me started on that ridiculous relationship."

"What, you don't like Mia?" Lexi smiled. She already knew the answer.

"No, Mia is fine. I don't like Mia for Meg. Meg can do better and she should. And I tell her that every chance I get. You should do the same. She'll listen to one of us sooner or later."

Lexi laughed at Jesse's boldness in being absolutely certain that she knew what was best for Meg. She really did sound like she was looking out for her kid sister.

"Listen, it sounds to me like you made the right decision. In not going." Jesse stopped for a second. "And in ending your relationship. I know it sucks, particularly when you want to be friends with someone and they want more. Never really works out."

Lexi hoped to God in that moment that Jesse was not trying to send her a message.

As if she could read her thoughts, Jesse reached out and touched Lexi's forearm softly, reassuringly. It sent a shiver through Lexi's whole body in a way she was sure was not intended. Jesse raised her eyebrows. "Believe me, I know. I've been there."

"Yeah?"

"Yep. I dated a girl, Lauren, for almost three years. Our families knew each other forever. We practically grew up together. We started going out when I was in law school. Our parents were totally infatuated with it. They all thought this was it, figured we'd be together forever. It was really the only time my mother was actually happy I was gay, because she approved of Lauren's family. So stupid." Jesse laughed wryly. "I think that's maybe why I stayed in it so long, because on paper it was perfect. And of course, Lauren is a great girl. She's beautiful and smart, but I was never in love with her. And I knew she was in love with me. It wasn't fair to either of us, really. So I ended it, and it sucked.

Everybody was disappointed. I was disappointed too. I wanted to be in love with her. I did. I just wasn't." She sighed deeply and leaned her elbows on the table, looking right at Lexi. "But my point is, it's still hard because I see her a lot. You know, our families are still friends. It's awkward sometimes."

"What's it like when you see her?"

Jesse raised her shoulders. "It's complicated." She crossed her arms over her chest and ran her hands up and down her toned biceps. She shrugged and spoke calmly. "We're friends. We have to be." She said it almost under her breath. "But there's tension." She shook her head. "It always comes back to the same thing. If I had just ended it sooner, when I knew I wasn't in it for the long haul, I think it would have been okay. But I let it go on for a million terrible reasons. If I had ended it earlier, I think we could have recovered. I think we might actually be real friends, the way we were before we got together."

Jesse rose and pulled a stack of menus from a cabinet. "So my completely unsolicited advice is that by not going, in the long run maybe you'll save your friendship with Julie. Maybe not." She shrugged again lightening the mood. "Either way though, I guarantee you there's less heartache." Waving the pizza menu in the air, she shifted gears entirely. "Anyway let's order. I'm famished."

The conversation flowed this easily all night. They moved seamlessly from talking about work to family, friends, movies, relationships. Nothing was off-limits. Jesse ranted more about her disapproval of the Meg-Mia coupling and it was clear she really did have Meg's best interests at heart. Hearing her concern for their mutual friend made Lexi see Jesse in a whole new light. The hours slipped by, and Lexi relished every second.

A few hours later, the pizza long gone, they sat in the living room, Lexi on one end of the lush sofa, her bare feet curled up under her, while Jesse leaned up against the other end, facing her as they talked. When Jesse got up to get them each another beer, Lexi crossed the room and stood on tiptoe to reach a framed photograph on the bookshelf. It was a snapshot of her moms, Jesse, and Mary Brown, their arms linked as they stood together on the grassy knoll outside the Commons.

"Oh my God, look at you guys." She held the frame close to her face, poring over a twentysomething Jesse. She looked a touch younger, yes, but more than that, she looked softer. Her broad smile held a kind of innocence that she couldn't quite describe. It was like she was looking at the prototype, the girl who had not yet evolved into the chiseled, charming individual walking toward her now.

"Funny, right?" Jesse came up behind her, peering over her shoulder at the picture.

"Aunt Mary's hair is so long," Lexi marveled, hoping to cover the fact that she had been focused solely on Jesse's image. "And Marnie, God, I remember when she dyed her hair that ultra-blond. This must've been right before I started my senior year of high school." She flipped it over but, of course, the frame obscured any date that might have been on the back of the photo. She turned it back to the front and ran her hand slowly over the glass. "God, they all look so young."

"I know." Jesse sounded wistful. "We were."

Lexi glanced back at Jesse. "Not you. You look the same." It was true. Other than looking significantly more sophisticated, Jesse had hardly aged at all. "My mothers, though, unbelievable." She shook her head, shifting the image back and forth in her hands, allowing the light to hit it as she examined each angle. "Could I borrow this?" She looked back at Jesse again. "Sounds weird, I know. But I'm putting together this thing for Mush's fiftieth birthday. This would be perfect."

"Mush?"

"Sorry. My mom, Chris. That's what we call her. Mush."

Jesse laughed. "That's cute. She is such a mush too."

Lexi had almost forgotten they'd all been friends, before they weren't.

"Yeah, of course you can take it."

"I'll give it back. I can just scan it and use the image."

Jesse nodded again, obviously pondering something. "Actually, I'm sure I have more. Hang on." Jesse disappeared into the den, loudly riffling through her things. When she came back, she held a leather-bound photo album. Dusting it off, she sat down right next to Lexi, opening the book in her lap so they could both see the pages.

Lexi's arm was stretched out on the back of the couch behind Jesse as they perused the pictures together, pointing and chuckling at the dated clothes and hairstyles. At one particularly embarrassing shot of Jesse dressed in some kind of princess getup at a Bay West

Halloween party, Lexi turned to Jesse as she teased her. Up to that moment, Lexi hadn't realized how close they actually were. Then she did the unthinkable. Dropping her gaze to Jesse's mouth, she licked her own lips, drawing her full bottom lip in with her teeth as she leaned in.

And on that hot April night, outrageously high on conversation, mildly buzzed from a few beers, sitting altogether too close on the couch, Jesse Ducane kissed her back.

They kissed for a long time.

Lexi was aware of Jesse's hands first on her face and neck, then slowly making their way down her entire body as she pulled Lexi onto her lap, sending the photo album spilling to the floor.

In all of her fantasies, things usually ended about here. Typically it involved Jesse stopping them dramatically with a fervent *no* or *we have to stop*—it had played out a multitude of different ways in her mind. Always though, it ended in the same conversation about why this shouldn't and couldn't happen. So it was no exaggeration that Lexi was absolutely astonished when no protest came at all. Rather, she felt Jesse's hands move under her shirt, sliding up her back where Jesse unhooked her bra and then shifted her hands around to the front, up and under the fabric, until a hand covered each of Lexi's breasts. They remained there for a few seconds, until Jesse kissed her way down Lexi's neck, lifting off her shirt and bra in one fluid motion. Only then did she speak, breaking them apart momentarily to utter a one-word directive.

"Up."

Lexi followed obediently as Jesse led her directly upstairs into the bedroom.

What happened next was surreal. With her mind in overdrive, Lexi tried like crazy to stay in the moment by focusing on every nuance—taking Jesse's shirt off and kissing her chest, Jesse's fingers unbuttoning her shorts and pushing them to the floor, the feel of Jesse's lips on her shoulders and arms, her belly, her thighs. She swore she could feel each individual thread of the cool sheets beneath her blazing body until she lost control completely, finally emerging from her fog with a short, sharp twinge felt all the way to her toes.

Oddly, instead of feeling spent, Lexi's orgasm invigorated her, supplying a welcome burst of energy. Swiftly, she pulled Jesse up.

Wasting no time, she kissed her way down Jesse's incredible body, grating her teeth open-mouthed over Jesse's unbelievably tight abdomen before reaching her ultimate destination.

Lexi had had a decent amount of sexual activity in her life. There had been the long-term high school boyfriend whom she had lost her virginity to; the short-lived college girlfriend to whom she gave her other v-card; plus a smattering of girls and a few boys she had messed around with over the years. Most recently there was Julie. In all of these encounters, not once did she ever experience anything remotely similar to what was happening now.

As she gratifyingly went down on Jesse, she felt her insides tightening up, rushing headlong toward an uncontrollable peak. She knew what was happening. She tried unsuccessfully to think about Margaret Thatcher or baseball, things she'd heard guys did in this situation. It didn't work. As Jesse got closer and closer, betrayed by both her rhythmic movements and gasping breath, Lexi's building orgasm intensified. She was very obviously and kind of audibly having trouble staying focused. Thankfully, Jesse used her hand to press hard at the back of Lexi's head, keeping her in place until they both came, Jesse bucking off the mattress as Lexi moaned into her.

Lexi couldn't move. She barely made it to Jesse's stomach, her thick brown curls splayed across Jesse's torso, before she completely passed out.

❖

When Lexi next opened her eyes it was nearly two hours later. No longer sprawled out across Jesse, she found herself tucked neatly under the covers on her side with Jesse's arm draped over her thigh. She felt divine. So good, in fact, that she cursed herself for having to get up to use the bathroom. Slipping out from between the sheets, she carefully tiptoed across the floor so she wouldn't wake Jesse.

She hadn't intended to leave. Only, when she stepped back into the bedroom she panicked. Jesse hadn't moved at all. Lexi didn't know how exactly to insinuate herself back into the previous position or if she should even try. Standing in the doorway between the two rooms, she could feel herself starting to sweat. Overwhelmed by insecurity, she snuck out of the bedroom, throwing her clothes on haphazardly as she moved quietly through the house until she clicked the front door closed behind her.

Lexi spent the entire morning wondering if that was the best or worst decision she had ever made.

At one o'clock that very afternoon, as she sat on her sofa upstairs in the living room rereading the same paragraph in her wills and estates textbook, letting her mind wander gratuitously back to last night, she heard a faint tap at the front door. She scurried down the steps hoping it was Meg, assuming it was the UPS man, and was stunned to find Jesse standing on the other side of the screen.

Lexi barely got the word hi out before her cell phone rang. Reaching into the back pocket of her jeans she grabbed it and saw the screen flashing *Mom*. She answered the phone and opened the door at the same time. She half stepped out of the house, keeping the door open by placing her body between it and the frame as she held up one finger to Jesse.

"Hi, Mom."

She listened to her mother and watched Jesse look around while she waited.

"Okay, Mom. Give me two minutes, okay? I'll call you right back." She rolled her eyes but kept the phone to her ear since her mother was still talking. Jesse smiled politely. "All right. I got it. Five minutes, Mom." But she didn't hang up. Instead she nodded her head and said, "Okay...okay."

Pressing the phone tight to her chest, she turned her attention to Jesse. "I'm sorry, can you just give me one second?"

Jesse nodded her head slightly. "You're busy." Lexi had to suppress the urge to drop the phone and jump her right there on her doorstep. "Don't get off the phone. I just came by to give you these. For your project." Jesse handed over an envelope that Lexi hadn't even noticed she was holding. With a small wave, and an even smaller smile, Jesse backed away, leaving Lexi with an envelope full of pictures, her mother on the phone, and about four million frazzled nerves.

CHAPTER EIGHTEEN

After waiting as long as she possibly could, Lexi knocked on the door of Meg's house, found the door unlocked, and walked right in. Scanning the first floor living area, she saw no sign of Meg. She was sure she was home—she had watched her enter the house a half hour earlier. She moved into the kitchen and noticed Meg's laptop open on the breakfast bar. Just as she was about to call up the stairs, Meg opened the laundry-room door.

"I thought I heard you come in." Meg grabbed Lexi for a quick hug as she passed behind her.

"Did you miss me?" Lexi asked in a spirited voice as she patted Meg's forearm, before unwinding from her grasp.

"Actually, yes."

"So, how was it?" Lexi hoisted herself onto one of the counter stools.

Meg opened the refrigerator and grabbed two Diet Cokes, handing one to Lexi as she cracked the other open.

"It was okay." Meg's voice was even as she searched through each kitchen cabinet, finally removing a jar of peanut butter from the last cupboard.

"That's it, just okay?" Lexi was certain from the flat tone that something wasn't right. "Oh no, you ran into her? Becca?"

Meg shook her head as she tossed two pieces of wheat bread on a plate, simultaneously pointing to them to see if Lexi was interested in a sandwich. "Nope. I actually didn't see Becca. I'd say that was the bright spot of the weekend."

Lexi declined the offer with a shake of her head. "What happened?"

"Nothing. It was fine," she added, less than enthusiastic. Seeing Lexi's concern, she lightened her tone. "I'm just being dramatic," she said, half making fun of herself as she reached into the fridge for the jelly.

"Tell me," Lexi said earnestly.

Meg obliged, and as she made up her sandwich she laid out all of the details of the weekend from the beginning.

The car ride up had been uneventful, but pleasant. Tabitha's was old and adorable and quaint. She and the girls spent both nights partying there for the cause. Of course there were tons of people from the development—even Kam Browne and Mary Brown made an appearance, not that Meg talked to them. She told Lexi about the house they had rented, which was fine, but she emphasized heavily that it was not the same without her. Meg confessed that she met up with Mia on Friday and ultimately stayed at Betsy's house both nights. Apparently Betsy actually owned the house that they'd stayed in but rented it out most of the year. Meg made a special point of mentioning that Jesse had been a no-show the entire weekend.

As she meticulously cut off all the crusts of her bread, Meg finally got into what was bothering her. The problem, she told Lexi, was that Mia had brought along her work partner, Amanda, and further divulged that Amanda was very obviously into Mia. Meg acknowledged that while she was pretty sure nothing was going on between them, Mia loved the attention. Meg claimed she didn't care about the flirting itself, she certainly wasn't jealous, but she could have done without the display right in front of her. She admitted that she and Mia had gotten into a pretty wicked fight about it on Saturday night.

Inspecting her sandwich for the exact right spot to bite, Meg finished her story. "Look, I know we're not girlfriends or anything and that's fine. Seriously. She can do what she wants, and I'll do the same—not that I do. But I just didn't need it right in front of my face. It made me feel like an idiot, you know?" She leaned against the kitchen sink as she chomped through her sandwich.

"So that's it for you guys?"

Meg licked some wayward peanut butter from the base of her hand. "No, we hooked up after that," she confessed. "It blew over. It just annoyed me, is all."

Lexi shook her head in mock judgment. "Jesse's right. That girl is no good for you." She pursed her lips to hide her smile.

Meg choked out a laugh. "I'm sorry. What was that?"

"I said, Jesse's right. Mia is trouble. For you, in particular." Lexi knew she was smiling wide now, but she couldn't help it.

Meg smiled back, looking a little puzzled. "Okay, I'll play along. Since when do you and Jesse discuss my love life? I thought everything was strictly business with you two." She threw up some air quotes and dropped her voice an octave, openly teasing.

"We talked about you a little last night," Lexi said in a lyrical tone, delighting in Meg's semi-engrossed reaction as she swallowed the last of her PB&J. Then Lexi dropped the bomb as casually as she could manage. "Yeah, I went over there for dinner and we chatted for a while, you know, before we had sex."

"Shut up!" Meg laughed harder this time, shaking her head in disbelief. Then her mouth dropped open. "Holy shit, you're serious. I can't believe you let me go on and on about my stupid weekend, when you were sitting on this. Tell me *everything*."

Lexi did, including the part where she skulked out of Jesse's house in the middle of the night.

"So, wait, you left?"

Lexi nodded silently, her exuberance fading fast.

"Why?"

Lexi still wasn't a hundred percent sure of her reasons or the logic behind them. Even though she knew it was nearly impossible to find the right words to describe how she had felt, she tried anyway. "I don't know what happened. It was weird. I couldn't figure out how to get back into the bed." In defense of how lame that sounded, she continued down a path she hadn't planned on discussing at all. "Plus something totally weird happened to me when we were having sex. I was sort of embarrassed. I think I just kind of ran away."

Meg looked intrigued. "What happened?"

"I don't want to talk about it, it's mortifying." Lexi buried her face in her hands.

"Just tell me. I'm sure it's not that bad."

Lexi lowered her hands, peeking her eyes out just above her fingertips. "It's bad."

"Hit me." Meg waved her on with both hands.

"I don't even know how to say it." Lexi paused. She slid her hands back over her face all the way up to her forehead, fanning out her fingers until they held her curls back off her face. "Okay. So we were having sex—"

"Where?" Meg cut her off.

"Upstairs. In her bedroom," Lexi answered, challenging the importance of that fact with her tone.

"I just want to get a complete picture."

Lexi took a long blink and continued. "Anyway, she went down on me."

"Wait, did you—"

"Yes."

"Okay."

"Then I, you know"—Lexi blushed a deep red—"was going down on her."

"All normal so far."

Lexi licked her lips and took a breath so deep that her shoulders rose and her chest puffed out before exhaling. Searching for the courage to continue, she squeezed her eyes shut and placed both her hands on the counter to brace herself. "I came," she mouthed.

"Uh-huh." Meg paused, waiting for more. She looked at Lexi and realized that she didn't have anything more to add. Confused, Meg questioned her. "That's it? You came? I don't get it."

"Meg, *I* came. While *I* was going down on *her*."

Meg crinkled her nose as she winced. "Ooh. She didn't?"

Lexi shook her off. "No, she did. It happened basically at the same time. But—"

Meg put both of her hands up. "So wait a second. That's your big embarrassing moment? That's why you ran out?"

"Yes."

Meg rolled her eyes and was about to say something when Lexi stopped her.

"It was mortifying." She cringed. "I was like a fifteen-year-old boy. Complete lack of self-control."

"Hold on a second here." Meg was trying to make sense of Lexi's freak-out. "If it happened at the same time she probably didn't even notice."

"She noticed."

In the middle of a long gulp of soda, Meg raised her free arm up in question.

Lexi dropped her head onto her crossed forearms on the counter. "Trust me, she knew." She lifted her head a touch. "I was loud." She whimpered and her voice filled with self-loathing. "Sort of…all over the place."

"It sounds fucking awesome."

"Meg!" Lexi jolted her head all the way up.

"What? It does." Meg laughed, finishing her drink.

Lexi disregarded her with a huff. "Well, right after that, I completely passed out. Like passed out, passed out. Unconscious. I didn't wake up for hours. The whole thing is humiliating. I can't believe I'm even telling you about it. I planned on taking it to my grave."

"I don't think it's that big a deal." Meg tossed her empty can in with the rest of the recyclables.

"Oh yeah? Has it ever happened to you?" Lexi asked the question sarcastically, but a hint of genuine curiosity came through.

"No, it hasn't. But if it did, you can bet I wouldn't be complaining about it." Sensing Lexi's imminent protest, Meg stopped her with a hand in the air. "Just hear me out on this. What I'm saying is if I was with a girl who was so into me and thought I was so fucking hot, that she actually got off from going down on me, I would think that was fucking awesome. Total turn-on." She saw Lexi's lips turn down into a frown and called her out on it. "Stop, I know where you're going, I see your pouty face starting. If it happened the other way around, I would be just as stoked that I had such fucking mind-blowing sex that I was completely knocked out. It's a win-win if you ask me."

Lexi appeared to be mildly considering Meg's take on the situation when Meg interrupted her thought process, pointing an index finger at Lexi and adding, "What I would be concerned with, however, is you bolted in the middle of the night. And you blew her off when she stopped by this morning. That's weird."

"Why?"

"Why is it weird? Um, let me think." Meg tapped her chin. "How about because you've been in love with her since…" She looked at the ceiling pretending to calculate. "Oh right, forever."

"Meg, it's not like we're going to be together now." Lexi sat upright and pushed her hair behind her shoulders. "I'm not one of those girls who thinks that just because you sleep together that makes you girlfriends or anything. I know it was a one-time thing."

"How do you know that?"

"Because it's Jesse. That's what she does."

"Says who?"

"Please, you don't think she sleeps around?" Lexi said skeptically.

"I don't know," Meg answered honestly. "But what difference does it make really?"

Lexi didn't even need to say anything. The look on her face revealed that she was completely unsatisfied with Meg's response.

Meg softened her tone. "Look, this is what I do know. Jesse was seeing someone recently, someone from her past, an ex or something. She wouldn't tell me who. But I'm pretty sure it's over now. And she told me she wasn't that into her anyway." Meg walked over to the kitchen island, took a seat on the stool across from Lexi, and looked right into her big brown eyes. "The other thing that I know, and this I'm sure of, is that you like her. You *like her*, like her. So stop pretending this isn't a big deal, Lex. Because it is."

They sat together quietly acknowledging the truthfulness of the statement before the loud ding of Meg's email jarred them both out of the moment.

Meg clicked the email open, speed-read through it, and sighed. "I am getting so tired of this."

"Who's A. Whitmore?" Lexi faked pomp.

"Anne Whitmore is my boss. In New York. Not to be confused with Mitch Sanford, my boss in London." Meg's voice trailed off as she reread through the brief message.

"If she's your New York boss, how come she's ordering you to London?" Lexi interjected reading along with her.

"She's actually giving me a heads-up. I still have to manage my caseload here, so she probably talked to Mitch and knows I'm going to have stuff coming up in the UK, so she wants me to be prepared on both fronts."

"At least it's not until the end of the month," Lexi offered optimistically as she reached the end of the email.

Meg hung her head dramatically. "Just means the next few weeks are going to be full of more stress and anxiety," Meg muttered, already feeling sorry for herself.

Resting her chin in her hands, Lexi sighed in full commiseration. "Welcome to my world."

CHAPTER NINETEEN

For the life of her, Meg couldn't understand why it was necessary to go back to London. She had relinquished nearly all of her London projects to actual London staffers. The only thing she still had a hand in at all was the Davis Pruitt job, and that was merely to satisfy the company's president who had balked at the suggestion of change. As a result, she was still expected to coordinate and participate in all the Pruitt conference calls and meetings. And now, another trip across the pond. When had European travel become such a drag?

Truth is, she didn't want to leave New York. She had been assigned three brand-new clients, which meant initial workups, assessments, preliminary meetings, and projections. It was a lot of work and her days were hectic. Meg performed the juggling act she had gotten used to, somehow making time for everything. Often it meant putting in twelve- and fourteen-hour days at the office. On a few occasions, she'd attempted to bring work home to avoid becoming part of the furniture at her office on Third Avenue. So far, that had met with mixed results because she rarely made it home without being stopped.

Spring was finally here, and her neighbors seemed to have come out of hibernation. Meg discovered this while fulfilling the promise she had made to herself to learn the ins and outs of the condo development. Even though she had lived there for months, she still didn't quite have the layout down pat. So each night after work, once she was inside the tree-lined perimeter of Bay West, Meg made it her business to take a different route to her house.

She was determined to follow, at least once, each of the various paths that encompassed, intertwined, and dissected the streets and recreational areas that made up the community. She was amazed at all the nooks and crannies she discovered along the way. There were hidden gardens with seats for lounging surrounded by beautifully manicured shrubbery, hammocks strewn between oak trees, and she even found a tiny gazebo tucked away behind the auxiliary parking lot.

On these nightly adventures, Meg continually stumbled upon one social opportunity after another. Just walking down the street she encountered scores of neighbors she'd never seen before, all just hanging out and about. Some did yard work or planted flowers, others tinkered with their cars or some other DIY project—there seemed to be no shortage of items in need of repurposing. On more than one occasion, she'd seen groups of women spanning multiple generations gathered on the stoop of a unit, talking about local politics or ways the residents could reduce the community's carbon footprint.

Meg was forever being stopped and called over. Everyone wanted to get to know her. She was still the new girl in town.

Sometimes these events turned into a spontaneous mini soiree, like the night she ended up sitting on Rose and Teddy's front steps until nine o'clock, shooting the breeze with the pleasant couple and their next-door neighbors. Other times the gatherings were a touch more planned, like two nights ago when Jesse invited her over for a last-minute barbecue with Betsy and some girl named Allison from Jesse's firm.

As soon as Meg accepted, she hung up the phone and called Lexi and tried to talk her into coming with. Meg knew Lexi had been desperately trying to *randomly* bump into Jesse and so far had absolutely zero success. She reasoned Lexi should simply tag along and act like it was no big deal, she was Meg's BFF after all. Plus Meg figured this was probably Jesse's bid to set her up with Betsy, and she could use a wingman. She could tell by the hesitation in Lexi's voice that she almost had her, but ultimately Lexi declined. Meg sallied forth without her, and even though there was still no spark with Betsy, Meg had such a good time hanging out with the three women, she'd ended up staying past midnight.

Even with these breaks for socializing, Meg managed to get all her work done ahead of schedule. She had hoped in vain that her efficiency would spare her the scheduled trip overseas. She pondered this idly as she sat in front of her computer, booking Monday's flight to London.

The ticket prices were astronomical. It didn't really matter, Sullivan & Son was footing the bill, but the economist in her kept looking for a deal. But there wasn't one to be had on this Wednesday evening, just five days before her departure.

Wednesday. She exhaled sharply and checked the time: 8:56 and not a peep from Mia.

Meg wasn't even sure she cared. Things had cooled off between them considerably since P-town, that was for sure. They'd seen each other last Wednesday and the week before too, but things were... different.

For starters, they had hardly talked at all and the scant conversation they'd managed had felt forced. Then after they'd had sex, Mia left right away, making up excuses both times that she had an early shift the following morning. It bothered Meg more than she wanted to admit. Not because she was brokenhearted, though. What she hated was their friendship seemed to be getting lost in the shuffle. They rarely texted anymore, unless it was to hook up. Honestly, it was all starting to feel a bit wham-bam to Meg. What she had appreciated the most about their arrangement was that through the course of it, they had formed a friendship, confiding in each other about the most random things. She had often thought of their situation as the true definition of friends with benefits. Now that the friendship was fading, Meg wasn't really interested in the benefits package after all.

When she got back from London, she was going to make things right with Mia. It was okay that their fling had run its course, but there was no need to abandon their friendship. She would make Mia see that.

❖   .

Meg pulled up her calendar on her phone as she grabbed a coffee from the hotel's breakfast buffet. She had a full day today, starting with a new client meet and greet in the morning, followed by what she hoped would be the final Pruitt meeting after lunch. The rest of the week appeared to be open. She shook her head and walked the short distance to the office.

The morning meeting went smoothly. Even though she still wasn't convinced she was needed at this function, the big-name marketing company execs directed many of their questions specifically to her.

They had followed her work with Davis Pruitt and seemed particularly impressed that she had effectively orchestrated the company's reorganization without reducing its staff.

Afterward, London-boss Mitch called her to his office to explain this was part of the reason he'd asked her to fly over. He was utterly impressed with her work and had made a point of telling New York–boss Anne the same, even though she wasn't a bit surprised. But the other reason he had insisted that she come to London this week was she had never received a proper orientation. To that end, he instructed her to come in the next day around lunchtime, prepared to party. She was going to have to squeeze into one day the level of debauchery that most associates accomplished in a week, but if her work ethic was anything to go by, he had no doubt she would succeed with flying colors.

It was a good time, her orientation. She knew all the staff by now, so there were no nerves at all, just a fun time with her UK cronies. The only person unable to attend was Sasha Michaels.

Shocker.

On Thursday Meg woke up around noon to the revelation that she had the entire day to herself. She wasn't expected at the office and her flight home didn't depart for another twenty-four hours. Luxuriating in the piping-hot shower stream, Meg decided she would spend the day sightseeing. For all the time she had spent in London in the last six months, she had yet to see a single landmark.

She had planned out the course in her head, allotting just enough time to see everything she wanted. Then as she strolled down a particularly bustling thoroughfare on her way to the Tube, she caught a glimpse of a girl with perfectly styled short blond hair exiting a salon, and something crazy happened. Without a chance to back out of her split-second decision, Meg marched herself through the salon door.

She panicked a little at first as she assessed the girl at the front desk. The girl's light brown hair was pulled back except for one long pink streak that hung down the side of her face. She was covered with a vine of floral tattoos along both forearms and her dark makeup and nose ring completed her impressive look. Meg knew she looked like a complete dork in comparison and was about to sound like one too.

"Hi. I, um, don't have an appointment or anything and this is probably weird, but I just saw some girl walk out of here"—she thumbed toward the door—"with really short blond hair. And I was kind of wondering if, you know, whoever did her hair, could maybe do mine?" She touched the ends of her hair self-consciously.

The girl leaned over the reception desk and gave Meg a thorough once-over. When she met Meg's eyes, her expression softened and a warm smile spread all the way up to her hazel eyes. "Sure, luv. Hang on." Her bangle bracelets clanked against the counter as she turned toward the back of the shop. "David. *Dav-id*," she singsonged.

David emerged from the rear and sashayed to the storefront. Meg was surprised he could move at all in the painted-on skinny jeans he wore. His T-shirt was equally tight, finished with a scarf purely for effect. As he approached the desk, the receptionist took another long look at Meg and began to explain.

"David, you've just cut Lizzie's hair, yeh?" She obviously knew the answer, but David nodded anyway. She gestured at Meg. "This here *adorable* American is looking for the same. Can you do?"

David stepped in front of the counter and circled Meg a full 360 degrees. He stopped in front of her face and held up both hands. "May I?" he asked.

Meg moved her chin up and down even though she wasn't sure what she was saying yes to.

Starting at the base of her neck, David ran his hands up through the back and sides of her hair, carefully making his way to the front, pushing the strands first to one side, then the other, before messing it up completely.

"Darling, your hair is fab. So thick." He was about her height, so when he stood in front of her, their eyes were exactly level. He put one finger up to his puckered lips and nodded. "When I'm through, you are going to be one fit lezzer."

His voice was so serious, Meg couldn't help but burst out in laughter. David and the receptionist chuckled with her.

For the next two hours, Meg watched her own physical transformation take place in stages. She stared calmly in the mirror as the bulk of her hair fell to the floor. It wasn't nearly as scary as she'd expected it to be, perhaps because David kept her occupied by firing question after question at her. He'd already found out where she was from, how old she was, and what she did for work.

"Your girlfriend is going to be shocked when you get home!"

Meg smiled, loving that he'd pegged her right away. "No girlfriend. But yeah, I think my friends will be surprised."

David leaned back in the direction of the reception area. "Nat, she's single," he called out.

"So where are you partying tonight, before you up and leave us for good?" he asked.

Meg was a bit embarrassed, but she answered honestly. Shrugging her shoulders she admitted the truth. "I was just gonna go back to my hotel. I haven't been out really at all since I've been here. I wouldn't even know where to go."

David stopped dead. Still holding a lock of hair in his hand, he called out, "Natalie, call the girls, we're going out tonight." He looked at Meg in the mirror. "Seriously, come out with us. We're normal people. Quite fun, even. Not a serial killer among us. Swearsies." He crossed his heart with the scissors he held.

"Why not?" Meg said lightheartedly. In the mirror's reflection she made eye contact with Natalie who smiled and lightly clapped.

When he finally spun her chair around for the first look, Meg's jaw almost hit the floor.

"Holy shit." Meg felt the back of her neck. She turned her head from side to side. She didn't want to mess too much with the product David had applied but she felt the need to touch her head. She could feel little nubs trimmed down to the base underneath the pixie cut, allowing for what David called a textured look. The highlights were delicate, creating just a bit of depth. Meg loved it.

Natalie came out from the back of the salon, walked over behind Meg's chair. "Meow!" She raised her eyebrows and bit her lower lip. Then she handed Meg a slip of paper containing the words *Club Fenimore 9 p.m.* in big bubbly handwriting.

That evening, Meg broke her cardinal rule and didn't show up until nine forty. She even had a drink at the hotel bar to try to relax a little beforehand. Her nerves were unwarranted. Natalie spotted her as soon as she arrived and dragged her over to the rest of the group, which included David and his boyfriend, who were lovely. Natalie's friends were nice, and they vied for her attention. Meg gave it almost exclusively to Natalie though, who was sweet and even a little shy.

Meg drank, she danced. She even made out with Natalie both on and off the dance floor. It was way more of a public display than Meg would ever engage in at home, but then, she wasn't home. She was clear across the Atlantic, partying with a group of people that she would, in all probability, never see again. She let her hair down, proverbially of course, and had a blast.

The next day as she crossed her ankles and relaxed into the aisle seat en route to New York, she thought about the last six days, the last six weeks, the last six months. She felt exhilarated. Smoothing her hands along the back of her newly exposed neck, she chewed the inside of her cheek and suppressed a smile, wondering if it was possible to feel like an entirely different person simply from a haircut.

❖

Still riding the high of the last few days, Meg headed straight for her sister's house after getting off the plane. She'd missed Shannon and Matt more than she'd thought possible in the last few months. She had souvenirs for them—purchased at the airport of course, but it was the thought that counted—and she was eager to spend some quality time with them. Deirdre would be turning one soon, and Meg felt like she had missed half of her niece's short life already.

It was so easy being in their presence that Meg ended up spending the entire weekend there, gorging on takeout, cheesy movies, and good wine. Shannon and Matt went crazy for her haircut, and they made Meg reenact for them exactly when and how she came to the decision to chop it off.

Once or twice over the weekend she considered telling them about hooking up with Natalie. At least it would keep them off her back about Lexi. Since the day they'd met Lexi shortly after Meg moved in, both Shannon and Matt consistently harassed her about why they weren't together. They were completely dissatisfied with the truth: while Meg and Lexi were both gay and attractive, they were simply not attracted to one another. They fit as friends. Perfectly, actually. It was an answer her sister and brother-in-law were routinely disheartened by. Meg knew it came from a good place, so she didn't blame them. They wanted her to be happy. Meg didn't dare tell them about Mia. As close as she was with Shannon, there really was no way she was going to tell her that she basically had a fuck-buddy.

In the end, she didn't tell them about Natalie, even though there wasn't much to tell—they'd only kissed. In a way, the secrecy of it was nice, kind of like having her own personal memento of London.

She finally went home after dinner Sunday night. She was in no rush; there was no feeling that she had to beat the clock. She wondered if this new sense of calm was because her work in London was finally complete, giving her the time and freedom to enjoy her home. She would be lying if she didn't admit she thought it was at least marginally possible that her new look contributed to her positive attitude change. Over the weekend, the thought had occurred to her more than once that perhaps by cutting her hair off, she had somehow chopped away all of the pent-up tension in her body. She knew it didn't make sense, but rather than analyze it to death, she simply went with it.

The Monday after she returned from London, she marched into Anne Whitmore's office with a speech fully prepared, ready to accentuate her accomplishments of the last half-year. She planned on pointing out she was well aware that Sasha Michaels made more money than she did. She was even going to be truthful as to how she came into that particular bit of knowledge.

Before she could even begin, Anne cut her off.

"Megan, your hair looks fabulous. Turn around, let me get a good look." Anne made a circular motion with her index finger.

"Thanks, Anne," Meg said through a smile, obliging with a quick spin, before she started. "What I really want to talk to you about today is my performance over the last six—"

"You want a raise, Meg." Anne beamed. "You deserve one. We've already discussed it. The partners voted on it at the last meeting, in fact." She wrote down a figure on a piece of paper and handed it across the desk. "This salary will be reflected in your next paycheck."

It was identical to Sasha's. Meg was thrilled. She was also more than a tad relieved to avoid an awkward negotiation.

"So what prompted this?" Anne asked, still focused on Meg's hair.

Meg folded the piece of paper over and over in her hand until it was a small square and slipped it into her pocket. "I don't know. Just something I've been thinking about doing for a while."

"Well, it looks great." The older woman crinkled her brow. "You really are a risk taker. But it absolutely pays off."

Meg knew she was referencing her work now, more than her

hairstyle. It was funny, Meg mused inwardly—she would never have described herself that way, but reflecting a little, she realized she had taken some unorthodox approaches with her projects and they had universally panned out.

Anne continued. "I knew you would be good at this. I really did." She nodded in agreement with her own assertion. "There was never a doubt for me. But I can't stress enough how proud I am of you anyway. Now come around here and give me a hug."

They had known each other for years. Anne was, without question, Meg's mentor. Her idol, even, in some ways. Meg stepped around the desk and wrapped her arms around her boss. Despite her best efforts to will them away, Meg felt her eyes well up with tears of pride.

Later that day, as she ambled her way home, Meg mentally ticked the items off her to-do list. Spend time with family, check. Ask for raise, check. Now all she had to do was work things out with Mia. That was going to be a tricky one. Even with her newfound self-confidence, she worried about her ability to pull it off successfully. She took a deep breath, drinking in the warm night air. She looked up at the rooftops and was drawn into the beautiful blood-orange sunset that lay beyond them. When she turned her gaze back to street level she noticed Teddy up ahead, sitting on her stoop, thumbing through a magazine and drinking a beer. As she got closer, Meg saw her actually do a double take before she tossed her glossy mag aside.

"Girl, come here."

Meg knew where this was going. None of her friends had seen her new look yet. Meg strolled over and leaned up against the handrail. "What?" she teased, faking ignorance at Teddy's reaction.

"Look at you. Wow." Teddy nodded, clearly approving the change. "Sit down, have a drink with me."

"Sure." Meg sat next to the brawny woman. "I think I'll pass on the drink, though."

"Water, soda, anything?" Teddy offered.

"Nah, I'm good." Meg waved her off.

Teddy leaned back into the step behind her and gave Meg a once over, not even trying to hide her assessment. She brushed over her own short black buzz cut that was speckled with gray. "I cut mine off when I was about your age," she pondered aloud. "Feels good, doesn't it."

Meg breathed out a small laugh. "Yeah, it kind of does."

They talked for easily half an hour about mundane stuff—the weather, summer plans, the Mets' chances at postseason play. Then Teddy nodded in silence, pushed her glasses up, and said through her thick Dominican accent, "You know, Meg." She gave a dramatic pause. "You look like you."

Meg squinted in question, but Teddy answered her before she could actually ask anything.

"Come on, you know what I'm saying. New do, sitting out here so relaxed, chatting away with me. This is you." She leaned over and mussed Meg's short locks. "It's like the real you was hiding under all that hair. Now it's gone, and I gotta say"—she hummed in agreement with herself—"you look like you." She smiled a broad toothy grin.

"Thanks, I think," Meg said cautiously, but she knew it was a compliment.

Teddy reached over and patted Meg's knee. "Now, when are you going to let me introduce you to my cousin?"

Meg rolled her eyes. She should have seen it coming. She leapt to her own defense. "It's not that I don't want to meet her, it's just that—"

"I know, I know. You don't want a setup. I remember." She took a swig from her beer. "Wait a minute, though. We're doing an open house next month. Over at the Commons." She tossed her head in the general direction of the center of the development. "That'd be perfect."

Meg eyed her suspiciously.

"You been to an open house yet?" Teddy asked.

Meg frowned. "Honestly, no. I'm not even sure I understand the concept."

Teddy licked her lips. She was clearly about to give one of her famous lessons. She was truly a trove of information on Bay West and Meg was grateful for it. Plus she loved Teddy's rich expressive voice. Meg could listen to her talk for hours.

"Well, you've been to a social, so you know what that's about. Really no different from going to The Kitchen." Teddy looked up at the sky searching for the best description. "Opens are completely different. For starters, they're only open to people who live here." She paused and shook her head. "Scratch that. What I mean is that all open houses are open"—with one hand she mimed quotation marks around the word—"to any resident of Bay West and their invited guests. You don't have to know the people sponsoring it. But you can't just walk in off the street, like you can at a social." She looked at Meg to make sure she was absorbing it all. "So what usually happens is that it's a much smaller crowd." She touched Meg's forearm lightly. "It's still a crowd though, don't get me wrong. Think of it as the difference between a big club and a neighborhood bar. It's a much more chill vibe if you ask me."

Meg tried to grasp it all. "Why are you having one?"

Teddy leaned back on her elbows and kind of shrugged. "We decided to throw one because our anniversary is in June." She nodded toward the house, where Rose presumably was. "But really it's just an excuse to have a party with our friends. People have them for all sorts of reasons, or no reason at all. See, it started back in the beginning. All of us who lived here were having actual open-house parties. Then Kam Browne came up with this idea." She took another long drink from her beer and wiped her mouth. "Listen, I know she did it as a moneymaker, but so what? For a few bucks, I'm happy to go to the Commons, throw a party for my friends. It's just gravy that I don't have to buy shit and then clean it all up. Worth every penny, in my book."

Meg thought it sounded pretty cool.

With her explanation finished, Teddy got right back to business. "So, like I was saying. Come to the open house in June. My cousin Reina will be there. It won't be a setup, you have my word." She thumped her chest twice with three fingers and then held them up stiffly in some kind of massacred boy-scout swear. "You two just meet each other, see if anything clicks. If not, no harm done." She looked out over the top of her glasses. "Deal?" Teddy held out her hand optimistically.

Meg smiled and rolled her eyes blatantly as she stood up. She returned Teddy's handshake even though she was still not sold on the idea.

"You roll your eyes now, Meg," Teddy said as Meg descended the few stairs. "But I guarantee you're going to love her."

Meg waved without turning around. "We'll see," she called out behind her.

From the corner of the block, Meg could make out Lexi standing in front of her own doorway. She picked up her pace in the hopes of catching her before she went in. As Meg reached her, she realized that Lexi hadn't moved. She was completely still in front of her door, clutching a half-crumpled piece of paper.

"Hey, Lex."

Lexi startled at her name and turned to Meg. "Hey." Having not seen each other in over a week, Meg expected a warmer welcome.

"Oh my God, you cut your hair." Lexi nodded with a sullen expression. "It looks really great, Meg," she added with sincerity, if not excitement.

"Yeah, thanks." Meg was certain Lexi was upset—she'd known her long enough to recognize the signs. "What's wrong?"

"Nothing. Nothing, I'm fine." She wiped at her eyes. "Just… nothing. Long day. I should go in." She motioned to her house. Without looking up again she asked Meg, "You around tomorrow? I'll stop by."

"Yeah, of course."

Meg barely got the words out before Lexi closed the door firmly behind her. Meg reached for her keys and wondered what the hell that was all about.

Chapter Twenty

L exi successfully avoided just about everyone for almost a week. She dodged Meg's calls in particular, employing excuse after excuse when Meg tried to pin her down. It had been tricky, but luckily Meg had a busy week at work, so that bought Lexi some extra time. Meg knew something was up, Lexi was sure of it. But now that she had finally made a decision, she would come out of hiding.

It was getting better. Today she hadn't cried at all.

But her strength was weakening each second she remained in her room. As a matter of fact if she didn't leave right now she was certain she would reread the letter again, break down again, change her mind *again*. No way. Today was a turning point. She had decided that when she woke up this morning.

Lacing up her sneakers, she called up the stairs, "Hey, Mush, I'm going down to the boardwalk for a run. I'll be back in a little while."

"Really? It looks like it's about to pour," Chris answered, her voice full of doubt.

Lexi frowned at the gray sky out the window, knowing her mother was right. She stood still for a second and considered the alternative. "I think I can get it in before it rains. I'm gonna try, anyway."

Chris dangled a set of keys over the railing to Lexi. "Here. Take the car in the driveway. I'm not finished with your gaskets yet, so this will have to do." Her mom was always doing that—hijacking her car to do some routine maintenance.

Lexi grabbed the keys and gave a small smile of thanks. In moments like this, the favor was marginally inconvenient but a small price to pay. Plus, Chris always provided a loaner. Lexi had to stifle a laugh as she opened the front door and checked out the two-tone maroon and tan 80s-model Ford in the driveway. The thing was the size of a boat.

She slid behind the massive steering wheel and resisted the urge to look over at Jesse's house. It had been over a month since they'd slept together and Lexi'd had absolutely no contact with her since then. No phone calls, no texts, not a single sighting.

There was only the letter she had received three full days ago, offering a permanent position at Stanton Ducane—the letter that wasn't even really signed by Jesse. Her signature had been imprinted on the page using the hand stamp Lexi had seen hundreds of times on routine correspondence that required both partners' signatures. At least Laney Stanton had bothered to take the four seconds out of her day to grab a pen and scrawl her name across the page in earnest.

That small detail spoke volumes. For days Lexi had pored over the letter, looking for hidden messages, clues that she wasn't crazy, she hadn't imagined all the little moments they had shared. And then out of nowhere, on what was probably her thousandth rereading, it hit her. Running her index finger over the names at the bottom of the ivory bond paper, it dawned on Lexi—Jesse didn't care about her, not even enough to sign her conditional offer of employment.

What had happened between them had simply been a one-time thing. She had been an idiot to think even for a minute that it could ever possibly be anything more. Last night that discovery had devastated her, leaving her sobbing quietly under her covers for hours before falling asleep. But this morning she had woken with new resolve. She'd made a mistake, yes. But there was no way she was going to let it destroy her career.

As soon as she got home she would stop procrastinating and call the firm to accept the position.

She was working through just what she might say when she called as she pulled into the lot at the beach. She was more than a little preoccupied and just missed the curb as she made the turn into the parking area. Exhaling a sigh of relief at the near miss, Lexi decided to park the huge car in the corner of the lot, a safe distance away from the few other cars there. She didn't need to cap off the week from hell with a fender bender because she wasn't used to driving a monstrosity.

Without stretching, she jogged through the parking area up to the boardwalk entrance, passing by people heeding the warning signs from the looming clouds and thundering surf and heading toward their cars. The sensible thing would be to turn around and go home, she knew it. But even though she had finally made up her mind about the job, she still didn't trust herself to go back to the house and not do a one-eighty. Even now as she strode up the wooden ramp, defiant in the face of the storm, she felt the nagging indecision edging its way into her mind.

She pushed back against it, running as fast as her legs would carry her, consciously forcing out all thoughts of Stanton Ducane.

Just over half a mile in, the sky opened up full force. There was no drizzle, no light mist. The rain came down hard, pounding into her face and chest. She took pleasure in the pain, imagining that it was the universe doling out her just punishment for being so goddamn naïve about everything. The lightning came next. She saw it make contact with the beach near the edge of the water. The rain was heavier by the second, the boardwalk getting slippery. Her sense of reason took over. Even though she was enjoying her run—the physical exertion was a welcome release after her week of obsessing—it was stupid to risk the lightning, however unlikely her chances of getting struck were. There was an exit ramp a hundred yards ahead. From there she could duck under the boardwalk and take cover until the worst of it passed.

As she approached the ramp, she saw a figure sprinting from the other direction toward the same ramp. If the rain hadn't been forcing her to run with her head down and her eyes open only the tiniest slits, she would have realized much sooner that it was Jesse.

They reached the ramp at exactly the same time.

"Come on." Jesse placed her hand on Lexi's lower back, guiding her under the boardwalk. Safely out of the torrent, Jesse doubled over to catch her breath. "This rain is something else. It's got to ease up soon—we should wait it out here." Jesse leaned against a support post, hands on her hips, and rolled her neck from side to side. "I guess we're the only two idiots out here," she said between breaths.

Lexi could not believe her fucking luck. For weeks she had manipulated her schedule a thousand different ways, praying for a chance encounter with Jesse, hoping for an opportunity to talk about what had happened. A scant few minutes to read her face and see if it was all in her head or if there might be something more between them.

But that was all before the letter.

With the letter had come the answers to those questions, she reminded herself.

So here she was, the proverbial deer in headlights, unable to formulate a cohesive thought, completely distracted by Jesse's dark gray T-shirt, soaked through and plastered to her body.

She wanted to stop staring but the goose bumps forming on Jesse's forearms caught her attention. She followed them all the way up to Jesse's breasts, which were no less affected.

Lexi felt her face getting hot and she shifted her glance, embarrassed by her natural instinct. And then she realized how *she* was dressed, which only caused more anxiety. She was wearing a white tank top, a terrible choice considering the weather. It was completely drenched and fairly transparent. At least she was wearing two sports bras. She sighed in moderate relief, thinking that today might be the one day she was thankful for her big boobs. At least the triple layer kept her areolas from showing through.

"Did you see that lightning?" Jesse broke the silence. "Crazy, right?"

"I know." Lexi tried to sound interested in normal conversation. She still could not believe the odds of this happening when she had finally given up.

Jesse looked past her down to the beach, seemingly oblivious to Lexi's distress. "Hey, turn around and check out the waves, they're pretty awesome." In a step Jesse was next to her, leaning on a beam, their forearms almost touching. "Look, look." Jesse touched Lexi's wrist and pointed out a huge breaker as it crashed to the shore. Lexi fixed her eyes on the shoreline, determined not to look at where Jesse's fingertips rested lightly at the base of her hand.

A million conflicting emotions rushed through her. She wished she could be cold and distant, blow Jesse off, prove she was unaffected. At the same time, she wanted to scream at Jesse for being interested in her brain over her body. More than anything she wanted to cry for being so completely caught up in it all.

What she should do, she knew logically, was simply talk to Jesse honestly about what she was feeling, what she had felt for months. Maybe she would have, she told herself, if this chance meeting had happened a week or ten days ago, before the letter.

Instead she talked about the weather.

"There's another swell coming in." Lexi attempted casual, pointing out a wave just gaining momentum. "That's going to be huge too." Thankful that her voice didn't shake at all, she continued. "Too bad we're not surfers, this would be amazing."

"Do they really go out in the rain like this?" Jesse looked right at her.

Lexi maintained the eye contact at first, but she was surprisingly caught off guard by the pale green eyes. She'd almost forgotten their effect on her.

"I'm not sure if they stay out during the actual storm itself. But I know they're always out here before it starts, anyway." She turned her attention back to the water as she answered. "So, did you get a good run in? I mean before the rain." Lexi glanced down at her sneakers trying to keep regular conversation going.

Jesse laughed heartily. "You could say that."

"How far?" Lexi continued, not really sure what was funny about the question or the answer.

Jesse shook out her soaked hair and brushed her hands through it haphazardly. "I don't know. Six or seven miles. Maybe eight. I'm not really sure. But obviously I should have turned around sooner." She held out her shirt for emphasis. "Wasn't paying attention, I guess."

"Where's your car, I didn't see it in the lot. Did you park somewhere else?" Lexi wondered aloud, immediately wishing she hadn't.

Jesse grinned. "I forgot you're always keeping tabs on me, Detective." She only had to lean slightly to the left to bump Lexi's shoulder with her own. "I ran down here," she answered, "from the development." Her smile grew wider as she said it.

Lexi found herself staring at Jesse's mouth before catching herself. "Oh, are you training for the marathon or something?"

"No." Jesse chuckled again, continuing the inside joke she was having with herself. "I just get in these moods. Consumed with what's going on in my head." She stuttered a little. "You know, uh, work and stuff." She looked at the sand and shuffled a splintered board with her sneaker. "I have a trial coming up. It's kind of convoluted, so I'm trying to write a good opening for it, and I keep getting stuck." She continued to babble a little in her justification. "I figured I'd just kind of run it out."

"Is that how you do all your openings and closings?"

"No." Jesse raised her eyebrows and gave a slight shrug. "Hardly ever, actually." Her voice was as husky as ever. "You just keep catching me doing it," she added shyly.

Lexi felt her mouth go completely dry at Jesse's obvious reference to their last encounter. "So did you figure it out? The opening?" Lexi choked out, barely maintaining her composure by reaching for something other than *that* night to talk about. She couldn't believe Jesse just threw it out there like it was no big deal.

"I don't know yet." Jesse's tone changed again as she shrugged and looked away. "I guess I'll figure it out later, when I sit back down to work on it." She turned back toward the ocean. "What about you? What brings you out here in this lovely weather?"

This was it. The opportunity she had been waiting for. Jesse had just given her the perfect opening to lay it all on the table—the awkwardness of their situation, what had happened between them, the job offer, everything. But Lexi balked. The whole thing was too embarrassing. She knew the truth anyway. Asking the questions out loud wouldn't change the answers. It would only make them both uncomfortable. And Lexi was certain she would completely fall apart if she talked about it. There was no way she would let Jesse know how much it bothered her. She avoided the topic entirely, answering as plainly as she could.

"Just needed to get out of the house." Although it wasn't a total lie, it felt like one to Lexi, so she added a disclaimer. "I've been studying like crazy."

"Yeah? How's it going?"

"Good, I guess. Who knows?"

Jesse touched her arm again. "You'll be fine. School doesn't teach you how to be a lawyer. You learn that after, through internships and actual work. Trust me, you are way ahead of a lot of people in that area."

Lexi watched as the rain dripped down between the wooden planks, making tiny craters in the sand. She was nervous that this topic of conversation would lead right back to talking about work and she wanted to avoid going there at this point. "Maybe we should start walking back. I'm parked up in the north lot. Hopefully it will have stopped by the time we get there, or at least let up a little. I can give you a ride back," Lexi said, steering the conversation in a safer direction.

"Good idea." Jesse pushed off the beam and faced the north end.

They walked the length of beach underneath the boardwalk, climbing over the pylons in their way. Lexi was proud of herself for keeping her composure, avoiding discussion of both their one night together and the letter. She was slightly surprised but also relieved that Jesse didn't bring up the job offer either, figuring that their reasoning was the same. She was pleased with how easily their conversation flowed. Lexi'd forgotten how comfortable they could be with one another. She was especially satisfied at how normal she managed to sound. Avoiding direct eye contact was the key, she decided, which was much easier now that they were walking. She actually found herself fairly relaxed, if a little disappointed, as they reached the beginning of the boardwalk.

Lexi peered out from under the wooden overhang at the continuous downpour. "I guess we have to run for it." She nodded her head toward the only car in the lot, the gigantic Ford.

"To that car?" Jesse said in disbelief. "That's not your car. Where's your little Camry?"

Lexi raised one eyebrow. "Hmm. Checking out my car. Keeping tabs on me," she teased. "Interesting." She wasn't really sure why she was flirting now, when the time for that had clearly passed, but she didn't stop herself. "This is my car today. Make a note of it, *Detective*." Lexi beamed ear to ear. She took off sprinting without giving Jesse a chance to say anything.

She hit the car several paces before Jesse did. She had only gotten the door open a crack before Jesse flew up behind her, coming to a stop with her front flush against Lexi's back, their combined weight and momentum forcing the door closed again. In one motion Jesse spun Lexi around and leaned in without any hesitation at all.

They stayed there pressed up against the car making out in the rain, like something out of a movie, for what felt like forever, until Lexi found the rear door handle and they slid into the backseat together, a sopping-wet mix of sweat and rain on top of the plasticky vinyl.

They kissed each other frantically, their hands all over one another. Without breaking contact, Lexi raised her arms and let Jesse lift her shirt over her head. She cringed a little, remembering once again that she was wearing two sports bras. It didn't slow Jesse down. Undeterred, she pushed both bras up as she worked her way down Lexi's body, tilting her backward onto the seat and leaning down on top of her as she positioned herself between Lexi's legs. Then out of nowhere, Jesse pulled back a little and slowed the pace, dispensing sweet baby kisses all over Lexi's face and neck. Her hand hovered at the waistband of Lexi's shorts, her index finger gently playing at the elastic. They locked eyes, and in the intensity of the moment Lexi knew without a doubt that Jesse was seeking some kind of permission, making sure it was okay to continue.

Lexi knew that she should stop it from going any further. She should take the out Jesse was giving. Really, what good could come from this? If she let it happen, where would that leave her with the job offer—the one she had decided to accept just this morning? She closed her eyes and breathed in, mustering the resolve to call it off. She reached up to Jesse's shoulders, fully intending to push her away, but something in her body took over. She grabbed the back of Jesse's neck, pulled her down, and kissed her so passionately, so possessively, that there was no mistaking her answer. She ran her hands down Jesse's back, found the bottom of her shirt, and peeled it off as she wrapped her legs around her.

The second she felt Jesse's hand inside her underwear she realized that for all of her hemming and hawing, she had just made the only decision that mattered to her all week. This was what she wanted. It was what she had always wanted.

She pushed Jesse's running shorts down and felt their half-naked bodies make contact. She moved her hand lower to touch Jesse and watched her react when Lexi pressed her thigh against the back of her hand to add support and pressure. For a minute Lexi internally marveled at how effortlessly they were able to maneuver in this confined space. She almost had to suppress a giggle as she acknowledged her newfound appreciation of the dated sedan with its enormous backseat.

Jesse looked at Lexi again, as intensely as before, their faces millimeters apart as she eased two fingers deep inside. Lexi gasped a little at first and then held her breath for a second. She knew it would be quick, she only hoped she would hold out long enough to get Jesse close too. They moved together slowly at first, until Lexi couldn't take it any longer, her body instinctively taking over, accelerating the pace until she came hard and fast.

Jesse's smile was sweet and a little smug as she kept her hand inside Lexi, feeling her pulsate. She pressed her forehead lightly against Lexi's and kissed her softly as she moved against her, slamming her eyes shut and breathing out several expletives as she finished.

❖

The short ride home was filled with the mundane. They talked about when the rain might have stopped, but neither of them was sure. Jesse mentioned that she always loved the way the steam came off the street after a good storm. Lexi offered something silly about the changing climate and global warming.

When they entered Bay West from the main road, Lexi immediately turned onto the exterior roadway, heading for the auxiliary lot, citing a lame excuse about how there was no room near her house for the big car. Which was bogus because obviously there was. Somewhere beneath the filler conversation on the way from the beach, Lexi had decided she couldn't take it anymore. She had to talk about the job offer, about everything. After what had just happened, there could be no avoiding it. She settled in one of the first spots in the back of the lot and turned off the ignition.

Before she could say anything, Jesse leaned over, put her hand behind Lexi's neck and pulled her in, kissing her so sweetly, Lexi nearly slid off the seat and onto the floorboards.

"I'll talk to you." Jesse looked her dead in the eye before she opened the door and was gone.

Lexi walked to her house feeling ecstatic, elated, and more confused than ever. Pushing open the front door, she called up the stairs. "I'm home. Going to take a shower."

"Hey, honey," Chris yelled back from the kitchen. "Did you get wet?"

Lexi smirked to herself. *You have no idea.*

CHAPTER TWENTY-ONE

Later that same evening, as Lexi was setting the garbage pail at the curb, totally oblivious to the world around her, Meg marched across the two lawns, grabbed Lexi's arm, and dragged her into her own house. She shut the door behind them and faced Lexi.

"What the hell is going on with you?" Meg crossed her arms, exploding again before giving Lexi a chance to answer. "And don't say *nothing*. It's obvious you're avoiding me. And I know for a fact you've been ignoring Sam too." She uncrossed her arms and held both hands out, expecting an answer.

Lexi gave a weak smile at Meg's concern. Squeezing herself into a tight hug, she sank into the door behind her. She shook her head and huffed. "I'm a mess."

"What's going on?"

Lexi slid down the wall and crouched on the tile. "What isn't going on right now?" she responded rhetorically.

Meg arched her eyebrows and waited.

"Hmm, let's see. Where should I start?" She tapped her forefinger on her puffy lips. "I got offered a job at Stanton Ducane," she said with a twinge of anger and annoyance.

"That could be a good thing, you know." Meg understood the source of her frustration and was about to give her a pep talk, but Lexi stopped her.

"I know. I'm supposed to be excited. Thrilled, over the moon, all that." Her voice started to crack. "It is a great firm and everything."

"Also, you get to be with Jesse every day."

Lexi pinched a tiny leaf that hung off the bottom of her flip-flop. She rolled it into a teeny ball between her thumb and index finger, staring at the floor. "I don't know, Meg."

Meg squatted in the middle of the floor just to be at the same eye level.

Lexi met her gaze briefly. "I thought I could do it. I really did."

"This happened, when? The other night? When I saw you standing outside your house?" Meg commented as she put the pieces together.

Lexi leaned her head against the wall. "I *have* been avoiding you."

"Yeah, I got that."

"Sorry," Lexi said genuinely. "Don't feel bad though, it's not like you missed anything. I've only been bawling ever since." She frowned. "And of course, freaking out."

"I'm not convinced that this is a bad thing."

"Come on, Meg."

"Did you ever think that maybe this is her way of trying to get close to you?"

"No," Lexi responded sharply. She wiped her hands against her shorts. "You know, I had actually started to accept it. Not the job, I'm talking about the fact that she wasn't interested in me." She drew her knees in close to her chest. She had a funny kind of smile and as she spoke her eyes welled up. "Obviously, I was totally bummed about it. But I was coming to terms with it, I swear. I went over and over it in my head, pros, cons, the whole shebang. Then, this morning, I finally decided to take the job." She nodded her head, the tears spilling in spite of her small grin.

"Yeah?"

She wiped her cheeks. "Yep. Swallow my pride. I have no other offers anyway. Decided to be a bigger person and the whole bit. I had myself convinced." Her voice caught in her throat, and her eyes refilled immediately. "I really believed I could do it. Honest to God." She sniffled, rubbed her face roughly with her hands, taking care of the new stream of tears. Her smile was bigger now, and she wore the look of someone who has just realized her own foolishness.

"You changed your mind?"

Lexi let out a laugh. "Well, Meg, then I went for a run down at the boardwalk."

"Okay." Meg waited.

Lexi pursed her lips, holding back a laugh. "And I ran right into Jesse."

Meg narrowed her eyes. "All right. That's good, right? I mean, did you talk to her?"

"Not so much."

"Huh?"

Lexi threw her head down between her knees and broke into hysterical laughter even as she wiped away more tears. Propping her chin up on her kneecaps, she puffed out her cheeks. "No, I didn't talk to her. I had sex with her. Again."

"What!"

Lexi nodded confirmation, looking a bit self-satisfied and disappointed at the same time.

"In my car." She thought for a second before correcting herself. "That's not even true. It was actually a stranger's car."

Meg's jaw was on the floor. She held up her hand. "Whoa, whoa, whoa. Back up."

"It's not as bad as it sounds," Lexi said through a chuckle. "Mush was fixing my car so she had me use a different one that she's working on." She registered Meg's shock. "I guess that doesn't sound too good either," she admitted after hearing it out loud. "But that reminds me, she wants to look under your hood. She said you were rattling a little coming down the street the other day."

"Jesse?"

"No, Mush."

"Okay, slow down." Meg put both hands out, halting the conversation. "Start over."

"My mom wants to check out your car."

"Got it. Done." Meg swirled her head dramatically. "Now get back to the part where you have sex with Jesse."

"That's it. We ran into each other at the beach. I offered to drive her home because it was pouring." She shrugged. "We didn't talk about anything. It just kind of happened."

"Are you okay?" Meg scrunched her face up sympathetically, knowing the answer.

"No, I'm a disaster. I have no clue what the hell I'm doing or what I'm going to do now."

"And now you're not going to take the job?"

"How can I?"

Meg chewed her bottom lip considering the possibility.

"Meg, I already slept with my boss. Twice. I mean, talk about office slut."

"I still think that maybe she offered you the job because she wants to be with you, you know."

Lexi looked at Meg like she was crazy.

"Not that you're not a good lawyer or anything. But let's be honest. You're young, you're hot, you've got these big puppy dog eyes—"

"I don't think that's it," Lexi snapped.

Meg took a minute. "Okay, I'm sure you've already thought of this, but I'm going to throw it out there anyway." She waited for Lexi to give her full attention. "Why don't you try talking to her? I mean, she lives fifty feet away, for Christ's sake."

"And how's that gonna go?" Lexi's voice brimmed with animosity. "I just walk over, ring her doorbell?"

"Pretty much, yeah."

"And then what, just launch right in?" She bent her head and put on a fake stern face. "Excuse me, Jesse." Her voice matched her expression, and Meg had a hard time keeping a straight face. "Sorry to bother you with this, but I'm having a little dilemma. See, I know you offered me a job and everything, but I'm kind of in love with you, and the random fucking is messing with my head. So I was just hoping we could discuss it a little, you know, just so I can make an informed decision."

"I mean I know you're not serious, but that does kind of cover it," Meg said.

Lexi rolled her eyes.

"What *are* you going to do?"

"I don't know. Stress out some more. Get drunk this weekend."

"Well, that's a solution," Meg said.

Lexi shrugged.

"Did you have any place special in mind? Or are you just going to Virginia Woolf yourself again, hole back up in your room?"

Lexi managed a smile. "It's Memorial Day weekend. The summer kick-off social is this Saturday. Figured I'd make an appearance."

"Good, I can keep my eye on you." Meg kicked Lexi's foot lightly.

"Meg?"

"Yeah?"

"Thanks for looking out for me."

"Sure."

"And Meg?"

"Yeah?"

"Your hair looks fucking incredible."

"Thanks, Lex."

"Come here."

Meg slid across the floor and hugged her friend. Lexi ran her hand through the back of Meg's hair before pulling back. "What did Mia say about it?"

"I haven't seen her."

"No?"

"Nope." She tousled her own hair. "Something's off with us. I can't really put my finger on it."

"I thought that's what you guys did," Lexi teased.

"Don't be gross."

Lexi raised her eyebrows and smiled. "Hmm, you tease me all the time. Not so much fun when you're on the receiving end, huh?"

Meg laughed at being called out so readily. "I know. I'm just kidding. I loved it."

"Seriously, are you guys fighting or something?"

Meg stretched her arms out over her head. "No. I think it's"—she let out a long breath—"kind of over. Run its course, you know." She crossed her arms definitively. "I should probably take my own advice and actually talk to her. I've kind of been putting it off. Not that I think she'll be upset or anything. I just want to try to stay friends, and sometimes I think that can be harder in a way. I mean look at you and Julie, right?"

"True."

"I know she's going to the social, maybe I'll try talking to her then." Meg wanted to suggest that Lexi do the same with Jesse, but she didn't. She knew Lexi would never do it anyway. So she filled the silence with the only thing she could think of. "It'll be okay, Lex."

Lexi rested her head on Meg's shoulder. They stayed that way, together in the quiet on the cold tile floor for a long time.

❖

Two hours later, after Lexi had long gone, Meg took the matter into her own hands. A rush of adrenaline surged through her at the thought of what she was about to do. She hurriedly picked up her phone, scrolled through her list of contacts, and selected Jesse's name. She started the text immediately before giving herself a chance to back out.

You going in early tomorrow?

Meg already knew the answer. She'd bummed enough early morning rides from her neighbor in the last few months not to know her routine by now. Fridays were a sure thing. Her phone dinged in response thirty seconds later.

Yeah you want a ride
Is that okay
No prob. C u at 530
Thx

At promptly five thirty the next morning, Meg rested against the rear bumper of Jesse's car under the purple sky, still trying to work out how she was going to bring the topic up and precisely what she was going to say. It was a waste of time. As Jesse backed out of her driveway and slowly headed down the street, she did the exact same thing she had done every single time Meg had taken this trip with her, and probably every time she didn't.

Jesse turned her head to the left and rubbed her chin against her shoulder, taking a long look at the façade of Lexi's house, still dark and quiet with night.

It was exactly the opening Meg needed. She threw her head back and let out a sigh of relief. "I fucking knew it."

Jesse tipped her head down and eyed Meg. "What?" She sounded serious, but continued playfully. "What do you know, Megan McTiernan?"

Meg picked up right away that Jesse was attempting to make light of it, but she wasn't about to let her off that easily. "You like her." Meg made the statement adamantly, nodding backward at Lexi's house fading into the distance. "Lexi. You really like her, don't you?"

Jesse looked at her from under her long, dark lashes with an expression that was more serious than Meg had expected. Meg met her gaze and waited for the denial, prepared to challenge Jesse when she brushed it off like it was no big deal. But she didn't. She simply shifted her eyes back to the road and blinked long and hard, all but admitting it.

"Why don't you just tell her?" Meg asked.

With a subtle shake of her head, Jesse responded, "It's not that simple."

"Why not?"

"Because." She stopped and pushed her turn signal down with more force than was necessary. "Because. I don't know. Just because."

It was obvious there was something she wasn't saying. Meg pushed her. "Because what? Spit it out."

Jesse shook her hand through her hair roughly. "Look, I'm not even sure that she's interested in me." She paused for a second and then continued. "The way I am in her." She looked over her shoulder as she merged into the traffic, the action somehow undermining the seriousness of the conversation. "I thought so at first. Now, I don't know."

"What do you mean?"

"Nothing," she started but then stopped for a second, before continuing. "It's just that—" Her eyes burned straight ahead through the windshield onto the highway ahead of them. When she spoke, it sounded like she was talking to herself as much as to Meg. "She used to look at me and I could see it in her eyes. I could feel it. I knew she felt it too. I knew it." Then she narrowed her eyes as she second-guessed herself. "At least I thought I did. God, it's been so long that I'd forgotten what that felt like."

As Jesse continued to peer out the window into the distance, Meg considered asking her what exactly she meant by the last comment. But as she studied Jesse's tense body language, she knew that she didn't need to. Jesse and Lexi's connection wasn't random, it wasn't a fling. Meg had suspected all along that there was something deep and genuine between her two friends, and in this moment she was sure she was right.

"I would have sworn there was something there," Jesse said, as though she could read Meg's mind. She shook her head, not even trying to mask her disappointment. "But then after we slept together, she took off. I've barely seen her since."

"The way I heard it, it was you who ran away last time," Meg challenged.

Jesse glanced over, looking more relaxed than Meg expected, particularly considering Meg had just called her out. "So you're obviously up to speed on everything." Instead of anger or annoyance, Jesse's voice held a note of clarification.

"Don't be mad at her for talking to me. She's stressed out and confused. She just needed somebody to talk to."

"I'm not mad." Jesse sounded defensive. "I just wish she'd talk to me."

"Well, I think she feels the same way. I know she wished you'd talked to her before you offered her the job. That really messed her up. I'm just curious, is that your move to get close to her?" Meg asked, testing her own theory.

"What are you talking about?"

"It freaked her out. The job offer. She thinks it means you're not interested in her."

"What job offer?" Jesse sounded angry and confused.

Meg spoke slowly. "At your law firm. The lawyer position, I guess."

"I didn't offer her a job."

"Uh, yes, you did."

"No, I didn't." Jesse's voice was firm. "I specifically did not offer her a job, as a matter of fact."

Meg shrugged. "Well, she thinks you did."

Jesse continued to drive in silence, cocking her head this way and that as she licked her lips repeatedly. Whatever she was trying to work out in her head must have clicked, because she suddenly pounded the steering wheel. "Shit." She leaned her head back on the headrest looking defeated as she muttered under her breath, "Fucking Laney."

For the first time it occurred to Meg that there might have been factors at play behind the job offer that she and Lexi hadn't considered. "So, wait. You *didn't* offer her the job?"

Jesse shook her head slowly in response.

"Well, what are you waiting for? Clear it up. Come clean. Tell her you like her. You obviously do."

Jesse bit her bottom lip. "That's just it. Once I tell her—everything, that is—I'm afraid she'll...I don't know." She trailed off, sounding nervous. "I'm worried she won't want to be with me. That is, assuming she does right now."

"Listen to me. I don't know what it is you're worried about, and I can tell you don't want to tell me, which is fine. Whatever it is," Meg said dramatically, "I honestly can't imagine it making that much of a difference."

Jesse pursed her lips and raised her eyebrows indicating that she wanted to believe Meg, but she still had concerns.

Meg tried to convince her. "Jess, I've been listening to her talk about you for months. Basically since I moved in here. I see the twinkle in her eye every time she says your name." Meg said it playfully, even though it was true. She put on a sugary voice and batted her eyelashes in a terrible impersonation of Lexi. "Then Jesse did this, then Jesse did that." She dropped the act but her voice was still light and full of optimism. "Trust me, whatever it is you're worried about, it's not going to matter. Lexi is into you. I'm sure of it." Meg finished with a smile.

The corner of Jesse's mouth turned up ever so slightly. "I hope you're right."

CHAPTER TWENTY-TWO

The weather Saturday was perfect—bright sunshine, not a cloud in the sky, and high seventies. By late afternoon, Meg had had enough waiting around. She called Lexi and demanded she be ready in five minutes. Lexi acquiesced, albeit grudgingly.

They entered the summer kick-off festivities together and, even though Lexi had told her what to expect, Meg still took a few minutes to absorb all the details.

In the expansive lawn area adjacent to the pool, a huge cookout was set up, complete with two Budweiser trucks that were sponsoring the day's event. The DJ was playing a nice mix of oldies catering to the afternoon clientele made up predominantly of women and kids who lived in the development, but Meg spotted a few fresh faces prancing around inside the gated pool area, their bikini-clad bodies begging for attention. She also spied a group of girls that she was pretty sure were new renters. They looked a tad unsure of themselves and Meg made a mental note to befriend them before the night was over.

Meg rubbed her hands together, sizing up the multitude of food stands lining the perimeter. "Thank God, I'm fucking starving." She looked over at Lexi, who was still sulking. "You eating?"

"I doubt it."

Meg dragged her along anyway toward the first in a row of barbecue stations. She kept moving once she saw its sole option was veggie burgers. She was equally dismayed to discover that the next booth specifically offered tofu selections. Continuing down the row, her choices were soy chicken, seitan burgers, quinoa and kale salad, and something flat and oval-shaped called vegan fry, with no additional explanation.

"Christ. Who do you have to fuck around here to get an actual hamburger?"

Lexi barely laughed. "I'm gonna guess that's Kam Browne."

"Seriously, does no one eat meat any more?"

"You do know you're a lesbian, right?"

"And so that means what? I can eat all the pussy I want, but God forbid my lips touch red meat, then all bets are off?"

"Don't look at me, I don't make the rules." Lexi inspected her fingernails as she matched Meg's sarcasm.

Meg shook her head, only slightly defeated, then grabbed a veggie burger and loaded it up with toppings. She was just finishing when she saw Mia and Amanda heading toward them.

"Ladies." Mia raised her beer to them.

Meg squinted, scrutinizing the contents of Mia's other hand carefully. "That almost looks like a real hot dog."

"It is," she said taking a bite. "I guess as real as a hot dog can get, anyway," she added between chews.

"But where?"

Mia chuckled lightly at Meg's amazement. "Around on the other side of the beer truck, tucked away in a corner." She popped the last bite into her mouth and raised a finger to her mouth. "Shh, I don't think we're supposed to talk about it, but there's some hamburgers back there too." She laughed at her own joke. "You want me to grab you one? I'm going over that way for a refill."

"No. I conformed and had a veggie burger." She frowned. "But I will come with. I could use another." Meg turned over her empty beer cup, shaking out the last drop for emphasis.

When they reached the Budweiser trucks, they flashed their plastic bracelets, indicating that they were over twenty-one, to gain entrance to the cordoned-off service area, and walked to the end of the drink line.

"So, I kind of wanted to talk to you," Meg started.

"What's up?" Mia asked passively, as she perused the crowd.

Meg dug deep to overcome her awkwardness over the topic. She could tell that Mia preferred that they left this alone, but it had been on Meg's mind too much to ignore it.

"Look, things have been totally weird with us since P-town."

"Can't we just"—Mia sighed heavily and rolled her neck—"I don't know, not make a big thing out of it?"

Meg took a step forward in the line. "It's not a big thing."

"Then why are we talking about it?" Mia accused in response.

"I just wanted to talk, make sure we're still friends. That's all," Meg said, defending herself.

"Fine. Just don't be all drama about it."

"I'm not." Meg could hear the swell of emotion rising in her own voice. She took a breath and regrouped. "Mia, all I'm trying to say is, I just want to be friends. I kind of miss that."

Mia fixed her cool blue eyes on Meg, slightly annoyed. "Yes, Meg. We're friends."

"Yeah?"

"Of course."

"I only ask because we don't text anymore, about anything. We don't call each other. We don't hang out. These are things that friends do. So you can't blame me for being kind of confused." She turned and looked up at Mia who stood more than half a foot over her. She waited for Mia to make eye contact again before she continued. "Look, we both knew what this was when it started. We knew it would end eventually." She shrugged and offered optimistically, "It's sort of perfect that we both got here at the same time."

"That's true." Mia nodded her agreement and took Meg's cup, handing it over with her own to the girl working the taps. She smiled her irresistibly wicked smile. Reaching out she tousled Meg's hair. "The hair works for you."

"Thanks." Meg quickly messed with it again, trying to put it back into its calculated disarray.

They grabbed their full frothy cups and each reached into their pocket for a tip. Mia licked the foam spilling down the side of her drink as she held the exit gate open for Meg. As they started back toward their friends, Meg couldn't help but notice Mia's smile.

"So all you miss about me is the texts, huh? Wow," Mia joked, pretending to wrench a knife from her heart.

"Oh, please. Don't look to me to pump you up," Meg teased. "You'll just have to get all your ego boost from Amanda now."

"Amanda? You're kidding, right?"

"I thought you guys were a thing."

Mia shook her head adamantly. "We flirt sometimes, for fun. But she's my partner. There are lines you just do not cross." She looked to Meg for approval. "See, even I have some boundaries." She puffed her chest out, a little too proud of her own restraint.

"Too bad. She's adorable."

"Yeah? I could put in a good word for you…"

"Mmm." Meg scrunched up her face. "That's a little close for me." She let out a laugh. "I don't really think I need you two sitting around all day comparing notes about me." She mock-shuddered. "Anyway, I think I'll just take it easy for a while."

They were steps away from the group, which now included Sam and Julie. Mia whispered into Meg's ear, "Hey, I'm glad we're friends." She placed her hand possessively at Meg's waist and drew her in close so their bodies touched in an oddly familiar way. "But I'm just putting this out there, in the interest of full disclosure. Down the line if there's a time, you know, that we're both single again and feeling it"—she winked—"who's to say what could happen?"

As the night progressed, Meg couldn't help but enjoy herself. The dreaded conversation with Mia was behind her. And even though she didn't entirely agree with Mia's final take on their situation, it was still kind of nice to know she had options, however abstract they might be. It seemed that everything was working itself out. Work was good and calm for a change, the company was no doubt pleased with her efforts, even her colleagues were beginning to appreciate her in her new role. And here at Bay West, she had everything she could have hoped for—long-term girlfriend notwithstanding—but that would come, she had faith. This community, these people—she loved this place.

Lexi, on the other hand, was struggling to stay upbeat. Despite her vow just a few days earlier to happily drink away her woes, she was having a hard time getting out of the slump. Meg knew Lexi's night would turn around any minute. She'd gotten that promise right from the horse's mouth yesterday when she'd sabotaged Jesse on the ride into work. By the end of their talk, Jesse hadn't been able to conceal her smile as she swore to clear everything up this weekend.

Until that happened, Meg was determined to keep Lexi from

wallowing. She stood at the center of the circle of girls, keeping the conversation upbeat. She regaled her friends with travel nightmares, which she had plenty of from her months of commuting to London. Even though the content wasn't that funny, Meg played it for laughs, embellishing at every chance. She had good timing and delivery and she was at her best when she made herself the punch line of the joke. It helped that tonight she was on. She credited her level of comfort to the fact that tonight, for the first time in a long time, she was completely herself, unencumbered by looming deadlines or relationship drama.

She was on a roll. The girls were chuckling, a few even downright laughing, waiting for the big finish. Meg was taking her time getting there, milking a story for everything it was worth, and out of the corner of her eye she noticed someone in her periphery approaching the group but was so in her groove that she didn't even turn.

"Meg McTiernan, as I live and breathe." The sharp, sassy cliché cut through Meg's silly wit, deflating her and the story instantly.

The sultry self-assured voice was unmistakable. She used to hang on it at every syllable. Blinking slowly, Meg half smiled, half grimaced, her shoulders dropping as she spoke the name aloud before she even opened her eyes. "Becca."

Meg shook her head in disbelief as she met Becca's gorgeous face. For all the times she had envisioned their reunion, she had never expected it to happen here at Bay West. Of course, she shouldn't be surprised—in some ways she had been anticipating this moment since they'd broken up. Nevertheless, she expected her shock was written all over her face.

Becca puckered her thin lips and gave Meg a thorough once-over. She didn't even remotely try to cover it as her smoldering gaze took in every inch of Meg, from her new haircut to her beat-up old Converses. When she finished her assessment, she jutted out her chin and raised a signature eyebrow. "I thought you fell off the face of the earth."

"Ditto." Meg wanted to say more. She wished she had the nerve or the quickness to come up with some clever barb about how she'd moved on, how great her life was now. But she wasn't that sharp or cunning. Mean-spiritedness just wasn't part of her core makeup anyway. In fact the opposite was true, and Meg felt a natural pull to be hospitable and friendly even after everything that had happened between them.

Against her will she felt the old feelings simmering to the surface, and she wondered if being civil would be her downfall yet, as she stood face to face with the girl she had completely given up on, the one she would have sworn she was over. Standing less than a foot away, with Becca's long red hair blowing lightly in the breeze and fiery green eyes as enticing as ever, Meg wasn't sure how long she would hold out before getting hooked all over again.

With a move Meg had seen hundreds of times before, Becca brushed her hair over her shoulders and gestured to her group with a subtle flick of her long light eyelashes. Becca's eyes were far and away her best feature. They were inviting and secretive at the same time, with their hooded lids and lashes that went on forever. She used them to get whatever she wanted. Right now, as ever, it was attention.

"Look at you. Still the funniest person in the room, I see." Becca cocked her head and ran her tongue between her lips, making the gloss on them shine. "No surprise there, I'll admit." It probably passed as a compliment to the casual bystander, but Meg knew better. Meg's sense of humor had been a sticking point between them. Becca had never missed a chance to criticize Meg's jokes for being inappropriate, crass, or just plain unfunny. Meg had always suspected her jokes only bothered Becca because, however fleetingly, they stole her limelight. And now here Becca was using it to her own advantage, playing on Meg's long-sought-after desire for her approval. Meg recognized the manipulation right away, but it threw her off just the same.

Trying to steel herself, Meg took a drink as she turned back toward her friends and inwardly dissected the comment. She choked out a laugh into her cup as she regarded the group who stood stone silent as they watched the scene unfolding before them. Their open mouths and wide eyes actually lifted her mood, giving her both courage and inspiration, enough to momentarily break free from Becca's mind games.

She reached back to Becca and lightly touched her forearm. "Sorry, these are my friends"—Meg gently nudged Becca toward them, pointing to each girl in turn—"Lexi, Mia, Julie, Sam, and Amanda. Everyone, this is Becca. My ex-girlfriend." She was pretty sure she could forgo the formality, but she said it anyway.

Not surprisingly, her friends were warm and welcoming. They dropped their collective gape and replaced it with sincere hellos, opening up their circle to make room for her. Then they turned to one another and picked up previous conversations, affording Meg and Becca at least the illusion of privacy.

"So, who are you here with?" Meg asked, hoping it didn't sound like she cared. The last thing she wanted was for Becca to think she was still interested in her.

"Heather and Jenna," Becca answered quickly tossing an absent look over her shoulder. "They went to the beer truck." She pouted a bit fingering her bracelet. "You know me, not a beer person," she added, crinkling her nose. "We just got here. I thought it was an indoor party, but apparently it's not open yet or something."

Meg nodded checking her watch. "The doors open at nine. I just saw the DJ moving his stuff up there, so it'll get going pretty soon." Meg glanced around and noticed some movement had started up toward the Commons. "They should probably do a better job advertising," she offered, giving Becca an excuse for her confusion. "See, it's really almost two parties," Meg continued to explain. "The afternoon is like a combination cookout slash tea dance, but at night everything moves up to that big building over there." Meg pointed in the direction of the Bay West Commons, where people were beginning to line up. "That will really be more like a club."

Becca didn't ask how Meg knew so much about the setup. "I've never been to one of these parties before, but apparently it's this whole big thing. You know, *Time Out New York* just did a piece on this place. People live here and everything. I mean it's impossible to get in, huge waiting list. But still, so cool, right?"

Meg tried to interrupt, but Becca wouldn't let her get a word in. It was typical—Becca always had to be the one in the spotlight. "The article called it something. Oh God, what was it?" She tapped her upper lip as she thought. "I think it was like Americana Lesbiana or something kitschy like that. The reporter said this place was the new wave of feminism, the hottest lesbian neighborhood in the country. Can you believe it, right in our city? You read it too?" she asked presumptively, still not giving Meg a chance to talk. "Is that how—I mean that's why you're here, right?"

Meg hadn't read the article but she had certainly heard about it. It had been titled "The New American Lesbian" and focused largely on Kam Browne and her innovation and business acumen in developing the community. The neighborhood had been buzzing about the story for weeks, critiquing the nuances the magazine got right versus the plethora it didn't. The biggest gripe had been that the reporter had been a man. A straight one, at that.

"No, I didn't read the article," Meg confessed, a confident smile cutting though. "I live here."

Becca rolled her eyes. "Cute, Meg," she responded dryly.

The corner of Meg's mouth turned up a touch. "I'm serious. I live here, on the next street over actually." She was enjoying the look of awe on Becca's face, but she spared her anyway. She nodded over Becca's shoulder. "Jenna and Heather appear to be searching for you."

Becca turned toward them and gave a quick wave, ordering them over. Apparently she wasn't done with Meg. She narrowed her eyes, twisting a long red strand in her left hand. "But how?" Her mouth hung open in absolute disbelief.

Meg shook her head and laughed. "I don't know." She shrugged. "It just kind of happened. I've been here for almost a year now." Thumbing at Lexi she added, as proof, "Lexi here is my next-door neighbor."

Almost on cue, Lexi turned to Meg.

"Sorry to interrupt." Lexi put one finger up apologetically. "Meg, can I steal you for a second?" Grabbing Meg's arm she surreptitiously handed over her cell phone and whispered, "Don't make it obvious, but check out this text I just got."

Meg forcefully hid her smile as she scanned the message from Jesse. *Lex, we really need to talk. I saw you at the party with your friends. Was hoping for a few minutes alone. Meet me at my place?*

"What do you think that means?" Lexi muttered through clenched teeth, trying to mask the equal parts of hope and fear that were coming to the surface.

Meg knew exactly what it meant. "I think it's all good."

"You think?" There was obvious anxiety in Lexi's sweet brown eyes.

"I do." Meg hoped her confident tone reassured her.

"Listen, I don't want to make a big deal about where I'm going, so I'm just going to slip out—"

"I got you covered."

Lexi mouthed *thank you* and slid away without notice.

Meg turned back to Becca just in time to overhear her giving the lowdown to Heather and Jenna. "See, this is really more like two parties…" she said, as though she'd known it forever.

Meg shook her head and ushered them up the hill to the Commons where the music was already wailing.

CHAPTER TWENTY-THREE

Lexi hurried down the walkway that led to the main sidewalk. She kept trying to slow down, particularly since she really wasn't sure what she was walking into at all.

She rounded the tennis court and kept along the straightaway that led to her block, imagining scenarios that were all over the spectrum. She was so caught up that she had completely forgotten that the rear of Jesse's unit overlooked her path until she heard her deep sexy voice from above.

"Hey."

Lexi looked up, and there was Jesse, looking totally at ease as she leaned on the railing of her bedroom balcony, drink in hand.

Although she was taken off guard, Lexi was also relieved that she didn't have to go around to the front of the house, where she would risk being seen by her parents. She swiftly cut through the three backyards between them until she stood squarely below Jesse.

"Come on up. It's open," Jesse said in a tone that was virtually unreadable. Lexi watched as she took a long sip from the short glass.

She slid open the rear glass doors and closed them gently behind her. If she thought she was nervous before, it was nothing compared to the walk through Jesse's living room and up the stairs to the second floor. She tried to ignore all the memories that flooded into her head from her previous visit. She hurried through the master suite, barely allowing herself to glance at the bed, until she stepped through the open balcony door where Jesse was waiting.

"Thanks for coming. I hope I didn't mess up your night." Jesse looked up from her drink. She took a sip of the amber liquid, stifling a wince as she swallowed. "I just wanted to talk. I thought we might have a little more privacy here." Her intense eyes were serious and breathtaking against the backdrop of the dark sky. "Hope that's okay," she added, jiggling the ice in the glass.

"Sure." Lexi stood pinpoint straight as she waited for Jesse to say God knew what. Logically she knew it could be the worst of her fears, but something deep inside told her that wasn't going to happen. In this moment, standing on the balcony a few feet away from one another, Lexi knew with one hundred percent certainty that she hadn't imagined their mutual attraction. Even with the sound of dance music and laughter in the distance, Lexi could feel the heat that was ever present between them, whether they chose to act on it or not. She watched Jesse stumble over her words as she ran her hands through the short mess of dark waves, starting and stopping over and over, and she knew in an instant that Jesse felt it too.

"I'm sorry. Do you want a drink?" Jesse finally managed.

"No. I'm fine." Lexi smiled, because she was. Whatever Jesse was about to say, Lexi knew that it wasn't going to be the end for them. Boldly, she placed her hand on top of Jesse's and brought the drink closer, closing the gap between them substantially. "I am curious, though. What are you drinking?" she asked, hovering over the glass as she absorbed its potent aroma.

"Bourbon." A small smile escaped Jesse as she said it, as if the answer signified to both of them the seriousness of the situation.

"That bad, huh?" Lexi said raising her eyebrows.

Jesse couldn't meet her eyes. "I'm a little nervous." Lexi thought she saw her blush, but the light from the moon and the overhead sconces that lit the path made it hard to be sure.

"It's okay—" Lexi started, but Jesse cut her off.

"Let me just say a few things." Jesse licked her lips. "The thing is, I know about the job offer."

Lexi's brow furrowed in confusion.

Jesse let out a deep breath. "Sorry. What I mean is, I just found out that I, that we, offered you the job, one of the associate positions. I didn't actually know about it before, at the beach," she stammered out. "And obviously I wouldn't have"—she gestured between them awkwardly— "you know." She cleared her throat and gripped the rail of the balcony next to her. "I think what I'm trying to say, completely ineffectively I might add, is that we are sort of in a weird spot now." Jesse sipped her drink checking over the rim of the tumbler for a reaction.

Lexi was about to talk, but Jesse beat her to it. "The thing is, I didn't actually want to offer you the position. Laney and I talked about it, and I convinced her Scott was a better choice. It was a hard sell, believe me, because you are a far superior candidate. But I used everything I could to convince her. Everything but the truth, obviously."

Lexi didn't know whether to be insulted or relieved, but she could tell there was more to the story, so she waited.

Jesse said, "But while I was away last week, Scott turned us down. So Laney sent you the offer. She never talked to me about it because it was a no-brainer, the kind of thing Laney and I have been doing for years. I can't even be mad at her for it." Jesse laughed to herself and shook her head a little as she absorbed her own words. "Honestly, Lex, I didn't want you for the job because I thought there might be something here. Something real." She took a half step sideways and put her drink down on a small wicker table in the corner. Stepping in front of Lexi, she put her hands lightly on each side of Lexi's waist and met her eyes. "Lexi, am I crazy or is this real between us?"

Lexi kept her in suspense for just a second, reaching over to place her phone down next to Jesse's drink. She had been holding it so tight that a pool of sweat had gathered in her palm. She rubbed her hands on the back of her jeans and found both of Jesse's hands with her own. Lacing their fingers together she bit her bottom lip and said aloud what she had felt from the very start.

"It's real."

She saw Jesse's slow sexy smile spread across her face right before she leaned down to kiss her.

"Good." Jesse touched their foreheads together lightly. "But we still have a problem."

Lexi looked up, a rush of fear shooting through her.

Jesse sighed. "The job offer—"

Lexi was immediately relieved. "I don't want the job," she blurted out. "Seriously, I'm not interested." She couldn't keep from laughing. "Sorry, I didn't mean that the way it sounded." She looked up and saw Jesse was smiling. "You know what I mean. Anyway, I applied for a legal position with the Department of Education a while back and they just called me for an interview." She was giddy. "So I guess I'm declining your offer. No offense or anything." Lexi giggled as she ran her hands up Jesse's arms and wrapped them around her neck.

"It's probably for the best." Jesse nodded, finding Lexi's lips again. "Because despite what you might think, I don't sleep with my coworkers, interns or not."

With her hands buried in Jesse's hair, Lexi pulled her down and teased, "Actually, from my recollection, there's been hardly any sleep at all."

Jesse kissed her deep and soft, lifting her up and wrapping Lexi's legs around her waist. Carrying her into the bedroom, Jesse whispered, "Trust me, there will be sleep tonight. When I'm done with you, you're gonna need it."

❖

Lexi awoke in a state of complete bliss. There hadn't been much sleep for either of them, despite Jesse's promise. They spent the night engaged in intimate conversation, taking breaks to indulge in each other's bodies, finally dozing off before dawn. Lexi was exhausted but content, curled into Jesse, her back to Jesse's front. Picking up Jesse's hand, she kissed each fingertip once, then doubled back to her middle finger gently nibbling it before taking the entire thing in her mouth.

Jesse purred in response. "Well good morning, Alexis."

"Morning." Lexi turned around and continued her onslaught, pushing Jesse onto her back as she kneeled over her, searching for more unsuspecting body parts to devour.

Jesse moaned. "We have to eat," she whimpered.

Lexi responded with a naughty smile and Jesse rolled her eyes but played along. She pulled Lexi's legs down, positioning her in a perfect straddle on top, and then leaned upward, pressing their bodies together. "I meant food," she breathed in Lexi's ear.

"We can do that too," Lexi whispered back.

"So we're going to do this, huh?" Jesse asked as she slid her hands along the back of Lexi's shoulder blades and kissed her chest delicately.

Lexi knew that Jesse's question went beyond the surface. She knew that Jesse was talking about the two of them, in a relationship, together.

"Uh-huh," she answered, biting her bottom lip and leaning all the way back so her breasts were level with Jesse's face.

Jesse met them with her mouth, her hair falling forward and grazing the top of Lexi's breastbone as she moved her tongue through the cleavage. She held back Lexi's hair and started up toward Lexi's neck. "Are we crazy?"

"Probably," Lexi cooed into her ear.

Between kisses along Lexi's jawline, Jesse teased, "You know, there is an age difference."

"Mmm, I know," she said, basking in Jesse's touch.

"What about your mothers?"

"What about them?"

"They hate me."

"But they love me." She said it seductively, trying not to lose the moment as she leaned forward to push Jesse down.

Jesse resisted. "I'm serious."

"Oh my God, you're really talking about my parents *right now*?"

Jesse looked at Lexi dead-on. "I know the timing sucks, but this is a pretty big issue, this thing with your parents. If we're doing this, and we both know we are, then this is something we should deal with. Sooner rather than later." She took Lexi's face in her hands. "I know you're close with your moms and I know they're not my biggest fans—"

"That's putting it mildly."

"Awesome," Jesse muttered sarcastically, flopping back on the bed.

Lexi stretched out on top of her, kissed her sweetly on the cheek, and traced the outline of her rock-hard abs with one finger. "Look, I meant what I said. My moms love me. They want me to be happy. And look." She turned Jesse's face toward hers and smiled. "Happy." She kissed her again. "They will see that. I promise. It will be okay."

"So you're happy, huh?"

"Mmm-hmm."

"Good." Jesse rolled on top of Lexi picking up where they had left off. She paused momentarily, crinkling her forehead. "Do you hear music?"

Lexi scampered out from underneath Jesse. "My phone!" she yelled, remembering that it was still outside where she'd left it last night. Hopping out of bed she dashed toward the sliders.

"Um, babe?" Jesse called out. "You have no clothes on."

"Shit. Shit. Shit." Lexi scanned the room and grabbed the closest thing to her, a maroon hoodie hanging off the bathroom doorknob.

"Need some help?" Jesse offered playfully, as she propped sideways on one elbow savoring every second that Lexi fiddled with the zipper trying to get it closed before opening the door.

"It's Marnie's ringtone." She looked frantically over her shoulder as she slid the door open. "I never told them I wasn't coming home last night."

Lexi grabbed the phone off the table, a little breathless from her ordeal. "Hi, Mom." Not waiting for a response, Lexi jumped right into an explanation hoping to defuse the situation. "I'm fine. Obviously I stayed out." She surprised herself when a nervous laugh escaped her. "Just forgot to text is all." She clenched her teeth, wincing at the lack of detail she gave. She knew Marnie would pick up on it and question her, so she didn't give her the chance. "Anyway, I'll be home in a little while. 'Kay?"

There was silence.

"Okay, Mom?" She paused and waited, her heart starting to pound a little. "Mom?"

"Lexi." Marnie's one-word response was clipped and her voice had a strange tinny sound to it, like an echo. It took Lexi only a second to realize what was happening, but it was still too late. Almost in slow motion, Lexi looked down to see her mother stopped dead in her tracks on the path, exactly where Lexi had stood less than twelve hours earlier. Butter was next to her, looking at the ground as though even he couldn't bear to witness the disgrace.

Lexi could feel Marnie's anger even though her voice was steady. She said only three words. "Get home. Now." Lexi knew it was not a suggestion.

She walked back into the bedroom, her euphoria gone.

Jesse sat up. "Everything okay?"

"Not exactly."

❖

The silence in her house was telling. At this early hour, Lexi knew none of her brothers and sisters would be awake, but she had hoped that at least Chris would be up to give her some support. She stood on the landing inside the doorway for a split second, deciding whether to go up or down. Even though she wanted to head downstairs to her room, she figured that wasn't a realistic option. Slowly she trudged up the stairs to the main living area, where she knew she would find Marnie.

"Mom, I'm sorry I forgot to call," she said with more attitude than she had intended.

Marnie's gaze was fixed straight ahead, as if boring into the hickory cabinets in front of her as she braced herself against the kitchen countertop. "Forgot to call." Lexi could see the muscles tighten in her neck. "Forgot to call," she repeated again into the air. She shook her head vigorously and grabbed a container of strawberries that were next to the sink. Choosing a knife that was entirely too big for the task, she started to hack away. "I can't believe you, Lexi." She had yet to look at Lexi, continuing to take her anger out on the strawberries. "I can't believe you let this happen."

Lexi stuffed her hands into the pockets of Jesse's maroon sweatshirt. "Mom, let me explain."

Marnie shook her head. "I don't want to hear it, Lexi. Go to your room. I can't even look at you right now."

"Fine." Lexi was more than a little annoyed that her mother was treating her like a child, but she was happy to put off this conversation for now. She really wanted to wait for the more even-tempered Chris to wake up before talking about it anyway, so she turned and started toward the stairs.

Marnie slammed her knife down onto the cutting board. "I knew she would do something like this."

It stopped Lexi in her tracks. "God, Mom. She didn't *do* anything. It's not like that."

Marnie met Lexi's eyes for the first time since she'd been home, and Lexi could see that she had been crying.

"Mom, listen to me—"

"No, you listen to me." She wagged the knife in Lexi's general direction. "I know you think you know everything. But that woman is a predator. She finds someone weak and naïve, she sets her sights, and then she waits to pounce."

"Oh my God, Mom, could you be more dramatic?" Lexi said

undercutting her mother's stern tone with her own irreverence. "That is not what happened."

Marnie grabbed a bowl from the cabinet. "Please, Lexi, I don't need to hear the sordid details of how she seduced you. You could spare me that image."

"You are such a drama queen," Lexi shot back, borrowing the phrase that Jesse had used months ago to describe Marnie. "She didn't *seduce* me. It's not like that."

"Don't tell me what she's like. Honey, I know her. I know what she's like. I know she can be charming and funny and I also know she doesn't respect boundaries. Clearly." She indicated toward Lexi with a wave of her hand.

"Right." Lexi nodded her head. "This is where you're going to tell me she had a crush on Aunt Mary, right? A hundred years ago, by the way."

"A *crush*?" her mother replied. "Is that what she told you it was?" Marnie huffed. "I shouldn't be surprised. This is exactly what I mean."

Lexi felt her heart drop into the pit of her stomach. She didn't have the nerve to admit to her mother that Jesse hadn't ever told her anything about Mary. The little information she knew was based on the things both of her mothers had said over the years and what she could puzzle out from those comments. All of a sudden she was sickeningly aware that she might not have the whole story.

Her mother plowed on. "A crush. Try an affair." If Marnie registered Lexi's shock it didn't stop her. "A ridiculous affair that went on for years and very nearly destroyed everything in its way. Everything. Mary, Kameron, this place." She gestured around the room but was clearly referencing the community that lay outside the walls. "Even your mother and I got dragged into it." Her disdain was palpable. "And then when it was all said and done, when it was finally over, that woman"—she pointed in the direction of Jesse's house—"that woman didn't even have the decency to leave."

Lexi fought back the tears with everything she had. She took all the anger and hurt she was feeling and directed it right at Marnie. "You're lying."

Marnie just shook her head.

"You hate her. And you hate me for being with her." Lexi abruptly left the kitchen, nearly knocking Chris over in the hallway.

"What's going on?" Chris asked, rubbing the sleep from her eyes.

Lexi bounded down the stairs without saying a word. She closed the bedroom door behind her and reached for her phone. She didn't bother wasting any time on choosing her words carefully. She typed as fast as she could.

Did you have an affair with Mary Brown?

The seconds ticked away and she held her breath waiting for a response, praying it would include a denial, something indicating it wasn't true, that Marnie was mistaken. Instead the betrayal appeared in writing as her phone sounded.

I can explain.

But Lexi didn't want to hear it. She silenced her phone completely, curled up on her bed, and buried her face in the pillow.

❖

Midmorning, Chris popped her head around the door of her bedroom. Lexi couldn't quite meet her mother's eyes.

"You awake?"

Lexi nodded, piling up a wad of used tissues from underneath her pillow onto the nightstand.

Chris sat on the edge of the bed. "Your mother loves you, you know."

"I know."

"She's just trying to protect you." Lexi had heard their mumbled voices going back and forth a while ago. She knew that by now Chris would be up to speed on everything. "She just doesn't want you to get hurt, Lex."

Lexi nodded again and wiped at the tears that kept coming.

Chris peered at the cell phone that lay on the bed between them. "That looks like a lot of text messages and missed calls," she offered, squinting one eye thoughtfully. "Maybe you ought to talk to her. Hear what she has to say."

"What could she say, Mush?"

"I don't know, sweetheart." Her voice was calm and even, as always. Chris rarely got worked up. It was probably why her parents worked so well together. "People make mistakes." She placed her hand on Lexi's knee. "Sometimes they have good reasons. Sometimes they don't." She looked back to the cell phone. "You won't know unless you talk to her." She patted Lexi's thigh gently and left.

Lexi tucked her hands under the pillow and pulled the blanket all the way up to her shoulders, considering Chris's advice. Her mother's presence had relaxed her even if that hadn't been her intention. Lexi finally stopped crying and drifted off to sleep.

❖

The light tapping on her bedroom door woke her with a start. Looking down at her phone on top of the comforter, Lexi realized she had been asleep for hours.

"Lexi, honey"—Chris's voice was soft as she opened the door— "Jesse's here." Mush inspected Lexi's face, waiting for Lexi's sign that she was okay before she headed back up the stairs, leaving the door wide open.

"Hey." Jesse's voice was husky as she leaned up against the door frame.

Lexi sat up and rubbed her eyes, still puffy from crying. "Hi."

"Can we talk?"

Lexi pushed back the covers and walked to the door, hooking Jesse's pinkie with her index finger as she guided them through the sliding glass door into the yard. She dropped Jesse's hand as soon as they were outside and walked straight back to the rear of the deck. She turned and looked up at Jesse, squinting in the bright afternoon sun. "Why didn't you tell me about Mary?" She spoke softly and seriously, her voice revealing both her curiosity and pain.

"I don't know." Jesse looked away momentarily before turning back to Lexi. "I guess I just…I don't know."

"Come on, Jess." Lexi looked up, almost pleading. "Talk to me."

Jesse swallowed hard, fighting back her own emotions. "I thought you knew at first. Then when I realized that you didn't—" Her shoulders slumped before she tried again. "I guess I just wanted more time. Time for us to be together, for you to see me for who I am now." She reached for Lexi's hand. "Honestly, Lexi, I'm not that person anymore." Her light eyes displayed genuine anguish. "I wanted a chance for you to see that." She shook her head a little, turning her face to the sun. "I know what you must think. God only knows what your parents have said about me. And I suppose they're not all wrong, but I wanted you to see for yourself I'm not a bad person."

Lexi tilted her head and wrinkled her brow. "If you had told me last night—"

"Lexi, what was I supposed to say?"

"You could have told me the truth." Lexi looked right at her. "I had to hear it from my mother."

"I'm sorry." Jesse cleared her throat. "I couldn't bring myself to tell you yesterday." She placed her hands gingerly on Lexi's waist, meeting her eye to eye. "Last night was amazing." She checked for reassurance that she wasn't alone in that feeling and must have seen it in Lexi's eyes. "We had just gotten past the stupid job offer fiasco. So, forgive me, but I wanted more time before we dealt with another major obstacle."

Lexi raised one eyebrow, not quite certain the explanation was cutting it.

"Try to see it from my perspective for a second," Jesse implored. "What was I really going to say?"

"The truth."

Jesse's voice cracked in frustration. "It was our first real...I don't know, not date even. But it was the first time we were really together. And I just didn't want to start our relationship off by telling you about the affair I had with Mary, who is like your parents' best friend—"

"She's my godmother."

"Great." Jesse looked defeated.

There was an awkward silence before Lexi spoke. "So, it's true, though?"

Jesse nodded ever so slightly. "It was a long time ago. I don't know what your parents told you, but they don't know the whole story. I'm sure of that." She sounded more vulnerable than Lexi ever imagined. "I was young. I made some bad choices, selfish ones." Her voice dropped into her throat. "But I was in love—"

"With Mary?"

"Yes, with Mary." She dug her hands in the pockets of her jeans and leaned back against the corner post. "She loved me too." She met Lexi's gaze. "I know this isn't what you want to hear. It's partly why I didn't want to tell you." She chewed her bottom lip nervously. "It was different back then. Mary and Kam, their relationship was..." She shook her head. "It doesn't matter." She shrugged. "I thought it would all end differently. I thought"—she breathed out heavily—"I thought we would be together. I honestly believed she was going to leave Kam." Her voice was low and she looked a little embarrassed. "At the time I thought that made the cheating okay. Of course it doesn't."

"Are you guys still…you know…do you still see each other?" Lexi was terrified to ask the question but she had to know the answer.

Jesse squinted at her, making sure she understood the question. "Not like that, no. I still see her around, obviously. But nothing like that. Not in years."

"But Meg told me you were seeing someone from your past and you wouldn't tell her who it was—"

"Lauren. My ex, from when I was in law school. I told you about her actually. The night you came to my house." Jesse revealed a slight smile at the mix-up. "We got back together a few months ago. Briefly. Wait, you thought—"

"Well, not until this morning, but yeah, kind of." Lexi pouted a little, scared of what she was about to ask next. "Do you still love her?" Lexi turned so she could see Jesse's immediate reaction. "Mary," she added at the last minute, so there was no confusion.

"No." Jesse pushed back off the post and took a half step so she was more or less in front of Lexi. She reached under Lexi's chin and met her eyes. "I don't love her. You know that."

"I don't—"

Jesse put her finger on Lexi's mouth, silencing her. "You do. You know it." She smiled at the ground abashedly. "I didn't want to say it. It's so soon." She laughed at herself. "We haven't even gone on a real date yet." She laughed again, looking deep into Lexi's eyes. "I love *you*. And you know it. I have since the beginning, since the second you came to work for me, maybe even before that. Quite possibly since the day I saw you walking your dog down the street right before you started at Stanton."

Lexi's eyes widened in shock that Jesse remembered their brief exchange so many months ago.

"I thought maybe you were interested in me too, at first. I couldn't figure out why else you would want to work at my firm. And then, God, I tried to get you to give me something, anything, during our first meeting. But"—she frowned playfully—"nothing."

Lexi grinned. "I was a mess during that meeting."

"You were cute."

"I was dying."

Jesse folded her hands over the railing. "And then Lucy Weston came along, thank God. That was my chance and I jumped all over it." She brushed against Lexi with her biceps. "I should have given that case to Allison or even let Paul finish it. But I wanted it so badly. Just so I could be near you."

Lexi was smiling ear to ear. Jesse was completely forgiven, but Lexi let her go on anyway.

"I was so afraid they could all see right through me. Laney, Allison, even Lucy."

"Oh, Lucy knew."

"What?"

"She called me on it."

Jesse's eyes narrowed waiting for the lowdown.

"One day in your office, she asked me how long we had been together. I denied it. Told her she was way off. But she knew, she saw through both of us." Jesse threw her head down and laughed. Lexi loved the way Jesse looked right now—sexy, strong, and a bit shy— and she almost couldn't believe it was all real. "Do you think everyone else knows?"

Jesse raised her eyebrows at Lexi. "If they don't, they will soon. You okay with that?"

"More than okay." Lexi slipped between Jesse and the railing.

"So we're good?"

She knew there was more to discuss about the past, about Jesse's relationship with Mary. Questions she wanted answers to, timelines and details about how it had started, when it had ended—all of it, really. But now wasn't the time. Right now was their time, their beginning, and Lexi wanted to enjoy it.

"We're good." Lexi answered with a smile as she toyed with the hemline of Jesse's shirt, brushing the skin underneath with the tip of each index finger.

Jesse leaned down and pressed their lips together, then pulled back. "Let's go out tonight, just me and you."

"On a date, you mean?"

"Something like that." Jesse leaned in again, but stopped just shy of making contact. "Just one thing, Lex." She grinned. "Will you please tell your parents before you leave that you won't be coming home tonight."

Lexi met her smile and pulled her into a long, slow kiss.

CHAPTER TWENTY-FOUR

L exi let the screen door fall shut behind her and immediately the smile spread across her face. Even though things were far from okay with her parents, she couldn't help being thrilled.

Earlier, after Jesse'd left, she'd explained to her parents in very limited detail that, for now, they were simply going to have to accept that she and Jesse were together. When Marnie refused to understand, Lexi told her calmly that was fine, but she was off to take a shower and then she would be going to Jesse's. Matter-of-factly she'd added that she wouldn't be home that night. She registered the look of fury in Marnie's expression, both that this was happening and that she was powerless to forbid it. Chris had placed a hand on her wife's shoulder and told Lexi with her eyes that it would be okay.

How could it not be? Her parents loved her and she loved Jesse.

Glancing down the street before she crossed, Lexi spotted Sam sauntering over from the rental section. They met in the middle of the street.

"Just coming to see you. On your way out?"

Lexi noticed that Sam was dressed in sweats and an old T-shirt that she recognized as Julie's. Lexi knew she still crashed there a lot, so it wasn't that odd, but still.

"Yeah, I am." Lexi felt herself blush as she inadvertently looked past Sam at Jesse's house.

Sam tweaked her head following Lexi's gaze and put her hands in the pockets of the worn-out sweats. "So. You and Jesse, huh?" She phrased it as a question, but it was clear she knew the answer.

Lexi immediately felt guilty. "Sam, I wanted to tell you," she started. "It's just, well honestly, there wasn't really a whole lot to say until now."

Sam shook her off with a smirk. "Dude, it's okay. You don't owe me an explanation." She playfully nudged Lexi's flip-flop with her own. "I kind of figured it out anyway. I have known you forever, I can read you like a book."

"Are you mad?"

"No way." Sam winced a bit, as if disappointed Lexi would doubt her support. "I'm happy for you. It's what you always wanted."

"It is."

Sam shuffled nervously as they stood there. "Actually there's something I wanted to tell you too." She shifted awkwardly. "I'm moving into Julie's place."

"Oh." Lexi's face dropped. "Oh, are you guys like—"

Sam cut her off right away. "No. No. It's nothing like that. We're just friends," she insisted, but Sam's face had turned pink and she deflected her eyes as she continued to explain. "One of the girls is moving out, so there's a spot open." She made eye contact again. "Things at my house suck. My parents are constantly up my ass. And hello—Bay West—how can I pass that up?" She looked at Lexi as if to gauge her reaction. "I know it might be a little weird for you, with Julie and everything."

Lexi knew that Sam wanted her approval and she gave it right away. "It'll be fine." She took a second to assess her friend before she teased, "Look at you—a renter."

"Me? What about you?" Sam played back. "Totally in love with the infamous Jesse Ducane."

"I guess we both got what we wanted." Lexi reached over for a hug, feeling guilty for how neglected their friendship had gone over the last few months.

Sam hugged her back. "Looks like." She looked down at Lexi. "You know I was coming by to see if you were interested in The Kitchen tonight." She jerked her head toward Jesse's unit. "Any chance I could persuade you and your girlfriend there? It's supposed to be fun. Holiday special, all drinks half off..."

Lexi crinkled her nose. "Not tonight."

"All right." Sam gave her a break, not even trying to convince her. "I'm going to see if Meg's in, then." She backed away, calling out to

Lexi as she was almost at Meg's front door. "Hey, Lex. I love you." She grinned, completing the corny phrase with two finger guns.

Lexi turned and smiled. "Me too."

❖

Meg squeezed through the crowd, juggling a round of drinks for herself, Julie, and Sam. It was crazy that the bar was this packed on the Sunday night of a holiday weekend when the city was usually deserted, but Meg guessed that word of the drink special had really gotten out.

As she cleared the archway into The Kitchen's back room where she had left her buddies, she was genuinely caught off guard when she was confronted with the same sexy green eyes that she'd seen less than twenty-four hours earlier.

"Need some help there?" Becca crooned as she rested against the inside wall without actually reaching out to assist.

Sam came to her aid, so Meg shook her head and passed two drinks over to Sam, who disappeared back into the farthest corner of the room. Meg stayed in front of Becca, taking a sip of her crisp Ketel One and club soda.

"Twice in two days. What are the odds?" Meg asked, not really expecting an answer.

Becca's offended look surprised her though, so Meg continued. "Come on, Becca. I don't see you—I mean, at all—for almost a year. Now it seems I can't get away from you."

"Is that what you want, Meg, to get away from me?"

Meg picked up on the signs immediately. Becca had never been subtle about what she wanted. "Don't play games with me," Meg responded. But Meg heard a slight invitation in her own voice.

"Who's playing games?" Becca teased, fingering the edge of her glass as she used her tongue to draw in the thin red straw. She leered at Meg over the top of her glass as she sipped her drink.

"You are."

"Am not," Becca said, flicking her hair over her shoulder.

It was totally predictable, classic Becca. She had employed the same tactic of preying on Meg's vulnerability just last night. But somehow Meg had been impervious to it then. Perhaps it was because there had been so much else going on. With Lexi and Jesse gone most of the night, Meg took it upon herself to spend time with Betsy and Allison, who'd both decided on coming last minute, thoroughly expecting Jesse to be there. Meg entertained them willingly—she liked them both, so it was easy to hang with them. She'd also spent a serious chunk of the night breaking Teddy's chops that her mysterious cousin who was allegedly all that missed every major Bay West social. Teddy gave it right back to her, commenting that Reina was in high demand, and since when did Meg care so much. Meg had even found time to chat up the new renters whom she'd learned were a trio of nursing students at the local college.

Meg had felt so at home and so on her game, that even when she talked to Becca, which she had done intermittently throughout the night, she hadn't fallen victim to her overt advances.

But tonight, she'd come out with just Sam and Julie. And as much as the two of them went out together under the guise of looking for girls, they usually spent the majority of the night contentedly talking only to each other. Meg felt like a third wheel. Bumping into Becca was almost a welcome distraction, and if she was being honest, she was kind of enjoying Becca's attention.

Meg smirked and raised her eyebrows mischievously. "Anyway, since we're talking, I have some questions for you."

Becca licked her lips. "Like?"

"Like where have you been?" Meg challenged. "I mean, we broke up eleven months ago." She looked at Becca critically, her tone getting more serious than she wanted it to. "I never heard from you. Not once. Never ran into you anywhere. And then you just show up out of the blue at Bay West." It sounded like a question even though it wasn't.

"I still can't believe you live there."

Meg blew past the comment, pretty sure it was the sole reason for Becca's renewed interest. "So what's the story?"

"There's no story."

Meg leaned in and breathed in Becca's ear. "Don't bullshit me, Bec." Meg was certain she knew the reason behind Becca's absence but she needed to hear it.

Becca puckered her thin lips, a sexy smile threatening to emerge. "I was with someone."

Meg sipped her drink and scoped out the bar as she waited for Becca to elaborate.

"Chloe."

Meg nodded knowingly. "From your office." She had met the girl several times when she and Becca were together. Becca had denied any attraction between them. Hearing her admit it now stung a little bit, but not as much as she would have thought. "I guess I'm not surprised. I figured something was up to not even bump into you here. So what happened?"

Becca rolled her eyes. "Straight girls. They're all the same. They're into it until they're over it."

Meg laughed in agreement. She scanned the room again and caught sight of Mia working hard to charm a cute brunette at the end of the bar. They made brief eye contact and each offered a small, easy nod of acknowledgment.

"...it's fine anyway." Becca was still talking into her drink. "Wasn't all that it was cracked up to be in the end. Not like me and you."

That got Meg's attention. She couldn't keep the surprise out of her voice. "What?"

Becca laid it on thick, batting her eyelashes as she fished the cherry from her glass. "Oh, please, Meg, you can't deny there has always been something between us."

Meg was filled with both disbelief and disgust, but when she met Becca's sleepy emerald eyes, what she reluctantly felt was desire.

Becca was all over it. "Meg, I know we didn't communicate the way we should have." She reached over and tugged at the bottom of Meg's shirt. "But honestly, what I learned from being with Chloe is that there are some things you either have or you don't. You and me"—she wet her lips—"we have chemistry. You can't make that up. It's either there or it's not." Meg felt Becca's cold fingers touch her stomach underneath the fabric of her shirt. "Me and you, we always connected like that."

She wasn't wrong, not about that. Their physical relationship had never been the problem. What Becca had failed to realize was outside the bedroom, when she routinely blew Meg off, constantly looking over her shoulder to see if something better was waiting there, when she repeatedly neglected to introduce her as her girlfriend claiming she wasn't into labels, when she held her at bay for two years—all of that had destroyed her. The day-to-day things that Becca did to belittle their bond far diminished any sparks that existed between them in the dark after a few drinks.

She could have said all of this to Becca, cut her down right then and there, but what would be the point? She put aside that jumble of thoughts and remembered she'd gotten through it on her own, emerging stronger and more independent. She was a different person now. She didn't need to make Becca pay for the damage she'd done or, worse, give her the opportunity to take some kind of credit for her transformation.

Instead she took hold of Becca's hand at the wrist and removed it from under her clothes.

"No." She said it evenly, trying very hard to conceal her emotion. She took one last look at Becca's beautiful eyes, swirled the remainder of her drink, and swallowed it in one gulp. "I gotta go." Meg took the few steps to the bar and placed the empty glass there before slinking through the crowd and slipping out the back door.

She was slightly drunk and super horny. She didn't want to give herself any chance to change her mind, so she flagged down the first cab she saw. Sitting in the backseat, she shot off a quick text to Julie and Sam, saying she was tired and on her way home. She knew they wouldn't be mad—heck, they were probably psyched she was gone so they could ogle each other openly. Meg giggled at the thought as she opened a series of picture messages from Lexi. There was a beach scene at sunset and then a selfie of Lexi and Jesse in front of it. There was no description. It wasn't necessary, anyone could see how in love they were. Meg was happy for them. Leaning into the cracked leather seat she laughed to herself.

She never thought she could be this happy to go home alone.

CHAPTER TWENTY-FIVE

Meg was on all fours in the corner of her tiny front lawn, so she had to crane her neck at the signature squeak of Lexi's front door. She leaned back and wiped sweat from her forehead, never letting go of her gardening spade. "How's things in the war zone?"

"Same." Lexi looked back at her house before sitting down squarely in the middle of Meg's lawn. "You're really turning into Martha Stewart these days," she commented, avoiding the touchy subject and focusing instead on Meg's incessant home repairs.

It was true that in the past few weeks Meg had been nesting like crazy. She had completely finished the interior makeover, including the floors, painting, even putting up new moldings throughout her house. Today she was tackling the front yard. Already this morning she had installed a window box just below her big kitchen window. Currently she was gloved-up, weeding and trimming the lawn edges to increase her curb appeal.

"You guys are still going out tonight, right?" Meg asked, pulling a thick root by the base. There was a new microbrewery opening up in Brooklyn, in Meg's old neighborhood, right around the corner from the one-bedroom high-rise apartment she'd briefly considered purchasing a year ago. It was widely known in the community that the two female co-owners were gay. While the place hadn't been designed exclusively as a girl bar, it was certainly a friendly, welcoming environment.

She knew Lexi and Jesse were coming—she was really just making small talk. She and Lexi had been talking about it all week. It was going to be Lexi and Jesse's first night out as a couple, and Meg thought this new place would be the perfect venue. All the regulars would be there. The place had been hyping its opening for months and it seemed a new place had the air of a fresh start, so Meg thought it appropriate for her friends. Selfishly, of course, Meg was just excited to hang out with them.

"We're definitely going."

"You nervous? To see Julie? I mean, since you're with Jesse now?"

Lexi spread her legs wide and began to stretch. "I guess a little." She bent forward over her right knee, then her left. She twisted her head to the side, keeping it parallel with the ground. "Let me just ask you a question," she started. "About her and Sam."

"I'm not sure," Meg answered before Lexi could even get the words out.

"How do you know what I'm going to ask?"

Meg looked at her. "You want to know if there's something going on with them, right?"

"Is there?"

"Would that bother you?" Meg asked, working at a patch of dandelions.

Lexi sat upright and stretched her arms above her head. "No. Not really. I know it shouldn't." She moved her shoulders in small circles. "It's a little weird, though."

Meg speared her small shovel into the dirt. "Look, I'll tell you this, because I'm your friend. If it bothers you, get over it." She looked right at Lexi. "Because whether it's happening now or not, I don't know. But if they're not hooking up yet, it's just a matter of time, trust me."

"You think so?" Lexi sounded surprised but not upset.

"You said yourself a million times that Sam always took Julie's side over yours and stuff."

"True." Lexi considered the concept.

"I've actually thought about this a lot." Meg pushed the handle of the gardening tool back and forth in the ground. "I think what probably happened was Sam realized pretty early on that she was into Julie, but you guys were already, you know, whatever, so she had to back off." Meg paused. "But now, you're with Jesse…" Meg took off her gloves, drying her damp hands on her dirty shirt. "You don't really care, Lex, do you?"

Lexi nodded. "No, you're right, I don't. I was just…I didn't see it coming. But I'm happy for them, if it's what they want." She finished with a shrug of her shoulders and stood up, shaking out her whole body.

"I can't believe you're going running in this heat," Meg said from her position in the grass, but she was distracted by one of the new renters waving at her from down the street.

"Gotta stay in shape," Lexi said, backing toward the sidewalk. "In case you hadn't noticed, my ninety-year-old girlfriend has a slamming body."

❖

Meg hitched a ride to the pub opening with Lexi and Jesse. She hadn't been out at all since Memorial Day weekend and was excited for the potential of tonight. She loved Brooklyn. She loved her new home too, but she had missed her old stomping ground more than she'd realized during the last year. She was happy to be out with her two best friends, happy for them that they were together, and she was secretly hoping her new friend Taylor might make it to the opening as well. Meg had told the new renter about the event when she stopped by while Meg was fixing her yard. The girl seemed genuinely enthusiastic, but she'd also informed Meg she was enrolled in summer session and had a big exam on Monday, so her presence tonight depended entirely on how much work she was able to accomplish in the afternoon.

Still, Meg was optimistic. It certainly beat her other prospects. Becca had been calling her steadily for a week and a half, emphasizing with each message that they needed to talk. Meg had dodged all the calls, letting them go to voice mail, and left all the texts unanswered. She suspected Becca was still shocked Meg had turned her down at The Kitchen two weeks earlier. Becca was not one to take rejection without a fight, and for as much as Meg was proud of her restraint and completely confident in her decision, she figured it likely Becca would be here tonight, and she wasn't wholly confident that after a few drinks she would always be so strong.

She was three-quarters of the way through her second drink, enjoying the pleasantly tame conversation between Lexi, Jesse, Julie, and Sam, who were all being overly nice to one another, when she noticed Mia's head above the crowd. It offered the perfect diversion, and Meg was genuinely excited to check in with her and find out what she'd been up to lately. She was just about to excuse herself from the group when Mia spotted her, and Meg saw something in her face change. And then Meg noticed Mia clasping someone's hand. It took Meg a second to recover, and she knew her surprise showed, as much as she wished to God it hadn't, as she watched Mia drop Becca's hand.

Both Mia and Becca stared at her blankly before they turned back to each other. Mia whispered something to Becca, and Becca nodded agreement. Meg watched them interact; she couldn't tear her eyes away. They were so familiar with one another, their subtle touches not those of the recently acquainted. She saw it then, the intimacy between them, and recognized it as something she'd never experienced with either of them. Meg felt the lump in her throat even before Mia started over.

Mia hung her head more than she needed to. "Meg, I'm sorry," she offered with a look that was more pity than remorse.

"Yeah, it's fine." Meg looked into her glass, disappointed to find it was mostly ice by now.

"We didn't mean for it to happen." Mia lifted her shoulders. "It just did." She glanced behind her, checking on Becca's status at the bar, part of their staggered approach. Meg witnessed her concern for Becca and almost gagged on the spot. Turning back to Meg, Mia added, "We actually kind of owe it to you." She smiled awkwardly.

It had probably come out wrong. Meg could tell Mia was uncharacteristically nervous—she was overtalky and her voice had a kind of shrill shake to it. It didn't make Meg feel any better. "You've got to be kidding me, that's what you're going with?" Meg's anger was there in force.

"I'm sorry. I don't know, Meg. I don't know what to say."

Meg took a sip of her nonexistent drink. "You can stop apologizing, I'm not *that* surprised. Becca's beautiful. And let's be honest, you never pretended you weren't shallow."

Mia took the shot in stride, blinking heavily. When she opened her eyes they were glassy, and Meg thought she might be genuinely distressed over the turn of events. Mia quickly looked over her shoulder again for Becca, using the opportunity to swallow her emotion. "Look, I know you're hurt."

"Don't worry. You guys can relax. I'm pretty sure I'll survive." Meg didn't even try to mask the animosity in her voice.

"Come on, Meg. Don't be like that."

"Like what? Pissed off that my ex-I-don't-know-what"—she gestured at Mia with her empty drink—"is with my ex-girlfriend? Sorry, but it's frustrating and annoying and, truthfully, just a bit high on the ick factor for me."

"I am sorry."

"Yeah, you said that."

Meg was looking for an escape and caught Jesse's attention. Jesse beckoned her with two fingers and Meg heeded the silent advice, barely nodding as she walked away from Mia, and putting on a forced smile as she passed Becca.

Jesse put an arm around Meg's shoulder and grabbed Lexi's hand. She leaned in between them. "Let's get out of here. I know a great little spot, perfect for the three of us."

A full week later, Meg had completely recovered. Honestly, she was pretty much over it that very same night, when Jesse had taken her and Lexi to the quaint Mexican joint hidden amongst Brooklyn's pre-war factories that lined the water's edge. There in Red Hook they'd sat two stories high in the open air, overlooking the harbor as they sipped margaritas, noshing on empanadas and hashing out the situation.

Meg wasn't heartbroken, as Mia had suggested. She was more embarrassed than anything. She felt like an idiot, imagining Mia and Becca initially connecting over her as their common denominator and ultimately finding happiness with one another where neither of them had found it with her.

Jesse and Lexi had let her vent. They both seemed to genuinely understand where she was coming from and they'd commiserated with her. To their credit, neither threw out any I-told-you-sos. On the contrary, they'd let her yammer away, getting drunk and listing each girl's shortcomings in full detail.

In her heart, Meg knew she didn't want to be with either of them. They could have each other, and Meg imagined they did so, often, in their new bliss, the thought eliciting only a slight pang as it occurred to her. There was too much good in her life to let it really get her down. The past year had been amazing, complete with twists and turns, unexpected triumphs, and unforeseen hurdles, chock full of the moments big and small that change your life forever.

Never again would she settle for the shell of a relationship she'd had with Becca—she deserved more. And she wanted more than the mindless frivolity she'd shared with Mia. In some ways it was ironic: she wanted what she had so clearly seen they had with each other. She laughed inside, registering how annoying that was, but there was also a part of her that was kind of happy for them. Not happy enough to want to see them or anything, which was why she was glad that tonight's party was an open house and not a social. She knew they didn't have an invitation.

Meg sat quietly on her deck relishing this thought, finding solace in knowing that she didn't have to endure their lovefest just yet. She leaned back in her chair and closed her eyes, soaking up the last few rays of the setting sun. She was more than content, and the night, with its myriad possibilities, had yet to begin. Her phone dinged with a message, and she swiped it quickly to see if it was Teddy with some final update or Taylor checking one last time that it was okay for her to attend an open house when she didn't even know the sponsor.

To her surprise, it was neither. Even though she had a hard and fast rule against doing any kind of work on Saturdays, Meg couldn't resist what s.michaels@sullivanandson.com might have to say.

She tapped open the email whose subject line said only *thank you*.

Dear Megan,

I can't thank you enough for all the projects you completed for me in the last few months. I realize this email is incredibly overdue, but I felt a touch awkward about the whole situation and didn't rightly know what to say. Thank you seems to fall far short, considering the amount of time and effort you've put in.

I don't know if you've heard, but I am transferring to the New York office after the holidays. I look forward to finally meeting you and to having the opportunity to repay you in person for single-handedly saving my career.

Sincerest thanks,
Sasha

Meg really wasn't prepared for such a genuine note. She must have had quite the reaction as she read it, because as soon as Lexi stepped out onto her own deck, her friend noticed.

"What's with the face?"

Meg shook herself free of it and got up, meeting Lexi at the railing. "Weird email."

"From who?"

"Sasha Michaels."

"*The* Sasha Michaels? From your job?"

"The very one."

"What'd she say?"

"Thank you, basically."

"Hmm. Didn't see that one coming. Not after everything you told me about her."

"Yeah, me either."

Lexi squinted into the dying sun. "Maybe she's not all bad?"

"Maybe not. We'll find out this winter." When Lexi looked perplexed, Meg explained, "She's moving to New York. Coming to work here."

"Interesting."

Meg shrugged. "We'll see." She put her phone down on the smooth top of the shared railing that divided the two adjoining decks. "Anyway, you guys ready for tonight?"

"Ready as we'll ever be." Lexi breathed out heavily. "We should be at the open house about nine, you know, provided we're still alive by then."

Meg laughed. "It'll be fine. Where is Jesse, by the way? I thought I saw her crossing the street before."

"She's inside, in the bathroom. I caught a glimpse of you out here, staring at your phone with that bizarro expression." She shrugged. "I was intrigued."

"So you left her in there, by herself?" Meg said with another laugh.

"We're all going to be at the same dinner table for the next two hours," Lexi said, deadpan. "What's another five minutes?"

They both turned toward the sound of the sliding door as Jesse passed through.

"Are you crazy?" Jesse started, but she clearly wasn't mad. She came right over and looped her arms around Lexi's waist from behind.

"I'm not sure I'm even ready for this dinner tonight. Do *not* leave me alone with your parents, please."

Lexi laughed, placing her hands on top of Jesse's.

"What's your game plan, kid?" Jesse looked right at Meg.

"Going over to Sam and Julie's for a pre-party thing beforehand, and then heading over to the open house with them. I'll probably get there the same time as you guys." Her phone beeped with a text and she clicked on it, aware that a slow smile emerged as she read.

Lexi raised her eyebrows, waiting to be informed of the texter's identity.

"Taylor," Meg provided, a little shyly.

"Is she coming tonight?" Lexi asked.

"Yep."

"This is the nurse? The new renter, right?" Jesse added for clarification.

"She's not quite a nurse yet," Meg corrected with a smile.

Jesse crinkled her forehead. "Aren't you getting set up with Reina tonight?"

Meg hung her head and chuckled. "It's not a setup. We're just meeting each other." She looked from Jesse to Lexi. "I would like to remind you that it's entirely possible we won't be remotely interested in one another." She nodded emphatically. "And besides, there is absolutely nothing going on with Taylor. She's new here. I'm just being friendly."

Jesse and Lexi exchanged a look as Jesse spoke. "You buying it?"

Lexi shook her head in playful response and Meg rolled her eyes and laughed at her friends, who were so obviously teasing her.

"Who knows, Meg. This could be your night. One of these girls could be the love of your life." Jesse smiled, dropping a kiss on top of Lexi's head as she said it.

"Well you certainly have options, that's for sure," Lexi added with her dimpled smile.

"Get out of here, you two." Meg waved them off, watching as they linked hands before entering Lexi's house.

Meg picked up her phone and leaned back against the rail, taking a long look at the very top of the bridge just visible over the tree line. She turned and headed for the shower, replaying her friends' last words over in her mind, wondering if they just might be right.

About the Author

Maggie Cummings is a new author with Bold Strokes Books. A lifelong New Yorker, she currently lives in the borough of Staten Island with her wife and their two children. She has degrees in English, theater, and criminal justice, and works in law enforcement in the NYC metropolitan area.

Totally Worth It is the first novel in the Bay West Social series.

Books Available From Bold Strokes Books

Cold to the Touch by Cari Hunter. A drug addict's murder is the start of a dangerous investigation for Detective Sanne Jensen and Dr. Meg Fielding, as they try to stop a killer with no conscience. (978-1-62639-526-8)

Forsaken by Laydin Michaels. The hunt for a killer teaches one woman that she must overcome her fear in order to love, and another that success is meaningless without happiness. (978-1-62639-481-0)

Infiltration by Jackie D. When a CIA breach is imminent, a Marine instructor must stop the attack while protecting her heart from being disarmed by a recruit. (978-1-62639-521-3)

Midnight at the Orpheus by Alyssa Linn Palmer. Two women desperate to make their way in the world, a man hell-bent on revenge, and a cop risking his career: all in a day's work in Capone's Chicago. (978-1-62639-607-4)

Spirit of the Dance by Mardi Alexander. Major Sorla Reardon's return to her family farm to heal threatens Riley Johnson's safe life when small-town secrets are revealed, and love may not conquer all. (978-1-62639-583-1)

Sweet Hearts by Melissa Brayden, Rachel Spangler, and Karis Walsh. Do you ever wonder *Whatever happened to...*? Find out when you reconnect with your favorite characters from Melissa Brayden's *Heart Block*, Rachel Spangler's *LoveLife*, and Karis Walsh's *Worth the Risk*. (978-1-62639-475-9)

Totally Worth It by Maggie Cummings. Who knew there's an all-lesbian condo community in the NYC suburbs? Join twentysomething BFFs Meg and Lexi at Bay West as they navigate friendships, love, and everything in between. (978-1-62639-512-1)

Illicit Artifacts by Stevie Mikayne. Her foster mother's death cracked open a secret world Jil never wanted to see...and now she has to pick up the stolen pieces. (978-1-62639-472-8)

Pathfinder by Gun Brooke. Heading for their new homeworld, Exodus's chief engineer Adina Vantressa and nurse Briar Lindemay carry game-changing secrets that may well cause them to lose everything when disaster strikes. (978-1-62639-444-5)

Prescription for Love by Radclyffe. Dr. Flannery Rivers finds herself attracted to the new ER chief, city girl Abigail Remy, and the incendiary mix of city and country, fire and ice, tradition and change is combustible. (978-1-62639-570-1)

Ready or Not by Melissa Brayden. Uptight Mallory Spencer finds relinquishing control to bartender Hope Sanders too tall an order in fast-paced New York City. (978-1-62639-443-8)

Summer Passion by MJ Williamz. Women loving women is forbidden in 1946 Hollywood, yet Jean and Maggie strive to keep their love alive and away from prying eyes. (978-1-62639-540-4)

The Princess and the Prix by Nell Stark. "Ugly duckling" Princess Alix of Monaco was resigned to loneliness until she met racecar driver Thalia d'Angelis. (978-1-62639-474-2)

Winter's Harbor by Aurora Rey. Lia Brooks isn't looking for love in Provincetown, but when she discovers chocolate croissants and pastry chef Alex McKinnon, her winter retreat quickly starts heating up. (978-1-62639-498-8)

The Time Before Now by Missouri Vaun. Vivian flees a disastrous affair, embarking on an epic, transformative journey to escape her past, until destiny introduces her to Ida, who helps her rediscover trust, love, and hope. (978-1-62639-446-9)

Twisted Whispers by Sheri Lewis Wohl. Betrayal, lies, and secrets—whispers of a friend lost to darkness. Can a reluctant psychic set things right or will an evil soul destroy those she loves? (978-1-62639-439-1)

The Courage to Try by C.A. Popovich. Finding love is worth getting past the fear of trying. (978-1-62639-528-2)

Break Point by Yolanda Wallace. In a world readying for war, can love find a way? (978-1-62639-568-8)

Countdown by Julie Cannon. Can two strong-willed, powerful women overcome their differences to save the lives of seven others and begin a life they never imagined together? (978-1-62639-471-1)

Keep Hold by Michelle Grubb. Claire knew some things should be left alone and some rules should never be broken, but the most forbidden, well, they are the most tempting. (978-1-62639-502-2)

Deadly Medicine by Jaime Maddox. Dr. Ward Thrasher's life is in turmoil. Her partner Jess left her, and her job puts her in the path of a murderous physician who has Jess in his sights. (978-1-62639-424-7)

New Beginnings by KC Richardson. Can the connection and attraction between Jordan Roberts and Kirsten Murphy be enough for Jordan to trust Kirsten with her heart? (978-1-62639-450-6)

Officer Down by Erin Dutton. Can two women who've made careers out of being there for others in crisis find the strength to need each other? (978-1-62639-423-0)

Reasonable Doubt by Carsen Taite. Just when Sarah and Ellery think they've left dangerous careers behind, a new case sets them—and their hearts—on a collision course. (978-1-62639-442-1)

Tarnished Gold by Ann Aptaker. Cantor Gold must outsmart the Law, outrun New York's dockside gangsters, outplay a shady art dealer, his lover, and a beautiful curator, and stay out of a killer's gun sights. (978-1-62639-426-1)

White Horse in Winter by Franci McMahon. Love between two women collides with the inner poison of a closeted horse trainer in the green hills of Vermont. (978-1-62639-429-2)

Autumn Spring by Shelley Thrasher. Can Bree and Linda, two women in the autumn of their lives, put their hearts first and find the love they've never dared seize? (978-1-62639-365-3)

The Renegade by Amy Dunne. Post-apocalyptic survivors Alex and Evelyn secretly find love while held captive by a deranged cult, but when their relationship is discovered, they must fight for their freedom—or die trying. (978-1-62639-427-8)

Thrall by Barbara Ann Wright. Four women in a warrior society must work together to lift an insidious curse while caught between their own desires, the will of their peoples, and an ancient evil. (978-1-62639-437-7)

The Chameleon's Tale by Andrea Bramhall. Two old friends must work through a web of lies and deceit to find themselves again, but in the search they discover far more than they ever went looking for. (978-1-62639-363-9)

Side Effects by VK Powell. Detective Jordan Bishop and Dr. Neela Sahjani must decide if it's easier to trust someone with your heart or your life as they face threatening protestors, corrupt politicians, and their increasing attraction. (978-1-62639-364-6)

Warm November by Kathleen Knowles. What do you do if the one woman you want is the only one you can't have? (978-1-62639-366-0)

In Every Cloud by Tina Michele. When Bree finally leaves her shattered life behind, is she strong enough to salvage the remaining pieces of her heart and find the place where it truly fits? (978-1-62639-413-1)

Rise of the Gorgon by Tanai Walker. When independent Internet journalist Elle Pharell goes to Kuwait to investigate a veteran's mysterious suicide, she hires Cassandra Hunt, an interpreter with a covert agenda. (978-1-62639-367-7)

Crossed by Meredith Doench. Agent Luce Hansen returns home to catch a killer and risks everything to revisit the unsolved murder of her first girlfriend and confront the demons of her youth. (978-1-62639-361-5)

Making a Comeback by Julie Blair. Music and love take center stage when jazz pianist Liz Randall tries to make a comeback with the help of her reclusive, blind neighbor, Jac Winters. (978-1-62639-357-8)

Soul Unique by Gun Brooke. Self-proclaimed cynic Greer Landon falls for Hayden Rowe's paintings and the young woman shortly after, but will Hayden, who lives with Asperger syndrome, trust her and reciprocate her feelings? (978-1-62639-358-5)